ESCAPE IN TIME

Visit us at www.boldstrokesbooks.com

By the Author

Never Enough

Escape in Time

to/ Jo

HAPPY DIVA LIT FEST 2017!

ESCAPE IN TIME

Enjoy my words!

Robyn Nyx

by

Robyn Nyx

2017

05.11.17

ESCAPE IN TIME

© 2017 By Robyn Nyx. All Rights Reserved.

ISBN 13: 978-1-62639-855-9

This Trade Paperback Original Is Published By
Bold Strokes Books, Inc.
P.O. Box 249
Valley Falls, NY 12185

First Edition: April 2017

THIS IS A WORK OF FICTION. NAMES, CHARACTERS, PLACES, AND INCIDENTS ARE THE PRODUCT OF THE AUTHOR'S IMAGINATION OR ARE USED FICTITIOUSLY. ANY RESEMBLANCE TO ACTUAL PERSONS, LIVING OR DEAD, BUSINESS ESTABLISHMENTS, EVENTS, OR LOCALES IS ENTIRELY COINCIDENTAL.

THIS BOOK, OR PARTS THEREOF, MAY NOT BE REPRODUCED IN ANY FORM WITHOUT PERMISSION.

Credits
Editor: Cindy Cresap
Production Design: Susan Ramundo
Cover Design By Sheri (graphicartist2020@hotmail.com)

Acknowledgments

Thank you to all the background staff at Bold Strokes Books who create these little paperback treasures. To Cindy, who patiently exorcises my Anglicisms, fine-tunes my efforts, and teaches me something new with each manuscript. Thank you to Gemma with a G, who inexplicably chooses to voluntarily read my manuscripts back to front like some Satantic ritual and always manages to find something I've missed (and to Larny, for letting her!). To my mum and dad, whose support and love is, and always has been, unwavering and constant. And most importantly, my eternal gratitude to Victoria, whose knowledge, encouragement, and love keep my fingers tapping and the creative juices flowing.

I'd like to give a special thank you to the team at Ravensbrück concentration camp in Germany. My visit was made all the more visceral and potent by the museum, the solitary confinement cells of each nation whose women were murdered there, and the video diaries of the camp survivors. They combined to create a painful but poignant reminder of how easily women (and humans generally) are able to persecute each other, and how quickly we can perpetrate such atrocities against the different and the unfamiliar. What lies in these pages may be fictionalized, but they have a solid base in the actions and events of real people at Ravensbrück, some acting on orders, others acting for "sadistic pleasure." Such scenes don't make for pleasant reading, but nor should they. They are our history. And they should remind us, constantly, that compassion for others is our most powerful characteristic, and apathy is our most dangerous.

Dedication

For my lady, Victoria
Your presence in my life reminds me daily
how lucky I am to have found you. I've never known
peace like this before, and I cherish every moment
we're together. I promise never to let go.

For all the Jewish and LGBT people, and all the other
communities who suffered throughout the reign of Hitler.
Your loss should always be felt and never forgotten.

For my secondary school English teachers, Jack Crawford
and Ingrid Farrell, whose time, dedication, and care to
their profession stoked my literary fire as a youngster.
Mr. Crawford, I finally accede to your greater knowledge—
you were absolutely right: you have to sit your ass
in the chair and carve out the words even when
writing is the last thing you want to do.

Prologue

2049—Cartagena, Colombia

Landry Donovan had to prepare for her team of operatives to join her. As the extractor and team leader, Landry had coordinated the final stages of their mission, and all they had left to do was get out of their deep cover posts in the military base without raising suspicion. She kicked open the jeep door, climbed out, and jogged across the desert road to the tree where she'd hidden the people retrieval unit high in a deserted bird nest of some kind. She was already looking forward to getting back to her sanctuary in San Francisco. Off the Pulsus Island and temporarily into a normal life, away from rescuing the future by saving the past one person at a time.

She climbed the big tree easily, grasped the PRU, and dropped the five feet to the ground. As she straightened up, someone grabbed the back of her jacket and threw her hard and fast against the gnarly tree trunk. She was unprepared for the attack. The air rushed violently from her lungs, and her nose cracked audibly as her unguarded face smashed against the hard bark. The PRU fell from her hand and skittled away in the dirt. *Fuck.* Damage to that could mean never returning home.

Disoriented and breathless, she began to turn to face her assailant but was tossed to the ground like a discarded toy by an angry child. She reached out to break her fall and felt another crack in her wrist as her hand caught awkwardly between some rocks. A powerful kick struck her in the pit of her stomach before she could recover. The force lifted her from the ground, and she slammed into the tree once more.

Another three kicks to her ribs and chest and pain ripped through her body like an explosion tearing apart a building. Her head was pulled up painfully by a handful of her hair, and she finally glimpsed the guy putting a beating on her before his balled fist smashed into her face too many times to count. It was the same guy she'd just allowed to escape because his wife had begged for his life.

His steel-toed boot connected with her ribs for a fifth time. She felt and heard the bones crack. The sixth kick sent the splintered ends into her lung and pierced it. Being beaten to death by this asshole was unexpected. Landry knew the dangers of time travel and the risks of missions like these. At least no one was home waiting on her return, depending on her to come home.

The guy fell to the ground beside her, and even through the intense fog of agony that cocooned her whole body, she managed to smile at his dead eyes…and the serrated tip of a hunting knife that protruded between them.

"What the fuck, Landry?"

She could just make out her colleague and operative Delaney through her rapidly swelling eyes. She spat out some blood and grinned. "I had him on the ropes."

"Sure you did." Delaney pulled open Landry's shirt and leaned in to listen to her labored breathing. "You've got a punctured lung. I'm going to have to deal with it."

Landry nodded as Delaney retrieved a health kit from her pack and pulled out a hefty syringe.

"This might sting a little."

Landry's laugh turned into a painful cough. "Do it."

Delaney thrust the syringe through Landry's chest wall and released the pressure. Landry struggled to suppress a scream. Delaney waved the PRU at her. "Now let's get the fuck out of Dodge."

With Delaney's help, Landry held the PRU at arm's length and traced a large circle in the air. The inside of the circle became blurred until it looked like a half-shredded photo, its pieces still clinging together. She held the PRU to its center, and three thick luminescent blue light threads reached out and hovered mid-air. Delaney took hold of a thread and wrapped it around Landry's wrist, pressed the end into her fist, and folded her fingers over it.

"Hold tight."

Landry watched as Delaney and Joyce did the same. They'd enter in body mass order—Joyce first, Landry second, and then Delaney. Landry pressed the retrieve key. She glanced back at the dead man at the base of the tree and gripped her ribs to ease the pain. As they were pulled into the time circle to travel back to their future, Landry was glad her mom would be able to fix the damage to her body. Her mind was another matter entirely.

CHAPTER ONE

December 19, 2075—Pulsus Island

Landry leaned back in her armchair and let the soft leather comfort her freshly repaired body. The patch-up team had their work cut out when she returned. The pre-jump altercation had resulted in some pretty serious damage: three cracked ribs, a broken nose, and a punctured lung. She was thankful for the quick and efficient intervention of Jacqulyn Delaney, an operator she worked with fairly frequently. And often played with.

She briefly thought about the man they'd left behind. His death hadn't been part of the mission, but it turned out to be necessary. Brutal and vicious, but necessary. That was their duty. That part of the job wasn't so different from the work she used to do for the government before she joined the philanthropic organization Pulsus Vita.

She lifted the burning cigar but didn't raise it to her lips. Seeing how much ash she could get before it fell into the ashtray was a game she played. Watching the smoke rise and curl toward the extractor fan on the wall was almost hypnotic. It was a similar habit with the shot of bourbon she'd poured over ice, enjoying watching the cracks appear in the frozen cubes as the two temperatures battled for supremacy, before cold always succumbed to warmth. She thumbed the droplets of condensation and swirled the viscous liquid around the glass with zero intention of it passing her lips.

Tradition. Routine. Things she needed to ground her whenever she returned from a mission. To return her to her reality, short-lived though it was. Tomorrow, she'd pack up and head to her mainland home for two weeks. Immerse herself in real life, far away from this community bubble, in an effort to enjoy time in the present and attempt to really live rather than exist.

She replaced the cigar and switched on the laser machine beside the armchair. The slide in the cartridge was the same each time she returned from a mission, but she pulled it out and checked anyway. No one had been in her apartment since she left it two months ago. Two months here, eight months in the past. Nothing compared to the seven years the operatives had given up for their part in the mission, but still, it took its toll. She had a limited window to affect the change, to find and rescue the target, to alter the course of history. Past history. For the future she *lived* in. Her job was high risk and specialist. An extractor had to be an extraordinary human being with off-the-scale intelligence, unlimited resilience, and exceptional strength. Tactical, intuitive, charming…every good thing a human could be. And every bad thing: isolated, detached, void of emotion, and remorseless. Every time she jumped, she became someone else. It would be so easy to lose touch with her real self, and she'd seen it happen with another extractor. She wasn't sure she'd ever discovered who she really was. Life, loss, these things had happened to her before Pulsus, and now she was making things happen. But it was other people's lives, not her own. The greater good was a greater sacrifice.

She held the slide to the light, and as she inspected the drawing, she smiled slightly. Preparation time for missions varied greatly, but the removal of her tattoo was the last thing she did before the jump. She couldn't have any unusual marks or features during missions, nothing to draw attention to her, or arouse suspicion. But as soon as she returned, it was one of the things she had to do before she rested. One of the ways she pulled herself back to the present.

Landry replaced the slide and positioned her right wrist in the clamp beneath the laser pen. The tattoo used to be all she had to remember her mother by, her last drawing before she was raped and murdered, leaving Landry alone at seventeen. Until Pulsus came knocking.

"Begin." She watched the machine re-create the delicate lines, the twisting, gnarled branches of the tree, and imagined her mother's hand tracing a pen on her forearm. The clamp repositioned Landry's arm as needed, and within minutes, the outline was complete. She recognized herself again. No matter which angle she caught a glimpse of her forearm, she could see some part of the design—a wisp of a branch, the veins of a leaf, all hints of her mother's brilliance. She stretched out her fingers and took a deep breath as the machine worked in hues of red to occupy the space around the top tree, shades of blue in the tree below. Color was the most painful part of this operation since it had to go deeper into the tissue to settle properly. It was an old machine she'd restored, because newer models didn't use color as it was considered too risky. Landry didn't care for the new rules—no one was draining the color from her life.

By the time the tattoo was once again realized, Landry was jonesing for her own bed. That was another habit she'd adopted soon after joining Pulsus to combat a life in the military, moving from one war-torn place to another, never really knowing where you might be bunking down next.

Now she could dream of the possibilities of tomorrow and its delightful uncertainty. It was the start of her one-month down time, to live as if she didn't affect the future, and interact with people she knew as if just four months had passed. Everyone else from Pulsus stayed on the island during their vacation time, saying it was less complicated and that it was too problematic to navigate the "natives," as they'd taken to calling the rest of the world, without tripping up. But for Landry, this time among regular people leading regular lives was invaluable to her sanity. Spending so much time saving other peoples' lives left her little time to actually occupy her own, so as always, she'd make the most of the next two weeks. It occurred to her that she'd get to celebrate Christmas and New Year's while she was off the island. *Merry fucking Christmas*.

Chapter Two

December 19, 2075—Pulsus Island

Delaney threw herself onto the overstuffed couch in her living room and pushed her face into a soft cushion until her lungs overrode her brain, and she came back up for air. She squeezed her eyes tightly shut and pressed her hands over her ears. Landry's pain had been too much to witness. The sound of her bones crunching as that bastard's boots connected with her ribs, her wounded grunts as he smashed his fist into her face, and her pained wheezing as Delaney performed the emergency intervention—Landry would never have survived the jump with the untreated punctured lung.

Delaney's patch-up had been relatively easy in comparison to Landry's. No physical damage, just seven years of living to reverse. The PU team could repair cells, but they couldn't undo the effects of the job on the brain. She couldn't unsee the look in Landry's eyes as he pounded on her, nor could she blot out the many days of torture she'd personally had to mete out to innocents. Restoring the body was easy, but mending the mind was proving impossible.

Which is where you come in. Delaney pulled the glass from the table and took a long drink. It coursed down her throat, burning as it went. It would take every drop in the adjacent bottle to haul her into unconsciousness. Years of seeking mental obliteration this way meant it took more and more to have the desired effect. While the rest of the island, the world even, barely touched alcohol any more, it was Delaney's savior, and the only way she could live with the circular story her life had become since joining Pulsus.

She eased herself back into the couch. "Music. Playlist one." Something the world had once known as rock, filled her ears. "One hundred and twenty decibels."

"Volume not recommended." The electronic female voice chastised her from the speakers all around her, but the level increased regardless. Landry had reprogrammed the machine and overrode that particular command before she installed the system—no one had told her to turn her music down since she was a kid learning to play the drums, and she wasn't about to let some software start now. With noise above eighty decibels subject to legal recriminations, the world was simply too quiet for her. Without her music this loud, she'd have to listen to the records playing in her head, the ones with crying voices from the years she'd lived in the past. She'd worked for Pulsus for just three years, but already completed twelve missions and lived ninety years more than her biological age of thirty-six. It was hard on the mind, living in a past and existing in the future. The time between missions was becoming increasingly difficult to navigate, and with no one to share it with, Delaney was beginning to wonder how much longer she could last.

Landry had joined at the same time in 2072, in the more senior position of extractor, and Delaney wanted her immediately. She was a thrilling combination of muscle and brains, with tanned skin, dark hair, and hazel eyes that blazed like a forest fire. Landry Donovan was a five feet ten inch package of the very best nature had to offer in a woman, and Delaney wanted it all.

But Landry would only give her body. They'd return from a mission, and in the one-month down time, Landry would disappear to the mainland, and Delaney wouldn't see her. Landry never fraternized with the island community until she returned for the pre-mission training. And in that time, they'd hook up relatively frequently. Always at Delaney's place, and she'd always be gone before Delaney woke. No matter how hard Delaney tried to stay awake after they'd had sex, she failed, and would wake to an empty bed, the soft impression of Landry's hard body still fresh and warm on her mattress.

Delaney emptied and refilled her glass. She didn't bother with ice; the liquor wasn't in there long enough for it to make a difference. She lay back and closed her eyes, trying to visualize the last time she and Landry made love. *Made love? Did she even know how?* Their sex was violent and frantic, like Landry was trying to fuck away her feelings. Just once, Delaney had tried to slow things down, and she'd felt Landry shut down instantly. Sure, she made the right noises, but she was barely in the room, and on that night, she didn't even wait for Delaney to fall asleep before leaving with a lame excuse about the following day's training.

As she drained and refreshed her glass once again, her mind began to drift to the last mission, to drug taking, and to the rape and torture she'd been party to. She recalled the jumping in she'd endured to gain access to the gang. Pulsus was a humanitarian organization with a big-picture view, but the geeks had no idea what they really sent operatives to do. And when the PU team had fixed their bodies, and the psych squad had evaluated their minds, they alone were left to deal with the years they'd just experienced. Sometimes just one, other times, ten. Though the operatives had been individually handpicked by the founder of Pulsus, Jenkin, or JJ as she liked to be called, even a woman of her immense intelligence couldn't possibly fathom the accumulative effects of a life lived five times over. *All in a good cause, Delaney*. That's what Landry always told her, but the longest she had to live in the past was months, not years. And yes, she had to do awful things too, but hers were usually directly for the change they were there to affect. If Landry had to kill someone, it was invariably someone who deserved it. Delaney had been chosen because her military record reflected her unswerving ability to follow orders, despite their questionable morality. The problem was, the more decades she lived in the past, the more she found herself questioning that ability in the future.

CHAPTER THREE

December 20, 2075—Pulsus Island

Landry didn't have to check caller ID to know who was calling at eight a.m. on the first of her vacation days. Her mom was more reliable than any alarm.

"Landry?"

"Mom."

"Are you going to the mainland again?"

She asked the same question after every mission, obviously hoping for a different answer. Landry never said the words she knew her mom wanted to hear.

"I am." Landry was still getting used to having her around after being alone for eighteen years. But then, she remembered she hadn't actually been alone all that time after all. "We'll spend some time together while I'm training."

The chance to save her mom in 2058 was her first mission. It was the carrot Pulsus dangled to get her to say good-bye to the military, which had been her home for over a decade. Landry had felt completely helpless when she lived through 2058 the first time. Helpless and fueled by an anger that inexplicably lived with her still. Being given the opportunity to go back and take revenge on the men who'd killed her mother sounded almost too good to be true. Except, when she did jump back, there was no revenge to be taken because her mom was still alive. Military training kicked in beyond the emotional rationale that beseeched her not to kill in cold blood, and she coolly dispatched the would-be murderers, and left her mom safe and sound on the beginnings of this island with her university companion and Pulsus founder, Jay Jenkin.

Still, when she jumped back to 2072, it was quite the mindfuck to find both her mom and JJ waiting for her in the PU room looking two decades older.

Nor had she been prepared for the flashbacks and the instant development of memories from a life she felt like she hadn't really experienced. The successful mission meant Landry *didn't* become a full orphan at seventeen. Her mom had still encouraged her to join the military, so she still ended up with the very special skill set Pulsus needed, but the edge had been taken off her anger at the world. Her brain held tight to the old orphan memories that shouldn't rightly exist, and they viciously competed with the new ones. It was strange, like she'd experienced two lives in parallel. Once the brain developed a memory, it simply didn't let it go.

"That's not real time. You know you're always too busy then. Can't you delay your trip and spend one day with me?"

As she gave in for the very first time, Landry shook her head. "Why don't you come over for breakfast? I'll catch a later train, but I have to get in by this afternoon to see the game." She'd considered pro basketball instead of the military after her mom had *not* died, but talked herself out of it. Now she just loved to be courtside, imagining a different life along a path unchosen.

"I'd like that. And I want to make sure your lungs are fully healed. You were in a bad state yesterday."

She was still getting to know her mom through experience, rather than recollected memory, but her worried voice was easy to spot. "Questioning your own workmanship? I spent the necessary hours in the curatio tank just like you told me. Your machines are flawless, Mom, you know that."

"You're my daughter. I can't help wanting to make sure you're okay."

Her words made Landry smile. The military had been her family for a long time, but she was beginning to believe there was nothing like the real thing. "So, stop chatting on the phone, and get yourself over here then."

❖

Her mom had come straight in, medical kit bag in hand, her homage to the traveling doctors of old, and proceeded to give Landry a full medical in her lounge. When Landry got back from a mission, she found it mortifying to receive a physical examination from her mother, and Landry was sure her team members found it highly amusing. It was like being twelve again and examined for head lice in front of the whole class. She would've much preferred to be checked over by one of the hot female patchers. Hell, even a male one was preferable to her mom. But given that her mother was the inventor of regenerative technology, no one was about to argue with her insistence on being present for every one of Landry's return jumps. At least no one was watching *this* humiliation.

"See? I told you I was okay. Your fancy machines haven't failed me yet." Landry pulled her tank top back on, expecting it to smart just a little, but there was no pain. She thought she might not survive at all while the guy was mashing her into the ground. After Delaney had intervened—Landry wasn't comfortable with the term rescued—she'd presumed there would be pain for a while when they made it home. Going on her vacation in top shape was a pleasant bonus.

Her mom tenderly traced the branches of Landry's tattoo. "I love that this is the first thing you do when you get home."

Landry smiled. "It's been my reminder of you for a long time. I guess I don't need it anymore for that reason, but I still love it. 'As above, so below,' but sometimes I struggle to understand myself—the universe has no chance. And I need stability when I get back. This tattoo gives me that." Landry checked herself. She was being maudlin, and she didn't like it. Almost being killed before she was even born had obviously affected her more than she wanted to admit. *A change of subject is in order.* "Anyway, you fixed me up and I'm good to go."

"What happened, baby? You've never come back like that before."

"There are always risks, Mom. I'd just been lucky until yesterday...sixty years ago." Landry laughed, trying to make light of the situation and disguise the truth. In the debrief, she'd been too disgusted with herself to admit it, but getting attacked was her own fault. She'd allowed a moment of weakness to stop her from finishing the perp when she had the chance. His expression had begged silently to spare him, and his wife had loudly pleaded for her clemency and compassion. His death wasn't part of the mission and would have been incidental, collateral damage. There was no real need for it, so she made the decision to let him live. Before Pulsus unmade her orphan status, that decision would've been different. *It's a mistake I won't be making again.*

"Luck's had nothing to do with it. Your training and your preparation keep you safe." She clearly wasn't convinced.

It riled Landry that her mom could know her so well when she felt she'd only *really* known her for three years. Regardless of the science, her memories still didn't feel like she'd lived them. "Sometimes the prep isn't enough. You can't predict human behavior."

"That's where you're wrong, baby girl. Only one time in a million do human beings do something random or unexpected."

"I disagree. We're capable of infinite arbitrary and spontaneous actions."

"You sound like your father. He was a romantic too."

Landry thought she picked up a hint of derision in her mother's words. She scoffed. "I'm no romantic." She thought of the many dalliances she'd had to cultivate during her missions. An extractor had no time for love, and that suited her just fine. "But I would've liked to have had the chance to discover my dad's romantic side." There was anger in her voice and she regretted letting it free. Pulsus wouldn't authorize a mission to save her father from death on active duty. Quite apart from the ethical and financial considerations, her mother had remarried and given birth to her half brother, Michael, who by some absurdity had rescued an influential politician from certain death. It had saved Pulsus a job, so they had no interest in changing that element of the past.

As if knowing what was going through her mind, her mom took Landry's face in her hands. "We can't change the past for the sake of our own future. That's never what this was all about."

Landry closed her eyes and let her head rest against her mom's firm caress. "I know. But I miss him." She kept her eyes shut tight, lest the threatening tears saw their opportunity to escape.

"I know you do, baby girl."

Chapter Four

December 20, 2075—Pulsus Island

Delaney woke to the sounds of playlist one on repeat, and the throbbing in her head reminded her that she alone had emptied the bottle of bourbon that rested in her hand. She placed it on the table, got up, and headed to the kitchen to see what hangover cure the fridge might be harboring.

"Music. Playlist six. Sixty decibels." The soft sounds of Sade began to sooth her troubled mind. It wasn't just her dehydrated brain that hurt. *All this effort to fix the past when the present could benefit from a little attention too.* She pulled a bottle of protein and spinach elixir from the fridge door, took a dirty glass from the sink, and filled it with green gunk.

After the excitement of the first missions and the novelty had worn off some, she began to comprehend the horror of her new job. Delaney's vacation time now started with a drink. It was a few shots at first, to calm and resituate her mind in the present. But the things she'd done in the past began to revisit her often, and it failed to quiet their voices or dampen the vivid images. A few shots quickly turned into the full bottle. A bottle on the first night turned into a bottle every night...unless Landry was coming over, and then she'd just settle her nerves with the one shot. Sex with Landry was better than any alcohol, and her pussy was the one body part she didn't want to numb.

Delaney picked up her phone and her thumb hovered over the speed dial to Landry. She looked at the time and figured she'd already be heading for the mainland. Just hearing her voice provided some comfort though, so she pressed it anyway and waited for Landry's perfunctory message.

"Hey, Delaney, what's up?"

Landry's voice startled her. *She shouldn't be home*. "You shouldn't be home." She snapped her fingers to mute the music.

"Yeah, well, I somehow managed to invite Mom over for breakfast. She wanted to check on me after the state I got back in yesterday. It would've been a lot worse if you hadn't stepped in."

Delaney knew that saying "thank you" didn't come easy to Landry, but she teased her anyway. "Stepped in—that's an understated way of saying 'saved my ass,' don't you think?"

"What do you want, a medal for doing your job, hotshot?"

"You're the extractor. You're supposed to be the hotshot, not me."

"I'm no island, Delaney. You know I appreciate your backup, and I wouldn't want anyone else by my side."

Landry's voice had softened. No one else would've spotted it but her. Delaney smiled ruefully and was glad Landry was only on voice and not full facial hookup. She didn't just want to be by her side on missions. But they were soldiers, and soldiers didn't admit that kind of thing to each other. "Are you heading to the mainland soon, or do you have time for coffee?"

The lengthy silence from Landry told Delaney more than any words she could've spoken. "I'm already late. There's a game I've got to see. The Warriors are playing the Clippers in their first game since Coach Durant got fired. I want to see how the team reacts."

"What's so fascinating about watching ten women run from one end of a court to the other and back again for forty-eight minutes?" Delaney knew her ridiculous question would defuse the awkward quiet that had settled on their conversation.

"You can't be serious? Quite apart from the fact that they tend to be pretty fucking sexy women AND they get all sweated up and glistening within minutes, there's the fine matter of the beauty of the game."

"Fuck that. There's hardly any skill to it. Bounce, bounce, score. Give the ball to the other team. Bounce, bounce, score. Let's talk about football if you want to talk about a beautiful game."

"I'll grant you, football has its merits, but a basketball game is more intimate, more intense. There's nowhere to hide on that court—as opposed to football, where you substitute an entire team to play a different part of the game."

Delaney smiled, knowing that Landry would be emphasizing her point with her hands, even though nobody could see her. *Chop my hands off and I'd be mute*. She'd heard Landry say it a hundred times. *Chopping your hands off would be a travesty to lesbians everywhere,* was Delaney's stock response.

"So speaks someone who could never make the football team." Delaney's teasing deflected her own longing for an entirely different conversation.

"I never tried out for the football team. I decided early on I wanted my brain intact, and I've always been too fond of speech to play a game where I'm all but guaranteed a concussion every few weeks."

"Not if you're so fast that they can't catch you."

"Are you calling me slow? That guy came out of nowhere. I'd left him way behind, begging for his life. How could I know he'd come after me?"

Delaney could tell from Landry's tone she hadn't yet reconciled the reason behind her run-in with the meaty guy on their last mission. Delaney hadn't even brought it up, and she wasn't going to. Things like that didn't make it into the debrief. It was an unspoken soldier's oath. "You didn't. Forget about it. You didn't say anything, did you? 'Cause I didn't, Landry. That shit stayed there as far as I'm concerned."

There was a different reason for this new silence, and Delaney wanted to fill it with words of affection and tender comfort. But she held back. Landry wouldn't entertain that on a regular day, let alone one where Delaney felt she was actually getting a glimpse of her vulnerability.

"What if Elena hadn't invented regenerative tech, Dee? I'd be dead."

Vicious images of Landry's broken body assaulted her. She swallowed hard, trying to head off the bile she felt rising to the back of her throat. Landry dead. It was a thought she couldn't...wouldn't entertain. "What's the point in torturing yourself? She did invent it, and the world has you to thank for that. You jumped back and saved your mom, and now she gets to save us. You had an error in judgment, that's all. It happens, apparently even to the best of us. I'm pretty fucking sure you won't make the same mistake again." Delaney was beginning to wonder if Landry was having the same doubts she was about their work. Did she want out? She'd been close to death when they jumped. Had nearly dying made her reconsider how she was living?

"You're right. I was being stupid. It's time for a hard-earned break."

Delaney detected her change in attitude. The woman shut down faster than an Olympic sprinter could outrun a zombie. *Stopping a zombie apocalypse, I wonder when we get that mission.* "So I guess we'll see you in two weeks."

"Count on it. Have a great vacation, hotshot."

The line went dead before Delaney could respond, and she tossed the phone across the kitchen counter.

"What exactly does a great vacation even look like, Landry? A never-ending line of baller fans desperate for you to fuck them?" She drained the glass of its now warm liquid and threw the glass at the wall. It bounced off and landed at her feet, frustratingly still in one piece. Some clever fuck had invented non-breakable glass. Not all technological advances were welcome. Sometimes there was nothing that satisfied anger more than the sight and sound of smashing glass.

She had to get a grip and stop chasing Landry. She wasn't running, and it wasn't her fault she was emotionally unavailable. God, she hated therapist jargon, but she knew that kind of disconnect made their job easier. And that's how Delaney had been too, for the most part thanks to her family history. So why couldn't she have just stayed that way? Pulsus needed detached and unaffected operatives. They didn't need unpredictable and overly sensitive assholes. *Why can't I move on?*

CHAPTER FIVE

December 20, 2075—Mainland, San Francisco

Other than the service staff, the high-speed water train had been empty as usual. Pulsus had spent billions installing their under-ocean connection to the mainland, but it ended up serving mostly as its secondary usage, a freight train. As the program developed, Pulsus employees became increasingly nervous about interaction outside the island, and trips to the mainland for anything other than supplies decreased considerably. Landry was now the only one who consistently vacationed here.

She disembarked at the cargo platform where the other Pulsus staff began to load supplies from their dedicated container. They were working toward full self-sufficiency on the island, and they'd created electronic and communication devices and systems better than Apple or Google could even dream up, but there were some things they simply couldn't beat, like Twizzlers and M&M's. Those things had to be sourced externally.

"So we'll see you in two weeks, cowboy?"

Landry gave a wry laugh and nodded to the guy throwing cartons of Twinkies into the boxcar. "You got it, hoss."

"And you'll have some tales for me on the return journey?"

"Garrett, you are way too fascinated with my sex life. What'd your boy think if he knew?"

He grinned and winked. "My boy does know, and he *asks* me for the gory details. Everyone knows you fuck like a man and leave 'em wanting more. When I retell your stories, all we have to do is put a few extra body parts in the picture and it's a good night for everybody. You'd make a handsome man."

"I don't know what century you're living in," said Landry, shaking her head. "Where I come from, there have always been women that fuck like me. We're not all hearts and flowers, hoss. You may be from the South, but you should know better. And what do you mean *everyone*?" Landry impatiently pulled her bag onto her shoulder, slightly irritated. This was why she left the island on her down time. Everyone knew everyone else's business. It was like some never-ending TV drama that they all took part in so they'd have something to discuss by the water cooler, but it was news to her that *everyone* was enthralled with her sex life.

"Don't get testy, Donovan. You're a hero to a lot of people. Them being interested in you comes with the territory."

He had a point. Extractors were the island's version of movie stars. In a community mostly of soldiers and scientists, even they needed a champion. "I'll do my best not to let anyone down, then."

"That's more like it. You're one of the very few who still visit the mainland for anything other than supplies, cowboy. Everyone else leads a boring fucking life, seeing the same people day in, day out. Variety is the spice and all that."

She smiled. "Clichés and stereotypes. You're on form today, hoss. See you in two weeks."

Landry turned away and headed along the platform to the surface.

Her first view of San Francisco after a mission always comforted her. It was home in a way nowhere else had been since the death of her father. And though the landscape had changed irrevocably since the '60 earthquake had leveled the whole city, it still managed to remind her of a simpler time. This was the place her father had taken her to see the decommissioned naval ship, *USS Independence*. It was where she'd fallen in love with the idea of following her father's footsteps by serving her country. She'd chosen the army, before joining the Navy Seals, accepted as one of only a few annual interservice transfers.

Working with Pulsus was rewarding, there was no doubt about that. Knowing you were an integral part of changing the world for the better, saving people who would go on to save millions, was good for the soul. And the remuneration was generous, necessarily so to make up for the fact that any hope of a "normal" life was extinguished the moment you signed up.

She'd wanted to live in the Fisherman's Wharf area, the once thriving pseudo-center of San Francisco, but it had fallen into the bay with the quake. With the introduction of the *Handbook of the San Francisco Building Laws*, the rest of the city and the newly carved coastline had been repopulated with three-story buildings. The Neoteric Wharf was mostly restaurants, boutique shops, and coffee houses. It was the new place to be, and it was the place Landry had chosen as her home away from the island, away from Pulsus. Somewhere busy enough with tourists for her coming and going not to be noticed. Somewhere busy enough with tourists to keep her amused on lonely evenings.

The family was sitting at the table by the window, as she knew they would be at this time of day, sitting down to eat together after the usual lunchtime rush. As soon as they recognized her, they were out of their chairs and into the street, pulling her into a group hug. It hadn't been her plan to get this close to the people she was living above, but events on one of her early Pulsus vacations ended with the family's informal adoption of her. They gave her no choice.

"We've missed you, Lan Lan. You were gone long time."

Landry smiled at Priscilla, the small girl who'd wrapped her arms tightly around her right thigh, seemingly in no hurry to let go. The last mission had taken her back to 2015. The time travel technology was advanced, but they hadn't yet figured out how to stop it entirely. Jumping forward sixty years resulted in re-entering 2075 sixty days from the initial jump for the mission. Add that to the mission training time, and she'd been away from home for four months.

"Aw, my little sweet P, I've only been gone four months." Landry accompanied her words with a ruffle of her short blond hair. Priscilla scrunched her eyes up and smiled a beautifully innocent smile.

"That's a long time when you're three."

Priscilla's mom, Lizbeth, raised her eyebrows. "You're late today."

"Just a little delay, but back in time for the big game." Landry avoided the implied question. Lizbeth often tried to not so subtly mine for information, and Landry had grown skilled at gently eluding her.

"One day you're going to have to tell her what you do on these long business trips of yours." Lizbeth's wife, Caitlin, punched Landry lightly in the shoulder. "Take it from someone who knows—the woman never gives up."

"And *you're* damn glad I don't." Lizbeth released Landry, slipped her arm around Caitlin's waist, and kissed her softly.

"Are you letting her out to play?" Landry asked Lizbeth. She always had fun teasing them. When Landry met them three years ago, she'd quickly figured out who made most of the decisions. Caitlin was easygoing, and for the most part, would go along with anything Lizbeth wanted. It was a state of being in which Landry could never see herself, the thought of being tied down with a family of her own held no appeal. Her post-Pulsus plans didn't include restrictions or other people's wishes. Suiting herself had worked so far, and she saw no reason to change that approach as she grew older.

"Are you asking nicely?" Lizbeth looked at Landry the way she imagined she looked at Caitlin to capture her heart eleven years ago. If she didn't have strict rules about messing with a friend's wife, Landry would've happily spent a few days intimately discovering every dark contour of her shapely body.

"I always ask nicely." Landry's voice dropped to a husky whisper.

Caitlin cleared her throat loudly. "They've got a new point guard as well as a new coach—did you see the *Sports Illustrated* spread on her?"

Conscious of Priscilla's presence, Landry resisted responding with a sexually loaded retort. That, and Lizbeth had tilted her head in silent warning. "I've been away on business, not to the moon. And I have two courtside seats for precisely that reason. Block twenty-seven, right behind the team bench."

Caitlin's eyes widened, barely containing her excitement. "Beth? Can you and the boys handle tonight? We can call Josiah in. I know he's after extra shifts—"

"If you want to watch sweaty people running around all night, you should just work tonight. It's the Friday before Christmas. How quiet do you think we'll be?"

Landry was pretty sure Lizbeth was teasing and would acquiesce to her lover's pathetic plea when she'd groveled hard enough. "If you promise to do it in a tank and shorts, I might even forego the game."

Caitlin shoved Landry away. She stumbled back, holding her chest as if Caitlin had done damage. She scooped Priscilla up in her arms and lofted her high above her head. The little girl giggled.

It obviously gave Caitlin an idea. "Landry and I will decorate Priscilla's room ready for Christmas."

"Lan Lan make my room all pretty?"

She stretched her arms and pushed Priscilla higher, making her squeal in delight. "Sure." As she let her down, Priscilla latched onto her neck and squeezed as tightly as her small arms would allow.

"She suits you."

Landry shook her head at Lizbeth's attempted teasing and her glaring delay of a decision on the game. "I'll leave populating the world to more responsible adults like you two, thank you very much." Finding a long-term partner wasn't on Landry's to-do list. Having a baby wasn't even in the same stratosphere as her to-do list.

"Seriously, Beth. Can I go?"

"Of course you can, baby. I let Josiah know he was needed tonight the moment I saw Landry coming around the corner."

Landry laughed. "The games you girls play."

"Our games have got nothing on you, Landry."

Lizbeth gave Landry *that* look again. *Time for a cold shower.*

CHAPTER SIX

December 20, 2075—Mainland, San Francisco

Sitting in traffic on game night was part of the fun, but Landry's mind was on other things. She'd let Caitlin drive, partly because Caitlin had begged to get behind the wheel of Landry's Mustang, but mostly so she could concentrate on what was niggling at her. When she answered her phone this morning, Delaney had said "*You shouldn't be home*." It seemed a strange thing to say, but she'd dismissed it at the time, and taken it as her calling on the slim chance Landry might be available for coffee. *But she knows better. She knows I leave the island by nine a.m. after every mission.* Maybe Delaney had thought Landry would sleep in because of her massive patch-up. Maybe she was just checking up on her, given that she'd almost died pre-jump. There were too many maybes for it to be comfortable. It seemed like Delaney was drinking more and engaging less. Other colleagues told Landry they barely saw her while she was on vacation, and Landry knew it was because she was holed up in her apartment working her way through a crate of Widow Jane. Alcohol wasn't illegal, but most people had simply outgrown it. They'd found other, less damaging ways of dealing with their lives, like transposition booths where people exchanged their realities with movie stars, surgeons, or sex workers, where one person's life was another's escape.

They'd started having some rough release sex before the end of Landry's first year with Pulsus. It was like buddies working out, easing some of the boredom of the pre-mission training but with the added bonus of an orgasm. There was no emotion to it, for either of them, and that's why Landry never slept there. Their sex served a purpose, and it was easy. The last time they'd fucked though, Delaney experimented with some tenderness, and Landry made it clear she didn't appreciate it. That's not what they were supposed to be about, and maybe that's why Delaney wanted coffee, to clear the air and get back on track. At least that's what Landry was hoping.

Then there was the mistake with the big guy. That felt dangerously like weakness. Too much compassion—her mom being around had taken the edge from her anger. *But do I have to be angry to do my job properly?*

"Hey, are you okay?"

Caitlin's voice pulled her from her thoughts. "Sure, why?"

"Seems like you're not really here yet—still working in your head?"

Caitlin never pushed about Landry's work. After she'd intervened with the trouble Caitlin was having one night, it was like Caitlin had decided that whatever it was Landry did do, it was probably best that they didn't know. Could be that she liked the mystery of the woman living above their restaurant, so they could speculate about all the possibilities. CIA agent. Bank robber. Assassin. She knew that Caitlin was glad she'd been around that night and that her particular set of skills had probably saved her life.

"I guess I must be." Landry pushed back in her plush leather seat, stretched out her arms to the dashboard, and cracked her knuckles. *Let it go. I'm on vacation.* "Get me in the here and now. Tell me how the business is going. What magnificent recipes has your beautiful wife created since I've been gone?"

"She's working on a special dessert for Christmas. I've not been allowed to taste it yet, and she says she's on her fifth iteration. I'm kinda glad I don't have to try them all, or I'd end up the size of a house." Caitlin kept her eyes fixed on the road as she spoke. "We've been busy too. We've had to hire more than the usual temp Christmas staff. Seems like the neighborhood is getting more chic by the day. I keep expecting our landlord to raise the rent any minute. He should be asking for far more than we pay—the art gallery in the building next door pays four times what we pay for half the space. We haven't had a rent increase in two years."

Landry lowered the window to breathe in some brisk winter air. Caitlin had no idea she was the owner of their building. "What're you complaining about? Higher profits? You need all the money you can get your hands on so Priscilla can go to college. And it wouldn't hurt for you to go on a family vacation a little more often than you do. You have to enjoy your family while they're around."

Caitlin's puzzled look told Landry she'd said too much. She wasn't used to her dropping personal information so readily, and Landry heard the regret in her own voice. Caitlin would've been stupid to miss it. She was far from stupid. Landry's dad was heavily in her thoughts today.

"Jesus, Lan, you're making me want to turn the car around and go home to them right now."

Landry laughed. "Sorry, Cait, just reminding you life can be all too short."

"Don't I know that? Fuck, if you hadn't been around that night..." Caitlin's voice trailed off into silence.

"But I was." Landry noticed the tears forming in the corner of Caitlin's right eye and nudged her in the ribs. A change of tone was needed. "It all ended well. I hooked up with that hot SFPD officer—she was filthy."

Landry raised her eyebrows suggestively, and Caitlin grinned.

"You never did tell me what happened with her."

"You never asked. Besides, you've got enough excitement in your life with Lizbeth. You don't need to hear about my sex life."

"I don't *need* to, I just want to. I've always wanted to have sex with a cop. Did she use her handcuffs? Did she stay in her uniform? How was she filthy?"

Landry closed her eyes to recall the night they'd spent together. Her memories were movies in her head that she could recollect at will. With all that she had to do in her job, her sense of self and her vacation memories were vitally important.

"She was out of her uniform before we got past the hall. There's something incredibly arousing about a woman who's as comfortable naked as she was. Made me weak." Landry smiled as she pictured Officer Sanchez: five feet four inches, perfect hourglass figure with a nice full ass. "She took her time undressing me." Landry stopped abruptly. "Is this weird? This is weird. I feel like I'm telling you a dirty bedtime story to help you sleep."

"Damn right this'll help me sleep." Caitlin swung the car into a space, switched off the Mustang's throbbing engine, and turned to face Landry. "Go on, I'm living vicariously."

Landry released her seat belt and got out of the car. Caitlin was quickly beside her and handed Landry the key card.

"I don't trust myself not to lose it."

Landry slipped the small metal card into the breast pocket of her leather jacket. "Sure."

"So, you were saying…"

"She asked me to leave my boots and jeans on while I fucked her. She was wild, wanted it harder than I thought her delicate frame would take. And she was a screamer." Landry paused as they entered the arena and joined the line to go through security.

"You can't leave it there!"

Landry pointed to the young family in front of them. Mom, dad, and a boy who looked about eight.

"Kid's gotta learn. Who better than from you?"

"Really? So I'll be the one teaching Priscilla how to treat the ladies, will I?" Landry knew she was no role model. She was always up-front and honest about her lack of availability beyond the one night, but it wasn't the life she imagined they wanted for Priscilla.

"You might be the one she comes to if she's having trouble getting hold of one."

Landry laughed. It was nice that Caitlin saw her being involved with their little family in the decades to come. She was as settled as she'd ever been and had no plans to leave Pulsus or San Francisco. Coupled with her job security and exceptional health benefits, barring any more close calls like yesterday, it was an easy promise. Not that she'd ever say it out loud, of course. On the one occasion she made her father promise to return safely and always be there, he'd stepped on an IED and never returned. Just in case it might happen again, Landry didn't make promises to stick around. She knew it was fallacious logic, but other than this cute trio she'd been adopted by, she didn't really need to apply it.

After security, they picked up game snacks and drinks before taking up their spots courtside just in time for the pre-game dap. The Warriors came onto the floor in a flurry, with their new player, Jade Carter, nestled inside the group for the big reveal. Landry enjoyed this almost as much as the game itself. It was something the players did before the cameras went on so you could only see it live at the game, and it was all about the chemistry in the team. They parted for a flawless execution of kick-ass Brazilian martial arts, which ended with Carter running toward one of her teammates, being propelled into the air, and performing a double backward somersault. The home crowd rose to their feet and erupted into ecstatic applause.

"That's what I call an introduction!" Landry was on her feet with the rest of the appreciative fans.

The team hit their warm-up drills hard, and Carter was quick to show her skills, swishing three-pointers and sinking shots in the paint with ease. The Warriors had got themselves one hell of a point guard. There was also the added bonus of her being extremely hot. Her dark, shoulder-length hair was pulled back in a tight ponytail, allowing Landry to fully appreciate her olive skin, slender jawline, and model-like cheekbones. She was five feet eight, and with her sleek, lightly muscled physique, Landry estimated she was around 140 pounds. Carter was built for speed and agility, and she danced around the other players like their feet were cemented to the court. The way she finessed the ball, either to other players or to shoot, had Landry imagining those hands on her body.

"I don't remember if that article mentioned which team Carter played for, do you?"

"I'm pretty sure she came from the Knicks. I hear she wasn't impressed with the new megabucks owner wanting to make the coach's decisions," Caitlin replied, looking so serious that Landry shook her head and laughed.

"Not which basketball team, goofball! As in, who she likes to share a bed with?"

"See what happens when you're not around for two months? No one else I know talks like that. All I get is polite conversation about food and babies. It's not my fault it takes me a moment to readjust to adult conversation."

"Aw, poor married wifey. So?"

"You want to take a shot at the new MVP? How do you plan to do that?"

"That depends on your answer. If she's straight, my play will be different than if she's not." Landry winked, pulled out her phone, and Googled *Jade Carter gay or straight?* In her periphery, she saw the Lakers on a fast break. Their number twenty-seven peeled down the right flank and tossed a baseball pass toward her power forward. Carter flew in from nowhere and swatted at the ball viciously. She connected and it propelled toward the crowd—toward Landry. She slipped her phone to one hand and caught the ball in her right hand.

"Nice pickup. Wanna come down here and play?"

Landry looked up to see Jade Carter no more than five feet away. The big screen displayed a close-up of the two of them. Caitlin's mouth was open wide enough to have caught the ball in it herself.

"With you or the rest of the team?" *What the hell, this was quicker than Google on Li-Fi.*

Carter's full lips parted in a knowing smile, and she raised her eyebrows, perhaps acknowledging Landry's brazen approach. "How about the team now and me later?"

"The ball!"

The crew chief's shouting broke their gaze, and Landry was once again aware of over 36,000 pairs of eyes on her. She tossed the ball across to Jade. "I'll be here if *you're* game."

Jade returned Landry's challenge with a smile brighter than the arena lights and ten times as hot as their 1000-watt bulbs. She nodded slowly, turned back to the game, and jogged away.

"Now that's what I call an introduction."

Chapter Seven

December 20, 2075—Pulsus Island

Hitting the gym wasn't as satisfying as hard sex with Landry, but it was one of the things that kept Delaney sane between missions. Her fellow operative, Dani Simson, was a good training partner. She kept her focused and pushed Delaney beyond her limits. After one of their three-hour sessions, it wasn't unusual to be barely able to move.

"Your girlfriend left you all alone again?"

"Fuck you, Simson." Delaney pushed the weighted bar up and rested it on the pegs of the Smith machine.

"I wish you would. You know I'm not a big fan of your slavish monogamy to a woman who barely knows you exist."

They switched positions, and Delaney sank onto a flat weight bench, while Simson added another twenty-pound disk to each end of the bar.

"You sound jealous." Delaney was teasing. She and Simson had hooked up on many occasions before Landry got into her bed, and later, her head.

Simson was too concentrated on her breathing to respond immediately, but Delaney knew some pithy remark would be coming shortly. She watched her strong body propel the bar up before squatting down. The muscles in her legs were beautifully defined. She was bulkier than Landry. She was a certain kind of soldier they only sent on certain missions, ones where heads needed crushing to get the job done. Delaney thought she was an underused asset. She had brains too, but when she joined Pulsus, she told Delaney she was happy being an operative, a foot soldier who followed orders. She had no ambition or desire to become an extractor, the one everyone looked to for the big decisions, to lead the mission. She simply didn't want the responsibility.

"Jealous? It's your loss if you want to save yourself for your extractor and not have any fun while she's away. It's not like you're even a regular thing when she is around."

Delaney moved beneath the bar, stood up, and let the weight sit on her shoulders. She pushed up on her toes and stretched out her calves. "I'm not saving myself." Delaney wasn't sure if that were true or not. If Landry could go out and fuck anything that moved on the mainland, maybe Delaney should go back to Simson. She was warm and willing, and it was better than spending another night with a bottle of Widow Jane for company. *Fuck it.* "What are you doing for the rest of the day?"

Simson grinned, stood up, and pressed her body to Delaney's. "You."

❖

Delaney had forgotten how sexually aggressive Simson was. They'd only just started their workout, and she spent the next two hours as close to Delaney as she could get without messing with her form on the reps. Delaney could see one of the gym rat trainers desperate to intervene and maybe tell Simson to take a cold shower, but she had around fifty pounds of muscle on him, and Delaney didn't think he fancied his chances.

She had to admit though, it was nice to be wanted this much. Raw, intense sex was what she'd enjoyed with Simson before Landry. Fucking just for the sake of it, not for love, or emotion, or to prove anything to anyone. Sex with no strings, the way she used to do it.

It was Delaney who cut the workout short, knowing she couldn't keep the right side of respectable behavior much longer. They'd skipped the gym showers and jogged straight to Simson's place. Another refreshing change, fucking somewhere other than her own bed.

"God, Delaney, I've missed your hard body against me." Simson shoved Delaney against the outside wall of her house and used her other hand to gain access via fingerprint recognition. She grabbed a handful of her sweaty workout tank and pulled her into the house.

"I'd forgotten how rough you are." Delaney stumbled in before she steadied herself against the oak dining table in the open plan living space.

"Have you gone soft, soldier? That sounded dangerously like a complaint." Simson covered the ground between them in three long, purposeful strides. She took Delaney's tank in two hands and ripped it open to the hem. She grasped hold of her neck in one hand and pressed her other over Delaney's muscled pecs, forcing her back onto the table. "Was it?" She leaned over and tweaked her nipple hard.

Delaney hissed in pain. "I'm not complaining." She craned her neck forward to kiss Simson, but she pulled away, not allowing the contact.

She laughed at the attempt. "You don't get to kiss me."

She moved away from Delaney momentarily but only to flip her onto her front. The oak was hard and unforgiving, and Simson pressed herself forcefully against Delaney's body. She pulled the torn tank over Delaney's shoulders to her elbows and used the loose material to tie a knot in the small of her back, pulling her arms taut and powerless. Simson got up, and Delaney's hands snatched uselessly at the air behind her.

"You've got such a sweet ass, soldier. Have you kept it nice and tight for me?"

Delaney smirked, more to herself than Simson, since she couldn't see her face right now. It'd been a while since that particular hole had been breached. "You know how hard I work on my glutes."

Delaney jarred against the table when Simson smacked her ass. "That's not what I meant and you know it, smart mouth. Maybe after I've fucked this tight hole." She thrust the heel of her hand between Delaney's ass cheeks for an explicit demonstration of what she meant. "I'll show you what a mouth like yours is best used for."

Delaney sighed and felt herself melt against the table.

"I bet Donovan's not an ass girl, is she?" Simson pulled down Delaney's gym shorts and briefs in one movement. "Is that how you've stayed so tight for me?"

Delaney stiffened a little. She didn't want to think about Landry right now. "Don't—"

Simson pressed her weight against Delaney and sneered into her ear. "Don't what, soldier?" She pulled Delany's head back, sank her teeth into her exposed neck, and bit down hard.

Delaney shouted out in pain and struggled beneath her. "Don't talk about her. Just fuck me." Delaney pushed her ass back against Simson, and she laughed softly.

"Poor little soldier needs taking care of." Simson kicked Delaney's legs apart and forced her palm against Delaney's warm pussy. "You're soaked." She pressed harder. "Desperate for me." Her finger slipped tantalizingly over Delaney's slick clit. "Ask nicely."

Delaney took a deep breath. She loved this. Simson was her perfect foil. She knew exactly how she wanted to be taken. This sex was better than love. *It has to be*. "Please, fuck me. Fuck me hard." Delaney practically growled the words. She felt animalistic, she needed to have Landry fucked out of her system, and Simson was the only one who could do it.

She didn't need to ask again. Her thick, calloused fingers were inside Delaney before she finished the sentence. Her other hand gripped Delaney's bound wrists, and she held her down, not allowing her body room to respond. Slippery with Delaney's juices, Simson withdrew her fingers and glided them into her ass. Delaney groaned loudly as Simson picked up the pace and power, fucking her hard and fast like she knew Delaney loved. She released her wrists so Delaney could push back against her thrusting, and Delaney could hear her gentle, knowing laugh. She'd know she was giving Delaney what she needed. *And I don't need Landry.*

"That's right, soldier, ride me."

The combination of Simson's practiced rhythm and her dirty diatribe brought Delaney to the edge of her orgasm swiftly. She didn't know where this desire to occasionally be dominated came from. Could be it was something to do with her twisted upbringing. Or it could just be that her body responded to a damn hard fucking. Right now wasn't the time to analyze it. Right now was about enjoying the feeling of giving Simson complete control and celebrating it.

She let go, and as she came, Simson slipped the fingers of her other hand deep inside her.

"Oh fuck, yes."

Simson kept her tempo as Delaney rode her pleasure to its plateau. She pulled out of her and Delaney screamed in protest. "God no, don't stop."

Simson picked Delaney up, laid her on her back, and sank to her knees between her legs.

"I'm not stopping, soldier. We're on vacation. I've only just begun."

Chapter Eight

December 21, 2075—Mainland, San Francisco

Caitlin and Lizbeth had bought Priscilla a low-powered four-wheel bike so she could accompany them on their morning runs. They didn't serve breakfast at the restaurant, and Priscilla had no pre-school on the weekend, so Saturday morning was family time. Lizbeth had insisted on coming with Landry on the first morning run of her break. They could barely keep up with her, so she'd had to slow her pace some, but Priscilla's little bike meant she had no trouble staying alongside Landry.

Lizbeth's insistence was due to Priscilla being more enamored of Landry than usual. Even though Landry wasn't around all that much, the bond they'd formed felt like it was growing ever stronger. Lizbeth had convinced herself that Priscilla was developing faster than most kids her age and seemed ecstatic that her baby girl was forming bonds independent of her and Caitlin. Landry was baffled by her own connection with Priscilla. Her half brother, Michael, had twins and for some unfathomable reason, wanted her involved in their upbringing, but she had no interest in them at all. An early visit, which involved one of the boys peeing in her eye when she changed his diaper, had done nothing to endear them to her. So Landry expected to be a little unsettled by Priscilla's attachment, but it turned out she was more than comfortable with it.

"So what're your plans for Christmas? This is the first time in three years you've been home for it." Lizbeth decided it was rest time. She huddled on the best wooden bench in the Presidio, overlooking the Bay with a view of the very tip of the water tower on Alcatraz Island, though everything else had been submerged.

Landry took a moment to think before she responded. She hadn't expected to be able to have a real home with her new job when she'd bought the building. And yet, with each piece of furniture and art she purchased, it had started to feel less like a high-class hotel apartment, and more like, well, more like a home. It was somewhere she began to enjoy spending time, rather than viewing it as a base. And after every encounter with a new woman, she happily returned to her own bed, in her own comfortable surroundings. "I guess I hadn't figured that out yet." It was an honest answer. Time was so highly important and yet, of such irrelevance, that Landry *hadn't* given Christmas much thought. Her mom had laid a hefty guilt trip on her yesterday morning, and she had all but promised she'd join her and Jenkin for Christmas dinner. Landry hadn't quite accepted that they were now sleeping together. She wasn't sure she'd be able to stomach seeing someone being intimate with her mom. "*Your brother and his family will be there. Wouldn't it be nice if we could spend Christmas day together?*" Landry was slowly rediscovering the space in her heart where family had once resided, but her obnoxious half brother, irritating wife, and incontinent children were too much to stomach.

"Do you have…anyone?"

"Lizbeth."

Landry recognized Caitlin's attempt at a stern tone, and stifled a smile at the look she used to accompany it. Caitlin's effort at asserting what little authority she had was invariably lost on Lizbeth, and this time was no exception.

"What? I'm being delicate. She'll evade the question if she doesn't want to answer it, won't you, Landry?"

Landry nodded her affirmation of Lizbeth's astute assessment of the cat-and-mouse game they played when Lizbeth dug for personal information.

"So? Christmas? Family?"

"Christ, Lizbeth, maybe you should just leave her be sometimes."

"That's garbage, Cait. If I did that, we'd never know anything about our mysterious neighbor." Lizbeth wasn't to be dissuaded.

"Your lady has a point." Landry dropped to the floor in front of the bench and began a set of push-ups.

"My lady always has a point, and she often sticks me in the ass with it." Caitlin sat beside the shivering Lizbeth and pulled her in close. "I'm trying to help you maintain your shadowy secrets, and you're not helping."

"You make it sound like I'm secretly Wonder Woman."

Caitlin laughed and nudged Landry in the ribs with her foot. "She says, as she does twenty Superman push-ups without getting out of breath. You look like Wonder Woman."

"I don't have blue eyes or black hair."

"You're not an emissary to the world of Man either...although you do seem to be trying to get your particular message out to a lot of women, so maybe Caitlin's on to something."

Priscilla, who'd been amusing herself observing the squirrels, climbed onto Caitlin, and lay down across both of them. She smiled sweetly at Landry.

"You guys look like a Hallmark card."

"We model for them in our spare time. So, family? Christmas?"

"I haven't made any concrete plans yet. My mom wants me at her place." *Her place being on an island that no one knows about, where we're going quietly about saving the world, one person at a time.* "But I'm not interested in spending the day with my half brother and his ugly-ass family." *Or the inventor of the technology that sends me back in time to save said people.*

"Family's important, Landry. Even if they are annoying." Caitlin gently stroked Priscilla's hair away from her eye, and Lizbeth arched her eyebrow questioningly. "I'm lucky mine isn't," she added quickly to placate her.

"Garbage. If she doesn't want to be there, she shouldn't go out of some misplaced sense of loyalty."

Landry liked Lizbeth's take on the world. It was straightforward, forthright, and she took no shit.

Caitlin wasn't convinced. "What about a sense of belonging? Everyone needs roots somewhere."

"Baby, I love you. You know I do. But sometimes, you don't think before you start spouting. Where are my roots? Where do I belong?"

Landry knew Lizbeth was an orphan. She'd lived with twenty other parentless tykes in a children's home until she was sixteen. She was proud of what she'd achieved coming from her background, and rightly so. She shared her background freely and her profits—a portion of which helped to fund the same children's home she was raised in.

Caitlin looked suitably scolded and kissed Lizbeth's forehead. "I'm sorry, baby. I shoot my mouth off. Forgive me?"

Feeling slightly voyeuristic at the picture of family bliss, Landry dropped to the ground again for another set of push-ups. As she counted to forty, she heard feet pounding on the concrete. She looked backward beneath her to see the entire Warriors squad, led by Jade Carter, jogging toward them. She continued to fifty before rising to her feet. It wouldn't hurt for Jade to see what she'd missed out on by not coming back out on court after the game had finished.

Jade stopped a few feet from her, jogging on the spot while the rest of the team continued on. "This is a coincidence."

"Happy fates conspire." Landry tried nonchalance. Jade was incredibly hot, but she wasn't about to go fan-girl crazy over her. It was obvious why she hadn't come back out to the court last night, no doubt she had hundreds of women and men fawning all over her at every game.

"Sorry about last night. The girls hijacked me after cleanup to go celebrate the win."

She sounded genuine enough. *She didn't have to stop to talk.* "And your sixty-one-point game deserved celebrating." In her peripheral vision, she could see Caitlin gawping in much the same way as she had the previous evening.

"It's a team thing. I couldn't have scored that many without the girls around me playing out of their skin."

"Aren't you going to introduce us?" Lizbeth had extricated herself from beneath Priscilla and appeared beside Landry.

Before Landry could answer, Jade offered her hand. "I'm Jade."

"She's the Warriors' new player." Suddenly, Caitlin was alongside Lizbeth, with Priscilla in her arms.

"I can see that from the training gear. I'm Lizbeth. This is my wife, Caitlin, and our daughter, Priscilla."

High femme vibes radiated from Lizbeth as she claimed ownership of her little family, and Landry sensed her diving into protective mode.

"Your daughter's beautiful."

Priscilla looked away and nestled her face into Lizbeth's neck shyly.

"Thank you. So is our friend here." Lizbeth gestured to Landry. "And yet you still left her waiting like a fool."

Jade's eyes widened, and she looked a little taken aback by the brazen outburst.

"I was just explaining—"

"That you'd make it up to her by taking her to our restaurant tonight for dinner."

"Baby…" Caitlin looked mortified.

"I'm sorry. You'll have to excuse my friend. She and subtlety aren't particularly well acquainted." Landry stepped into the space between her and Jade, blocking the potential battlefield between Jade and Lizbeth.

Jade didn't miss a beat and sidestepped Landry to get a clear view of Lizbeth again. "What kind of restaurant do you run?"

"Vegetarian fusion. What kind of food do you like to eat?"

"I'll eat pretty much anything as long as it's well presented."

Caitlin and Landry exchanged exasperated glances. There was no stopping Lizbeth once she was in full flow, but it was nice to see Jade easily holding her ground.

"We've been a three-star Michelin establishment for the past two and a half years. Everything is exquisitely presented."

"And you're the head chef?"

Are you playing with her? Landry decided she'd ask Jade later, if this little dance didn't go disastrously wrong.

"I am. So you'll make up for your transgression *and* sample wonderful food at the same time."

It wasn't meant as a question. Jade glanced at Landry and smiled. Her teeth were as perfect as the rest of her. Landry's immediate visual had Jade nibbling her all over.

"I can't tonight, but I'm free on Monday."

Landry sighed. *This hookup is doomed never to materialize.* Lizbeth didn't open their restaurant on Mondays. But maybe that was a good thing, because Landry never brought women to their restaurant. For one, she didn't want to confuse Priscilla, and secondly, she didn't like anyone intruding on her life. The restaurant was her next place of sanctuary after her apartment. It was an extension of home.

"Shall we say seven?"

Landry kept her expression neutral. It didn't reveal the absolute shock at Lizbeth's apparent haste to matchmake. Nor did it hint at the slight panic of inviting a complete stranger into their neat but unusual family setup. She simply gave Jade a vaguely enticing look and half hoped she'd turn the invitation down. But she knew it was only a half hope.

"I have to be on the road for a game early the next morning, so I'll need an early night." She winked at Landry. "Could we say five?"

Landry liked what Jade was doing, but couldn't figure out if she was just messing with Lizbeth for fun, or if she was being honest. Either way, it was strange because ordinarily she could get a read on someone instantly. Consciously or otherwise, Jade was hard to read, and Landry's usually infallible profiling abilities were non-functional. She decided to put it down to being on vacation. Her mind was on vacation as well as her body, so she was letting her more base instincts run the show.

"Five will be fine. I'll cook up something healthy. I wouldn't want to slow you down for your game."

Lizbeth was looking at Jade, but Landry knew she might as well be talking to her. She certainly wasn't talking about Jade's basketball game.

"Yo, Carter!" The squad had circled back and were waiting a short distance away.

"I'd better go before they all freeze in their sneakers. Thank you for the…invite. I'm looking forward to tasting your cooking, Lizbeth." She turned to Landry. "Maybe you'll have more to say on Monday." She sprinted away before Landry could respond. It wasn't common for Landry not to have the last word in any encounter, physical or verbal. Jade had game and was so different from the women Landry usually entertained. She promised to be a very interesting conquest indeed.

Chapter Nine

December 23, 2075—Pulsus Island

Simson wasn't ugly. Plain would probably be the best way to describe her. Which was often useful on missions, as she blended in easily and didn't garner attention. She and Delaney had worked plenty of assignments together, and Simson always did whatever was needed *before* it was needed. She made Delaney feel safe. She was six feet tall, 180 pounds, and had been a champion in mixed martial arts before she'd done four tours with the army. Which was why her second duty at Pulsus was to train the extractors and operatives to fight.

Given that most of the recruits were from the services, they came in with some hand-to-hand combat skills. But the way wars were fought now meant they were rusty and underused, just another basic training unit. With the work Pulsus did, they needed the techniques Simson taught. And she had a very unique way of teaching, which was primarily kicking the shit out of each student until they could adequately defend themselves. In addition to doing that, she'd set mismatched pairs against each other. Big against small, no matter the gender. Sometimes, she'd ask a trained operative to step into the ring with her for an exhibition bout. When Delaney had sparred with her, Simson got so turned on that they'd fucked on the mats after everyone had left.

Today, she was finishing the training session pulverizing some fresh meat, an ex-Navy JAG Delaney recognized from their latest induction. Simson's crisp, white tank was already sprayed with his blood. He was a judgment jockey with a hot reputation, and Jenkin had pulled him in for an extractor position. He was just the sort of rookie Simson liked to make an example of by putting a hard beating on them to yank them down from any lofty position they had a misplaced sense of entitlement to.

Simson acknowledged Delaney, and the JAG tried to use the distraction to his advantage. His lunge was clumsy, and she evaded it easily, bringing her elbow down on his back. He crumpled to the floor, and she powered her boot into his stomach, sending him skidding into the ropes. Simson stalked across the ring and tugged him up by a handful of his hair before driving some khao chiang strikes into his ribs. He jerked around like a puppet on a string until she tossed him effortlessly across the canvas.

"You." Simson pointed to a strong-looking woman at one of the ring corners. "Get in here."

She swiftly did as instructed and cautiously approached Simson, who pulled off her gloves and strapped them onto the woman's hands.

"Show us what you've got. Finish him off then dismiss the class." Simson motioned to the JAG, who was getting to his feet with the help of the ropes and a fellow recruit.

The woman nodded and strode across to him. She waited until he was completely upright, holding on to the ropes for support, before she let loose with a flurry of punches to his body and face.

"She'll go far," Delaney said, passing Simson a towel to wipe the blood and sweat from her upper body.

"Yeah, you're right. She's got that killer instinct, doesn't ask questions, and just gets on with whatever you ask her to. She'll make a great operative."

"I've always wanted to know—are you harder on the extractors?"

Simson threw the towel at Delaney's head and laughed. "Of course I am. All of 'em come in here thinking they own the place just 'cause they've been headhunted for the extractor position. And besides, they're the ones responsible for the whole team when they start running missions. It's my responsibility to make sure they're ready for that."

Simson turned to walk out, and as she took Delaney's arm to follow her, Delaney saw the JAG fall to the floor, out cold. His conqueror began her parade around the ring, and the rest of the students whooped and hollered.

"Your girl could always hold her own though. Top of the class. I never got to putting a real beating on her, and I kinda regret that."

Delaney winced at Simson's phrasing. *If only she was my girl.* She pushed the intrusive thought away and tried to concentrate on the woman she was with, right now. "That's why she gets paid the big bucks."

"What does she do with all that money anyway? She's never here on vacation time. Does she hit the casinos hard? Is she a gambler?"

Delaney got into her car and waited for Simson to join her. "She's got property on the mainland. She wants to live as normal a life as possible outside Pulsus when she can." Delaney automatically trotted out the same shit Landry had given her when she'd asked the same question. *What the fuck was a normal life anyhow?*

"Yeah? Does she have a *normal* woman on the mainland too?"

Delaney clenched her teeth, started the car, and pulled off. She knew Simson wanted to know if Delaney was in love with Landry, but Delaney wasn't about to give that kind of information up. "Not that I know of. She likes variety, and I don't see her settling down while she works here. I mean, how do you even begin to explain the prolonged absences without contact? You couldn't even lie and say you were in the military. There's working away from home for a while, and then there's what we do."

"I'd get that if Donovan was an operative, we can be away for years, but extractors are off-grid far less time than us."

"It's still time away without being able to speak to her or see her. There's no job on Earth you can blame for that. Then you've got the things she sometimes has to do on the job, with other women, and who's gonna put up with that shit?"

"So she keeps it simple by having you as her fuck buddy on work time and fucking whoever she wants on the mainland when she doesn't need you."

Simson slid her hand across Delaney's thigh and squeezed her crotch. Delaney lifted her ass from the chair and shifted slightly, adjusting the seam of her jeans to a more comfortable position.

"I guess that's how she works." *That's exactly how she fucking works*. "Why are you so interested in Donovan anyway? Do you want her to fuck you?" Delaney decided to deflect the conversation to Simson, knowing that she would never entertain the notion.

She laughed raucously. "You know better, Delaney. I'm the one who does the fucking."

"Which is why we won't ever work."

"And yet, you're here today, back for more."

"You're a cocky cunt."

"And you're asking for it."

There was a short silence before they both laughed. "Bar?"

"Sure. Just swing by my place for a five-minute cleanup and—"

"A shave?"

Simson punched her arm hard enough to make Delaney swerve into the other lane.

"Did you not see what I did to that guy in the ring just now?"

Delaney smirked. "Please. That's your idea of foreplay."

Rik's Place was the only bar on the island to get alcohol in a social setting. The myriad other haunts only served smoothies, fancy frothy coffees, and herbal teas. Jenkin said she'd cater to what her employees wanted, and most of them wanted the soft stuff. At least she'd shown her sense of humor when she named this place, because there was no Rik behind the bar serving the parched patrons. This was self-serve at its best—flash the card and take the liquor. Just a few battle-hardened operatives frequented this spot and indulged in the wide range of age-old bourbons that lined the shelves. Simson had sprung for an eighty-one-year-old bottle of Jefferson's Presidential Select, and they sat in a booth toward the back of the bar, away from the one other habitué, with a bucket of ice and two chunky glasses.

Delaney had barely slept. Nightmares of her last mission were still vivid, and though she drank till she passed out, her memories refused to be dulled. Even a full day and night of rough sex with Simson had done little to give her sleeping brain something else to focus on. She'd hoped to be so exhausted from sex and the gym that the deep white matter responsible for her dreams couldn't possibly summon the energy to re-create intense movie-like scenes while she slept.

The only escape was to keep herself conscious, and in her sleep-deprived state, she'd drifted into considering the nature of the work they did at Pulsus. That hadn't led her to satisfying places either.

"You look like shit, Jaq. Couldn't sleep because I wasn't there holding you tight?"

Delaney emptied her glass and slid it across the table for a refill. "You know better than to call me that, *Sandra*." She caught the glass Simson pushed back at her, this time filled with a more generous shot.

"I should kick your ass for that."

"You should, but you know you can't. Don't make me ruin your reputation by putting you down." Delaney could see from Simson's puzzled look that she didn't know whether Delaney was joking. Just like Landry, she came into Pulsus more than able to handle herself, and she'd been able to handle Simson's training with ease. Neither she nor Landry were as big as Simson, but they were faster, high on stamina, and almost as powerful. Delaney liked rough sex with Simson, but she allowed her to be top because sometimes that's what she needed. Sleep deprivation though, impacted on her tolerance of Simson's sense of humor. They were both operatives, but their rank from previous military stations stayed with them, and being a colonel, Delaney outranked Master Sergeant Simson. When Delaney got serious, Simson quickly dropped her playfulness and assumed a far more intense persona.

"What's wrong, Delaney?"

"I'm not sure you want to know. We should just drink." Delaney downed the second glass in two swallows, and Simson topped it up again.

Delaney knew she could trust her. She trusted Simson with her life. Though they hadn't done every mission together, they'd teamed up for more than seventy years in the field. And in that time, Simson had proven herself again and again to be the soldier Delaney would always want beside her in the heat of battle.

But the things in her brain that were demanding to be heard. Delaney wasn't totally sure Simson would be interested in hearing. *I'm not sure I want to hear them either.*

"Jesus, Delaney, if you can't tell me, who can you tell?"

Delaney rolled the glass in her hands, studying the saffron colored liquid contained within, and contemplating what she'd gain by sharing her thoughts. She put the glass down, pulled the soft pack of Camel Lights from her cargo pants, and lit one with the Zippo Simson had brought back from one of their missions. It was the same Zippo that saved Delaney's life, stopping a bullet from a Chicom in a mission in Laos. Despite the hefty dent, it still worked perfectly.

"We're soldiers, Simms. Some stuff we just deal with and keep inside, where it belongs, y'know?"

"I get that, I do. But…I'm not sure you're dealing with whatever's going on. We've always liked to drink. It's always been our way of coping. But lately…"

Simson didn't finish her sentence. She didn't have to. Delaney knew exactly what she meant. Other than Landry, she was her closest friend at Pulsus, and right now, she couldn't talk to Landry about anything. Simson would have to have been blind not to recognize Delaney heading down a dangerous path. Trouble was, even though Delaney knew it herself, she had no idea how to stop it. Moreover, she didn't know how to handle the root cause of her over-reliance on the bottle, and it was beginning to consume her. She knew she needed to refocus her energies and reconcile her escapades.

"We're at war, aren't we?" Delaney spoke slowly and chose her words carefully. She needed to feel safe and know that Simson could get on the same page as her, but smacking her upside the head with the book wasn't the best way to go.

Simson's brow furrowed, indicating she was considering Delaney's interpretation of their work. "You could say that. No one else but us knows it, so it's pretty one-sided. But yeah, I see what you're saying. What about it?"

"And we do things…" Delaney glanced out the window and winced at the normalcy of their bubble of an island. People walking their dogs, jogging on the park track strangely placed next to the bar, workers collecting the trash. She lifted her glass but sipped at it this time. No matter how much she trusted Simson, she didn't want to be blind drunk when she was peeling open her brain for inspection. "Bad things, in the name of that war, because we believe what we're trying to achieve is morally right."

"The end justifies the means, yeah?"

"This isn't a normal war though. It's not government led. It's not supported by our nation, by any nation."

"Don't you think that makes it purer? Undiluted by politics and not muddied by agendas."

Delaney lifted her glass to her forehead and let the ice-cold droplets of condensation sooth her aching head. She filled the long silence with several draws on her cigarette and watched the smoke curl toward the open window.

"You follow orders. Do you ever actually think about them?" Delaney decided on a different tack. She didn't want to freak Simson out.

"Let's be clear. I follow orders until there are better orders. Or ones that make more sense. I don't follow blindly, if that's what you're getting at. I believe in what we do, but I don't necessarily like how we get there. Are you having trouble with some of the shit we're expected to carry out before the extractors come and save the day?"

"Do you think our focus might be too narrow?"

"I'm not getting you. Do you think we don't do enough on our missions?"

Crunch time. "No, not us. The board."

"Go on."

Simson hunched forward, reduced the space between them, and shifted her drink out of the way.

"What we've been doing for the past three years, it was a good start. They got their toes wet, and they've had time to iron out the kinks. But I think the board is too frightened to really do what needs to be done, what could be done." Delaney paused and finished her drink again. The flavor reminded her of the pecan pie her grandma used to bake whenever her mom left her there to get her out of the way of her drunken father. She ate a lot of pecan pie.

"What needs to be done?"

It was the question Delaney was waiting for. It was evidence that Simson was open to Delaney's point of view. "They should widen their focus. Instead of helping a few good people, why don't we take out the criminals, the evildoers, and the terrorists?"

"Won't that change too many things?"

"So what if it does? Surely that can't be any worse than leaving these people in play to decimate and destroy? Look at our next mission—we're going to Nazi Germany to save a doctor who was on her way to curing cancer. That will save millions of lives, I know that, but what if we went a few years further back? What if we just went back and executed Hitler? We still save Dr. Cancer Cure, but we also save the one hundred million others that died during that conflict." Delaney had become more animated as she laid out how she believed Pulsus should be developing. As she spoke, she could see Simson being pulled in, and why shouldn't she? It made complete sense.

"Why have all this power and use only a fraction of it?"

"Yes!" Delaney reached across the table and thumped Simson on the shoulder. "The board is too scared to make big changes for fear of the repercussions. But that's shortsighted. What they should be doing is making the big decisions and affecting big outcomes. We should get back from those missions, and let the board assess the changes to figure out new missions. With the technology they have at their disposal, what could possibly go wrong?"

Chapter Ten

December 23, 2075—Mainland, San Francisco

Five o'clock was two hours away. Landry wondered if Jade would show, given that she was pushed into it by Lizbeth rather than receiving a cordial invitation. Maybe she was too polite to turn her down or too chickenshit to say no to a woman like Lizbeth. Not that Landry would blame her for that, because Lizbeth hadn't come across as particularly friendly when she threw out the summons to her restaurant.

Landry had just returned from a solo run in Golden Gate Park. It'd brought back memories of her mission to San Francisco in 1978 to save the rising politician Harvey Milk from being assassinated. He went on to become mayor and brought the gay rights movement forward nearly forty years, with San Francisco being the first city to marry two guys in 1981. To get close to Dan White, Milk's would-be executioner, she'd spent time jogging the park with his wife, Mary Ann. Now, Sunset Boulevard was the park's new border to the Pacific Ocean. Visiting the past mostly made her glad of the future, but occasionally, it made her melancholy. Some things Pulsus hadn't managed to modify. Despite their continuous search, they'd still not figured out if someone in the past was on their way to solving global warming. No one in the present was anywhere near it still.

The hot shower washed away her light sorrow, but that was replaced by a bad case of nervous tension creeping across her shoulders and into her neck. After Jade had sprinted off to rejoin her team on

Saturday, Landry asked Lizbeth what the fuck she thought she was doing. Of course, she didn't swear because the angelic Priscilla was staring at her, clearly puzzled by whatever it was the *big people* had been up to. Landry didn't bring women back to her apartment, and she never entertained them downstairs in Lizbeth and Caitlin's restaurant. Landry tolerated Lizbeth's near-constant curiosity, but she'd pushed it too far with this stunt, and Landry was far from impressed.

"*I've got a good feeling about this one.*" Lizbeth was remorseless for her intrusive intervention.

"*This one? You've never met any of the others. How can you possibly know if she's any different?*"

"*You were different.*"

Not wanting to argue further in front of Priscilla, she'd sprinted off in the opposite direction from Jade, at a pace none of them would've been able to keep. Lizbeth's words were a constant refrain in her head. *How was I different?* She'd tried to ignore it and put it down to Lizbeth's blatant attempt to get her to settle down and have a nice family life. As if that's what everyone in the world needed, to find a nice woman and put down roots. All the world's evils would be resolved if everyone just fell in love. It was such stereotypical bullshit, from a nation obsessed with the perfect family of two parents and one flawless child. As long as both parents were adding to the economy, all was well with the world. Landry had more important things to do than contribute to capitalism, like saving the world one person at a time.

She sat on the marble bench in the wet room and covered her legs in shaving foam. It was the same ritual for every night out. Landry liked to be perfectly smooth, almost everywhere. She always left a tidy rise of dark hair between her legs but shaved the rest. She'd once slipped and ended up having to shave it all off rather than look uneven. It was an instant regret. She would've rather been uneven than feel like a pre-pubescent child. She'd often wondered how some women managed to make it look sexy. It was the same with a shaved head. Some women could carry it; others just looked like cancer patients.

While washing her hair, Landry was trying to decide whether she needed a haircut. Her bangs were falling over her left eye, and the back was beginning to reach down to the chain around her neck. She liked her neck naked, loved the feeling of a woman's hand wrapped around it as she fucked them, and the feeling of the sun beating down on it as she ran. Longer hair just made her feel…overheated and sluggish. She didn't know how it might need to be for the next mission Delaney had emailed her about, and she wasn't going to start thinking about it yet, so she'd ignored it. Delaney would understand why she didn't reply. They were close friends, but Landry preferred her two worlds to be kept entirely distant from each other, and Delaney was very much part of Pulsus.

Landry stepped out of the wet room and into the walk-in closet at the back of her master bedroom, then looked at her reflection in the full-length mirrors. She twisted this way and that, inspecting every inch of her body. She sought physical perfection and was happy with where she was right now. Between the training and the missions, the exercise, and the women on vacations, she'd carved the shape she wanted. And she loved the power and strength that came with it. As a child, she'd been skinny and suffered as a result. When her mom had been attacked and killed, she resolved never to be the weakest or smallest again, and set about building the figure she now appreciated. The figure other women also fully appreciated. There was nothing like that gasp of surprise from a woman when Landry picked her up and carried her to the bed, or the table, or the sofa.

She let herself air-dry while she brushed and flossed her teeth. She'd been paranoid about bad breath since a would-be boyfriend told the whole class her mouth reeked like a sewer because she had braces. A sixty-second mouthwash completed the routine, and she ran her tongue across her teeth, relishing the clean, ivory-like feel.

She sprayed her favorite scent, True Religion's Hustler, on her chest, stomach, and wrists before pulling on a pair of black Calvin Klein bikini briefs with a thick navy band and a matching black cotton bra. *T-shirt casual, smart casual, or evening smart?* Time for the all-important outfit decision. The girls didn't impose a dress code at their restaurant, La Azucarera, but Landry was old-fashioned about eating out, something she got from her father. She remembered he was always impeccably turned out whenever he wasn't on tour and took her mom on their weekly date night. Landry wondered what Jade would be wearing. So far, she'd only seen her in her team uniform and had no idea what kind of style she had. Landry had no doubt that whatever it was, she'd rock it. Jade's body was in beautiful shape, and Landry couldn't wait to explore it. She'd reconciled that it might not be tonight, given that Jade had an away match tomorrow. Landry shook her head. It was strange for her to be thinking about seeing Jade again before they'd met this evening. Maybe Lizbeth was right; maybe there was something different.

She ran her hand along the extensive selection of color-ordered, button-down shirts, enjoying the soft feeling beneath her fingers. She settled on the plain apple red and slipped it on. She could already imagine Jade slowly unbuttoning it. Landry picked out her snug black True Religion's and pulled them on, tucked her shirt in, and zipped them up. She went for a plain black belt and inspected her buckle drawer carefully before deciding on the round double snake design. She folded her sleeves halfway up her forearm, just enough so that half of her tattoo could be seen. It was an old play, but it usually worked. Women always wanted to see the rest of it, and she'd tell them the only way that could happen was to take her shirt off altogether. Landry smiled at her own cheesy lines. Her job was so serious that being this flippant in her personal life was both a necessity and a welcome relief. She completed the ensemble with chunky heeled boots, before looking over her watch drawer. She decided that the occasion merited wearing her favorite, the Audemars Piguet with the black rubber band. It was a gift from her mom when she returned from the mission that rescued her. She remembered her mom had bought her father an earlier model, and that he never wore due to its expense. Landry wasn't going to make the same mistake, but it was only for special circumstances, and tonight was that. Jade was a high-earning basketball player—Landry didn't want to look out of her league sporting a Casio.

It was 4:45 p.m. Enough time to fix her hair before heading downstairs to see if Jade would even show up.

Jade was already waiting at the bar when Landry came in. "How is it that you live upstairs, and I still made it here before you?"

Landry glared at Lizbeth, who was standing beside Jade looking delightful in her crisp, white chef's uniform. Caitlin, stationed behind the bar, shrugged at Landry in sympathetic apology.

"Is nothing sacred, Lizbeth?"

"Plenty. I can only tell what I know, and you haven't given us that much to go on in the past three years, so it's been a pretty short conversation thus far." Lizbeth flashed a look that meant she could do anything she wanted and be forgiven immediately.

Despite wanting to stay mad at her, Landry couldn't help but smile. "Damn, woman, someday soon you're gonna do something that I won't excuse."

Caitlin coughed loudly. "The usual, Landry?"

She nodded. Her usual was acai berry vodka over ice, drowned in Cherry Coke. Jade was holding on to a half full glass of blood red and orange liquid, which Landry figured was probably non-alcoholic. "Sex on the beach?"

"Isn't it a little cold for that? I don't think the coach would be impressed if I turned up sick."

Jade's left eyebrow twitched suggestively, and something much lower on Landry's body twitched in response. "I was talking about your drink…"

"Of course you were."

Lizbeth smiled conspiratorially at Landry. "I'll head back to the kitchen and let you get on with your apology, Jade. Caitlin will show you to your table." Lizbeth disappeared into the kitchen, and Caitlin began to come around from the bar.

"Don't worry, Cait—the window table on the mezzanine, yeah?" Landry asked without thinking. It was the best table in the restaurant and the one she always ate at. She suddenly thought it might be best to sit somewhere else. Jade was already in one of her refuges.

Caitlin tilted her head to the side, obviously thinking along the same lines. "Sure. The chef is cooking you something special off menu, so in the meantime, I'll just keep topping up your drinks."

"Thanks, Cait." Landry turned and gestured to the floating steps in the center of the room. "After you."

Jade shook her head. "You lead the way."

There was a half beat pause before Landry moved. She was hoping to get a nice view of Jade's ass as she scaled the stairs. Jade obviously had the same idea. "Are you that desperate to check out my butt?"

"What do you think?"

Landry held Jade's gaze for a moment before looking away. Jade's eyes were the color of a blue-gray agate, and her intense look somehow rendered Landry a little off-balance.

She walked up the steps, slow enough to give Jade the show she was after, but not too slow that she was milking it. It felt a little odd, and Landry wondered if Jade was just as predatory as she was.

Landry headed to the table and pulled out a chair for Jade. She walked beyond it, pulled out her own chair, and sat down.

"So you saved Caitlin's life?"

Landry sat down, took a slow drink, and placed her glass on the table. "Is that what she told you?"

"It's what Lizbeth told me. You're quite the hero in their eyes." Jade waited for more information.

"You would've done the same thing, I'm sure." Landry wished she'd come downstairs earlier and intercepted Jade before the girls could regale her with their tales.

"Taken on four armed men and women single-handed? No way. I would've called the cops, sure, but I wouldn't have taken them on. Sorry to disappoint you, but I'm just a basketball player. I bounce balls for a living, not heads. What do *you* do for a living that means you can deal with a crazy situation like that?"

I time travel and often have to kill people to save other people. "I'm in the military." It wasn't a complete lie. She *was* part of the militarized section of Pulsus. Saying you were in the services generally evoked one of two responses: either the woman would visibly swoon, or she'd get all political about conflicts, make her excuses, and leave. Jade did neither.

"So I'm guessing you're not a behind-the-scenes type with skills like Caitlin described."

Jade took a sip of her drink and tongued the corner of her mouth to catch an escaped droplet of juice. She had a look in her eyes that told Landry she knew exactly what she was doing.

Landry tried harder to concentrate on the conversation. "I think she exaggerates the story every time she tells it. People like the ones who attacked Cait aren't usually that dangerous hand-to-hand, and they were drunk too, which always slows them down. The sick fucks were so into what they were doing that they didn't hear me coming. I was right beside them before I even spoke, so they never really had a chance to draw any of their weapons."

"She said your joke made her laugh, even though her ribs were broken… '*Is this one of those bad jokes? How many assholes does it take to beat up one woman?*' Good to know you've got a sense of humor as well as being deadly."

Landry half-smiled, remembering her approach to the ghastly scene. The two guys were holding Caitlin upright while the women were taking turns battering her. They were laughing and taunting her with the guys sneering that they were going to break into the restaurant and rape her girlfriend. It was a robbery that had descended into a homophobic attack, and Caitlin was a bloody mess. "It helps to keep a sense of humor with the work I do…the work I can't really talk about." Landry needed to cut that line of questioning off before it really got going. When she met other women, it was easy to say she was a freelance photographer, but Landry had no idea what Lizbeth and Caitlin had already told her, and she also realized she didn't particularly want to lie outright to Jade. She could be economical with the truth and maybe leave things to interpretation, but she didn't want to blatantly deceive her.

"So, small talk is generally out then. The girls said you don't like to talk about yourself. You're saying you can't talk about your work. And you're clearly uncomfortable talking about your heroic escapades. What does that leave us?"

For a moment, Landry had no words. Talking a woman into bed wasn't usually this hard, but then she did tend to trawl the bars where loud music made it impossible to have any real conversation. *And I do talk about myself.* "Ask me anything—that's not about my work—and I'll answer. The girls can be melodramatic. I'm not a closed book."

Lizbeth materialized, as if on cue, and served their first course. "Chestnut, roasted butternut squash, and Bramley apple soup. Enjoy."

She left as swiftly as she'd appeared, and Jade tasted the soup, nodding appreciatively.

"Okay, let's see. Tell me about your parents."

"Wow, start with the hard stuff." Landry spooned a mouthful of soup before tackling the question. "This is really good."

Jade smiled and tilted her head, indicating for Landry to stop stalling and begin.

Which version do I give you? "My mom's a genius in the medical profession. My dad died when I was young, and she remarried. I didn't forgive her for that for a long time. Now she's playing at being a lesbian, and I'm not sure how I feel about that either. Next."

Jade laughed, and it made Landry buzz inside. She wanted more of that.

"Is that why you don't want to visit at Christmas?"

Landry tossed her spoon into the soup bowl. "Jesus Christ, what time did you get here? Have they told you everything they know about me? Maybe we should try small talk. What's your favorite color?"

"It changes. The color of the team I'm playing for." Jade winked, and it calmed Landry instantly. "How's this for small talk—is that the Royal Oak? I have the ladies' version." Jade pushed up the sleeve of her suede DKNY suit jacket and flashed her watch.

"That's beautiful. Is it a good sign that we have matching tastes?" Landry raised her eyebrow suggestively, and Jade smirked.

"As long as you don't want us to have matching tattoos, it's not a bad sign. Better?"

"Better." There was silence while they both concentrated on finishing their soup. Landry stole occasional looks at Jade and began to wonder if this was a good idea. She was insanely beautiful, and her body was off-the-charts sexy, but her mind was sharp and she had a wicked sense of humor. She was someone Landry could easily spend time with as a friend. Fucking her would spoil the chances of any friendship, but was a friendship what Landry wanted? *More than sex?* Did she even need a friendship? She was desperate to balance her work schedule with a normal life on vacation, and she'd been working on that for the past three years. Was a friendship with Jade the next logical step? She'd let the cute little family into her life, and it hadn't been a disaster. Far from it. And how normal could she be without friends?

Caitlin removed the soup bowls and replaced them with the next course. The restaurant had gotten busy, and Lizbeth was consigned to the kitchen for the rest of the evening. They'd continued with more small talk while enjoying the angel hair pasta primavera, which Caitlin had been instructed to point out would be good for Jade's energy at tomorrow's game.

"As wonderful as this evening's been, Landry, I have to get home for an early night." Jade dabbed at the corners of her mouth with her silk napkin and smiled. "The coach wouldn't be happy if you kept me up all night."

Landry's lascivious look gave her away. *I'd love to keep you up all night.* "When are you back in town?" She reminded herself she was contemplating a friendship rather than a one-night stand.

"I'll be back on Friday. After tomorrow's game, I'm heading to the East Coast to visit the family for a few days. Like I told you, there are a lot of us so it's a big deal. And it's my nephew's first Christmas, so there's a renewed interest for his sake. You know how adults get around babies."

Landry laughed gently. "Not this adult. I don't get the fascination—at least not until they can hold a conversation with you. Up to that point, they're just screaming shit machines."

"Another thing we have in common. If we keep going like this, in no time at all we'll have the white picket fence and the whole shebang."

Jade pushed her chair back, the naked flesh of her chest teasing Landry as she rose deliberately slowly.

"Do you want to get together Saturday?" Whatever this was going to be, Landry was sure she needed to see Jade again, and as soon as possible.

"I have a game Saturday, but I can be free Sunday after training. Maybe we can go meet your mother."

Landry let out a sharp laugh that startled the group at the table beside them, making one of them spill their drink. "Wow, your teasing is just endless, isn't it?" She began to get up, but Jade placed her hand on Landry's shoulder.

"No need, my chivalrous charge. My car is right outside on the curb."

She leaned down and kissed Landry, deep and hard. Her hair caressed Landry's cheeks as her fingertips traced a soft line from Landry's neck and along the hollow of her throat before resting on Landry's pecs. She pulled away and Landry followed, craning her neck for more, but Jade pressed her fingers to Landry's lips.

"Patience, baby."

Landry cleared her throat and settled back into her chair. "I'm not one for waiting, Jade."

She whispered huskily into Landry's ear, her breath as hot as Landry's desire for her. "You'll wait for me."

Chapter Eleven

December 27, 2075—Pulsus Island

"We admire your fervor, Operative, truly we do. But the risks are too great. There are too many calculations we're unable to make to ensure any operation of that magnitude could possibly be safe."

Gordon Carson was Pulsus's chief experiment integration engineer, and Delaney's dislike for him grew with every dispassionate word he spoke. Delaney stood at the far end of the boardroom, feeling insignificant against the eleven high-level, high-intelligence men and women who occupied the rest of the table. Jay Jenkin sat at the head of the table with Landry's mom, Elena, to her right. Delaney's close relationship with Landry meant that a quick conversation with Elena on Monday had the board pulled together by the end of the week for an extraordinary meeting. Delaney had presented her idea of development for their work in good faith, and now she felt like she was on trial. She'd expected some resistance, change is always scary, but she hadn't expected an outright no.

"Aren't the risks worth it? Instead of saving this doctor, why don't you send us back to assassinate Hitler before his fascist policies have the chance to gain any traction?"

"Let's say we did that." Jolene Dudley, the chief environmental psychologist, played devil's advocate. "At what point in his life would you have us intervene? Right after his mother gave birth—would you like to murder an innocent baby?"

Delaney threw her hands in the air in exasperation. "I wouldn't want to kill a baby, of course not, but we know there's no other path for him." She smashed her hand on the table to emphasize her point. "He's no innocent, and there are no major life occurrences that made him the way he was. He was simply evil."

Jolene continued her conjecture. "But the earlier we kill him, the less impact he has on others, yes? Or what if we ensure that his older brother, Edmund, doesn't die—what if that was the life-changing incident that resulted in his murderous anti-Semitism?"

Delaney ran her hand through her hair and shook her head. "That's just guesswork. If we spent the energy and resources on a mission that may or may not work, we would've wasted millions of dollars. Kill the man before he becomes a decorated war veteran, before he gets ideas of grandeur. We know that would stop the ethnic cleansing. Germany was beaten in World War One. Without Hitler, there wouldn't have been a Second World War. It was the deadliest conflict in history, and we have a chance to stop it from ever happening. Isn't that *our* responsibility? Aren't *we* monsters if we simply let it happen?"

"Jacqulyn, I understand what you're saying." Elena stood and walked the length of the table to sit on its edge beside Delaney.

She placed her hand over Delaney's, and Delaney saw a look of jealousy flash briefly across Jenkin's face. She *should* be protective of Elena. She was stunning; a more traditionally feminine, older version of Landry, and she'd featured more than a few times in Delaney's fantasies. Jenkin, however, was hard-faced, gray-haired, and had a God complex. Delaney couldn't understand her appeal, but she was never short of a younger woman fawning all over her. Elena was the first woman in her age bracket as far as Delaney knew.

"But we're only three years into this project, and hopefully, it will be many lifetimes of work. With the right leadership and genius, it will outlive all of us in this room."

Delaney saw something else in Jenkin's face, but couldn't place it. They had regenerative technology; theoretically, they could decide to live forever if they wanted to. *What's to stop you from becoming immortal?*

"We don't want to run before we can walk. The beauty of time travel is that if we do figure out how to make the kind of changes you're talking about, safely, and with minimum negative repercussions, we can do it later with the same effect. But right now, the board has already decided on a priority of targets and lined up the next ten missions. That's a lot of resource and no small amount of money. Time dilation to access the cosmic strings requires a metal that the earth only has a finite amount of, and we've already mined for and acquired all of it. Until such time as we replicate that ore or find more of it elsewhere in the universe, we're restricted in our ambitions." Elena took Delaney's hand in hers. "You're one of our finest operatives, Jacqulyn, and you've been on a lot of missions in your time with us. It's natural that you want to do more, given the time you dedicate to each operation. But you have to bear with us." She gestured toward the rest of the board. "Gathered in this room are the finest minds in their field, in the world. If it can be done, these are the people who can make it happen. You need to be patient." She released Delaney's hands and turned to walk back to her seat. "You need to continue to do your job and let us do ours."

Already lined up the next ten missions? Their priorities were obviously very different from Delaney's. Elena spoke of the potential to do things Delaney's way, but she wasn't sure it was sincere. And even if it was, Delaney wouldn't be around forever. She wanted to be part of bigger change right now. She couldn't wait. She wouldn't wait.

"In the meantime, perhaps you'd like to spend some time with one of my team before your next mission?"

The chief clinical psychologist, Lindsay Castillo, was the board member sitting closest to Delaney and had looked the most supportive to her plan. Now Delaney understood she'd misinterpreted—she was actually giving Delaney the sagacious therapist gaze of empathy and unconditional positive regard. It made her want to vomit.

"Thanks, Ms. Castillo, maybe I'll do that." *Or maybe I'll go gouge out my eyes with a spoon.*

"We do appreciate your input, Delaney." Jenkin sounded genuine, but somehow it seemed like she was looking straight through Delaney. "You're a valued member of our team, and your willingness to be involved at this level is welcome."

"Anything for the organization, Ms. Jenkin, you know that." Delaney went for a sincere tone too, though she was feeling anything but. They were blowing her off and their reasons weren't solid enough for Delaney. Elena had placated her with what she thought Delaney wanted to hear. It was easy to tell when she was lying—her tell, a quick chew of her bottom lip, was obvious, and it ran in the family. She needed to get out of there while she was able to maintain a visage of calm. "Thank you for taking the time to listen."

Delaney gathered her jacket and shoulder bag and headed for the door. She pulled it open a little too vigorously. It bashed into the wall and left a handle-sized hole in the drywall. "Sorry." Delaney left the room to their broken wall and their broken principles.

Chapter Twelve

December 29, 2075—Mainland, San Francisco

"I'm guessing your mom wasn't happy with your decision not to join the family for Christmas day?" Jade asked before leaning over the pool table and hitting an unbelievable shot, pocketing two balls. She'd invited Landry over to the team campus, where the players could relax like they would in a normal bar, but without the hassle of being bothered by fans. They'd been shooting pool for almost an hour, and with alternating views of Jade's chest and ass, it'd been hard for Landry to concentrate on conversation. The friend thing was harder than she'd thought it would be.

"She wasn't ecstatic, no. But she knows my reasons, and I did invite her to join me and the girls at the restaurant for Christmas dinner." Her mom hadn't been happy at all when Landry called on Christmas Eve to say she wouldn't be coming back to the Island. She'd tried to guilt-trip Landry into changing her mind, but the more she did that, the more Landry wouldn't budge.

Jade missed the next shot, and as Landry stood to take her turn at the table, Jade slipped her hand onto Landry's hip. "Have I told you how sexy you look in that shirt?"

"You did, but you can tell me again." Landry leaned into Jade's body and pushed her against the edge of the pool table. She ran her fingers through Jade's luscious hair and kissed her soft lips.

Jade broke off. "You look so sexy that it's taking all my resolve not to tear it open right now so I can get a good look at all that muscle you're packing underneath it." She ran her hand over Landry's shirt, feeling the rips in her abs. "It's all I can do not to think about how good you'd look in it while you fucked me on this pool table."

Landry took the cue from Jade's hands, making sure she caressed Jade's fingers as she did. They were unexpectedly soft considering her profession. Landry was desperate to feel them on her chest as Jade unbuttoned her shirt.

"I have a pool table at my apartment." *Because that's what a good friend would do, Landry, let you fuck her stupid on your fancy black pool table.* A wicked dirty look flashed across Jade's face, like that might be one of her fantasies. *And what am I doing, anyway? I've never invited a woman back to my place.*

"Lizbeth said you never have women at your apartment." Jade looked a little self-assured. "Are you thinking of making an exception for me just because I'm a famous baller?"

"Lizbeth shouldn't be so liberal with the details of my habits. Have you been talking with her since Monday, or did you just manage to get a ridiculous amount of information while you were waiting for me to come downstairs that night?" Landry definitely needed to ask Lizbeth to dial it down—she was acting like some crazy Cupid. Her prying into her private life was usually irritating in a fly around a horse's ass kind of way, but this was taking it to a new level of annoyance.

"That girl can get a lot of words out in a short space of time. Her heart's in the right place. She loves you and thinks you'll only be happy when you've settled down with the right woman."

"Is that what you think?"

"I'm only just starting to get to know you, Landry. All I see is you being content playing around with lots of different ladies. I don't think you're looking for a soul mate."

Delivered by any other woman, Landry felt those words would come with an edge, but not with Jade. She seemed to be just as much of a free spirit as Landry. *What happens when two predators come together?* "And what are you looking for?" Landry sank the eight-ball on her shot and forfeited the game. She was finding it hard to give her attention to anything other than Jade.

"I found out the hard way that relationships don't work for me. Not with this job. There's too much traveling involved, and I'm always training or playing to give any woman the care and love she deserves."

Landry placed her cue on the table, came back around to Jade, and flipped the chair around. She straddled it and took a long drink of her Corona. "What do you mean about finding out the hard way?"

There was a fleeting emotion across Jade's face that Landry easily recognized as sadness. Despite her breezy devil-may-care attitude, Jade obviously had some difficult history.

"I'd been with this woman, Hayley, for over a year. I'd just signed with the Knicks, and my career was really starting to take off. I earned more in my first week than I had in the full year before joining the team, and Hayley certainly enjoyed that aspect of our new life. I thought we were happy, but it turns out that other than the money, I wasn't giving her what she actually needed." She paused and tossed a handful of pretzel bites into her mouth.

"She was straight, wasn't she? A closet hetero posing as a respectable lesbian?" Landry's attempt to lighten the situation worked enough to make Jade let out a cute little giggle that Landry wanted to hear all night. *I want to hear her laugh, not scream out her orgasm?*

"I would've handled that a lot better—I mean, you can't help being straight, right? That wouldn't have been her fault. But I came home early from a world tour with an ankle injury. I hadn't called because I wanted to surprise her, but I came home to find her hog-tied, on her knees, with some dildo-brandishing dyke fucking her while she pulled on a chain around her neck."

Landry tilted her head and raised an eyebrow, unable to keep from imagining Jade in a similar position on her bed.

"Thank you for that *very* graphic description."

Jade shook her head in mock disgust. "Deviant."

"I prefer the term 'open-minded' actually."

"You're perving on my very damaging experience. I'm still emotionally scarred."

Landry stuck out her bottom lip in false sympathy and patted Jade on the head patronizingly. "Poor baby…did you scar the depraved dyke doing the fucking?"

Jade giggled guiltily. "I don't know that I scarred her, but I did give her a damn good beating."

"Did she enjoy it?"

"I didn't stop to check the moisture level in her underwear, so I wouldn't know." Jade tried to sound affronted, but her wide grin gave her away.

"Wow, you tough little baller." She gently tapped Jade on the chin with her fist, and Jade knocked her hand away.

"You're mocking me because you're some super dangerous Navy Seal or something."

"Not at all. I'd love to see you in action. I am going to admit that I Googled you a little after I heard you'd joined my team, on a professional level of course."

"Of course."

"And I never found anything about you serving time for battering an old girlfriend's lover."

Jade nodded and looked smug. "And no matter how deep you dig, you won't find a thing about it."

"Because you killed her and buried the body, along with the duplicitous girlfriend?"

Jade punched Landry in the thigh. "No! Because I paid them both to disappear, and the team doctor fixed her up so there are no medical records of it ever happening."

"So if they try to blackmail you now that you're an even bigger superstar, there's no evidence and they can't prove a thing?"

"Exactly."

The same look of sadness passed across Jade's face again, and her intense brightness disappeared momentarily. Landry could practically feel her melancholy and wanted to pull her into her arms to comfort her.

"You've not had a serious relationship since?"

"Nope. Anyway, you amateur head shrink, how about you give up some personal information of your own? When was your last serious relationship?"

Landry took a deep breath and another swig of the longneck she was harboring. *Are we really doing this?* "Would it scare you if I told you I'd never had one?" Jade raised both eyebrows, and Landry wondered if she was making a mistake sharing like this. "In a way, it's a similar thing to you. I don't have the availability a partner needs. My work takes me away—a lot, and for lengthy periods of time. I'm sometimes not around for months, and..." Landry paused, unsure how much she wanted to divulge, but sure she wanted to trust her. "There's always the possibility I might not come back at all." Landry searched Jade's face for a reaction and only saw understanding. "I can't expect anyone to wait around for me, and I wouldn't want them to either."

"Well, this conversation took a hard left turn to serious town, didn't it? Let's talk more about your estranged family life and lighten things up a little."

Landry smiled. She and Jade seemed alike in so many ways, and she couldn't recall the last time she'd felt this comfortable with anyone. She didn't want to lose it. *Could we manage to be the elusive friends with benefits?* "My relationship with my mom is complicated. It's a little like..." *Like I've lived two separate lives, one with her dead, one with her in my life, and I'm not sure which life I like best.* "Like we want to be in each other's lives, but we're not quite sure how that should work. You could say we're still in the design stage. Tell me more about yours. From what you said the other night, it seems pretty much the perfect American family."

Jade blushed a little, and her shyness made her all the more attractive.

"I've been really lucky. There are a lot of horror stories out there, but even though we were poor, I never wanted for anything. Both of my dads came from poor backgrounds too, big families who struggled to feed and clothe themselves. But damn hard workers. They'd always wanted to have big families of their own, but the poverty made that difficult. They decided to take a chance on having me but knew it'd be irresponsible to have more than one, because they wouldn't be able to support a bigger clan. Luckily, I started earning big pretty early on—big in our terms, anyway—and because they were really young when they had me, they still had plenty of time to have the family they'd always craved. I've ended up with two brothers and three sisters, and my brother's already got one of his own. They've all made their own way on their own terms. It's not like I'm supporting them all. I'm proud of every one of them."

Landry had watched Jade as she described her family. Her slight sorrow disappeared completely, and she began to exude a calm, centered glow.

"I can't imagine what that feels like."

"I'm sorry…I forgot about your dad."

Shit, I said that out loud? "No need to apologize. It sounds great, it really does, and I love hearing about where you've come from." *Surprisingly, I really do.* "Please, carry on."

"I don't know that there's much more to tell. We all get together for every holiday and birthdays where we can, but since there's so many of us, that's sometimes not possible for me. Thanksgiving, though, that's always been my favorite holiday—despite its unsavory history. Everyone getting together for no other reason than family, I love that."

"That's beautiful." *And I'm envious. I think.* "Two dads though, that's just greedy." Landry nudged Jade's shoulder playfully. This conversation was getting as heavy as its predecessor.

"Ah, the humor defense mechanism again when we start getting too deep."

"And you called me a shrink?"

Landry's phone vibrated on the table and buzzed for attention. A picture-perfect snap of the girls and Priscilla illuminated the display. Landry briefly considered not answering, but when she left her apartment to meet Jade, Priscilla hadn't been feeling well for a few days and had developed a fever. She wasn't sleeping well, and her eyes looked bloodshot.

"I'm sorry, I should take this. Do you mind?"

Jade caressed Landry on her forearm tattoo, and the sensitive skin tingled under her touch. "Of course I don't mind. Your chosen family is important."

Jade's words lodged into Landry's head, and she knew she'd have to muse over them later.

"Is everything okay…I'm still with Jade, why?" She looked up at Jade. *You're so beautiful.* "No, don't worry, I'll be right there." Landry offered an apologetic look in Jade's direction. "Honestly, it's fine…which hospital are you at…I'll be with you in twenty minutes… Lizbeth? I'll be there. Everything will be okay."

Landry ended the call, and Jade once again caressed her tattoo. The sensation traveled directly south.

"I have to go." *But I really don't want to leave you.* "I'm really sorry."

"Is it Caitlin or Priscilla?"

The genuine concern in Jade's voice was touching.

"It's Priscilla." Landry stood, grabbed her leather jacket from the back of the chair, and hastily pulled it on. "I'll call you tomorrow."

"Sure. Leave a message if I don't pick up. I'll be preparing most of the day for the game—but you know about that, given that you're a season ticket holder."

Landry nodded, leaned down, and kissed Jade on the cheek. Jade clutched at Landry's jacket as she pulled away.

"Drive safely."

Landry smiled and nodded again. "I do everything safely." As Landry left the bar, she took a quick glance back at Jade. Another player had already taken her seat at their table, and Jade was already in animated conversation. "Usually," she whispered.

Chapter Thirteen

December 29, 2075—Mainland, San Francisco

The emergency room was overflowing. Landry did a quick scan of the area and saw admin registration clerks darting from one person to another with bright colored clipboards, while teal-jacketed triage nurses trudged from one patient to the next with thinly veiled impatience. It was obviously a busy and tough night for everyone. She could see the girls sitting near a cluster of vending machines, with Caitlin cradling Priscilla in her arms. Worry was etched on their faces.

"Lan Lan." Priscilla looked up from Caitlin's arms, but a lack of energy prevented her from doing any more, and she nuzzled back down.

"Hey, baby." She stroked Priscilla's head. "What's happening?" Lizbeth stood, and Landry pulled her into a strong embrace.

She looked down at Caitlin, who smiled weakly. "Nothing's happening. We've been here three hours already, and they're trying to blow us off. They say she's probably just got a cold and not to concern ourselves until the fever's run for more than three days. They won't even take us through to the waiting area."

Lizbeth lifted her head from Landry's shoulder, where her tears had left abstract wells of water on her jacket. "I know something's really wrong, Landry. She's my daughter, and I feel her."

"Has the clerk seen you?" Landry asked of Caitlin, sensing that Lizbeth needed to stay in her arms.

"That's another problem. They're saying our insurance is invalid and the company is bankrupt, but that can't be. I showed her our card, and the payments are up to date. After the medical bills I had two years ago…"

Caitlin paused, and Landry could see she was trying hard to compose herself. Landry had pushed Caitlin to seek therapy after her attack. She insisted she was fine, but it was clear the experience was still affecting her deeply.

"We changed insurers on principle, and we made sure we had a good deal. They can't be right, Landry."

Landry shook her head. "They won't be. Hospitals make mistakes all the time. Sit tight, and I'll fix this." She let Lizbeth down to her chair, and Caitlin reached for her hand. She reluctantly uncoupled herself from Landry and slumped beside Caitlin, before beginning to stroke Priscilla's forehead gently and sing quietly to her.

Landry strode purposefully to the reception desk. The clerk didn't look up until Landry cleared her throat and placed her hands on the counter.

"Can I help you?" She was a middle-aged woman, with a tired looking face and aged complexion. Landry could see from her expression, she was both jaded and exhausted. She checked her nametag.

Landry smiled as politely as she could manage. This was Priscilla's health they were trifling with, and Landry's tolerance for that was, apparently, zero. "I really hope you can, Belinda. I'm with the Lovell family, and there seems to be a holdup. Can you clarify what's happening for me, please?"

"Are you family?"

Not your kind of family. "Yeah, I'm the aunt." *The aunt, not an aunt.* Landry smiled to herself at her willingness to become part of their family.

Belinda looked beyond Landry to Caitlin and Lizbeth and raised an eyebrow, looking a little skeptical about any family resemblance, but was convinced enough not to argue.

"Their insurance is no longer valid. The company went bust three months ago. We're not accepting any of their clients, I'm sorry."

Neither Belinda's words nor her tone genuinely expressed any such sorrow. Landry took her wallet from her jacket, pulled out a Platinum American Express card, and slid it across the counter. "This will cover anything you need to do for Priscilla."

Belinda nodded and put the card through her machine, smiling. "I'll send the triage nurse over as soon as he's finished with that patient." She motioned over to the short, skinny guy sitting beside a perfectly healthy looking woman in her mid-twenties. "She's a DFO—Done Fell Over—fainted at work. He won't be long."

Landry retrieved her card and slipped it back into her wallet and jacket before turning around. Luckily, the girls hadn't been watching Landry's exchange with the clerk. She saw the triage nurse heading their way, and he reached them at the same time as Landry.

"Would you tell me again what the symptoms are?" He was gruff and without formality. His energy made Landry bristle with aggression.

"She's had a fever for nearly two days and—"

"It's probably just a cold. Is this your first child?"

There was something about the way he said "your" that irritated Landry. Even in this age, some people still held on tight to their deeply ingrained homophobia.

"And her eyes are bloodshot…"

"Has she been sleeping?" His questioning was still as abrupt.

"The fever's been keeping her awake, but—"

"Then she's probably just tired. I'll put her on ES level four. As you can see, we're extremely busy. It'll be at least three hours before she's seen, but you're probably wasting your time. I'd recommend you just go home and put her to bed. She'll probably feel much better in the morning."

If you say "probably" once more, I might just ram that clipboard up your ass.

The nurse began to scribble something on his notes when Landry placed her hand on his clipboard and pressed it downward. He looked up at her, clearly assessing the threat level. She figured he was already considering whether or not to press his panic button. "She's an ES level two at the very least, and she'll go to the top of your list. Look around you. You've got a whole host of drunks, DIFFCs and DQs. These two aren't suffering from DPS. We'll follow you to a consultation cubicle, if you don't mind leading the way."

"And what are you, a doctor or a Jedi knight?"

"I've been a doctor, in the past, but I don't practice any more. Now I work for people far more influential than a fictional religious cult." Landry smiled and gave him the Federal Government Agent look. She knew she was clean-cut enough to fulfill the stereotypes this guy would have about female field agents, despite her jeans and leather jacket.

He glanced around him, and she could see from his changing expression, he agreed with her assessment of the Pit.

"Okay, follow me."

Caitlin stood and adjusted Priscilla in her arms, before whispering, "You were a doctor too?"

"Not exactly. I trained for a while, and it served a purpose at the time, but it wasn't for me long-term."

"What the hell is a DIFFC and a DQ?"

"They're medical acronyms, doctor slang. DIFFC is someone who drops in for a friendly chat and DQ stands for drama queen. There's no real emergency out here other than Priscilla."

"And what about DPS?"

Landry laughed quietly and put her arm around the still strangely silent Lizbeth. "Dumb parent syndrome, meaning parents who think there's always something wrong with their kid, or always know better than the doc."

"Wait here, please. The primary nurse will be with you shortly." The skinny nurse took one last look at Landry before disappearing along the corridor.

Caitlin laid Priscilla down. She looked so lost and tiny on the adult size hospital bed that it made Landry want to pick her up and take her to the island. *My mom could fix you.* Landry struggled to contain herself. "We need a doctor in here right now." She released Lizbeth into Caitlin's arms and marched out of the cubicle, returning moments later with a physician and a primary nurse.

"This is Dr. Stowe, Caitlin. She's going to examine Priscilla."

Dr. Stowe nodded and smiled at Landry. She'd been more than happy to follow Landry, who'd interrupted her coffee break and demanded that she come and assess Priscilla.

"So your daughter has a fever, yes?"

Lizbeth nodded, and Dr. Stowe touched Priscilla's cheek with the palm of her hand. "Nurse, take little Priscilla's temperature for me, please…the nurse is going to pop something in your ear, Priscilla, but don't worry, I promise she won't leave it there."

Landry liked this doctor already. She was far more interested than the rest of the hospital staff they'd encountered thus far.

"Has she been complaining of any pains or aches?" Stowe directed her question at Lizbeth and Caitlin, who were hugging each other tightly.

"She's been saying her hands and feet hurt," Caitlin responded when Lizbeth remained mute.

Stowe shone a small Maglite into Priscilla's eyes and ran her finger over Priscilla's lips. Landry noticed how cracked and dry they looked.

"Has she been drinking? Is she able to keep fluids down?"

"Yes, no different from usual."

"Priscilla, just this once, would you do something your mommies tell you not to do for me please?"

Priscilla nodded, her reddened eyes wet with tears.

"Would you stick your tongue out at me?"

Priscilla managed a little giggle, and Lizbeth broke away from Caitlin to hold her hand. The doctor nodded slowly and continued to nod when the nurse handed her the thermometer.

"We're going to borrow a little bit of your blood, Priscilla. Is that okay? Can you be a brave girl for me and let my nurse do that?"

Priscilla looked at Lizbeth and Caitlin for reassurance.

"We're here, baby. It's going to be okay. She won't hurt you."

Landry was relieved when Lizbeth finally spoke. She wasn't really one to be voiceless.

Lizbeth pulled Priscilla's favorite cuddly toy, a groaning teddy bear, from her handbag. "You can play with Oscar while they do that, okay?"

Priscilla managed a weak smile, pulled Oscar to her face, and kissed him. "Oscar makes everything better."

"We're going to need a urine sample," Stowe said to Lizbeth. "Would you take Priscilla to the bathroom and help her fill one of the sample cups, please? We'll be ready to take a blood sample when you get back."

"Of course...Priscilla, come with Mommy to the bathroom." Lizbeth picked Priscilla up and headed to the restroom. The nurse left to gather the required tools for the blood tests.

"Doc, you seem to have an inkling of what might be up with our girl. Do you want to share that with us?"

Stowe tilted her head, obviously trying to work out what the situation was with three possible mothers. "Are you her mom too?"

"No, Doc, I'm her aunt. Caitlin and Lizbeth are her moms. Your diagnosis?"

"It's a little too early to say without completing the tests—"

"Please, Doc, are we talking about something serious here?" Landry realized she was choking back her emotions and wrestling with a desire to grab the doc by her shoulders to shake the answers out of her.

Stowe looked at Landry, Caitlin, and then back to Landry, clearly contemplating her next words. "Potentially, yes. But I want to be absolutely sure I'm right before I say any more."

Stowe put her hand on Landry's shoulder, and she let out a small breath. There was a fleeting expression of arousal that could've easily been missed. Landry didn't miss it at all.

"Please understand I'm not blowing you off, Ms. Donovan. I wouldn't do that."

Landry put her hand over the doc's and smiled. It was a smile she used often, usually to get what she needed from someone who was less than willing to give it, but with a weakness for what Landry had to offer. "I can see that, Doc. But please, as soon as you can. Priscilla is their life and their light."

While Lizbeth held her tight, Priscilla only cried a little when the nurse took her blood. The ensuing thirty minutes spent waiting for the doctor to return with her test results crawled by desperately slowly with little conversation. Landry couldn't help but feel a slight sense of impending bad news. Stowe had refused to tell Landry what she thought Priscilla might be suffering from, even when she'd followed her from the cubicle and asked again. Apart from in the Pit, when Lizbeth had been certain something serious was wrong with Priscilla, she was being unusually reticent. Given that Landry had always experienced Lizbeth as a glass half-full kind of woman, she was beginning to surmise that their mother-daughter bond was telling her something about Priscilla's condition that science would soon corroborate.

Dr. Stowe pulled back the cubicle curtain and gestured for them to step outside, as two orderlies came in and began to move Priscilla.

"Ladies, walk with us. This is Dr. Burnett, and she's a pediatric cardiologist. We need to take Priscilla to the fourth floor to treat her condition."

"Which is?" Landry interrupted, rudely she knew, but they were all frantic for news they could work with.

"Her blood tests showed an elevated erythrocyte sedimentation rate, and we found white blood cells in her urine sample. We believe Priscilla is suffering from a rare lymph node syndrome called Kawasaki disease. We need to treat her quickly to stop any possibility of coronary aneurysm or a heart attack."

Landry saw Lizbeth's legs buckle but caught her before she fell to her knees. Caitlin stepped in and helped Lizbeth to keep walking.

"What's the treatment?" Caitlin asked. "Will she be okay?"

"The sooner we have her on an intravenous drip of gamma globulin and warfarin, the less risk there will be of heart problems."

"Warfarin? Not aspirin? Isn't warfarin associated with higher risk of internal bleeding?" Caitlin asked, her concerned laced voice shook.

"Only if the dose is too high. Aspirin is associated with Reye's syndrome in children, which can cause brain and liver damage. Dr. Burnett is one of the country's leading cardiologists. She's in safe hands, Caitlin, I guarantee it."

Dr. Burnett spoke. "I'll do an echocardiogram to check for existing aneurysms or any signs of heart disease. But because you've brought her in so early, you've vastly reduced the chances of that. I just have to be sure. When I've finished treating your daughter tonight, you'll need to bring her back to me in three weeks for another echo and watch out for any changes in her extremities, any peripheral edema—"

"Non-doc speak?" Landry asked Burnett. Stowe smiled, and Landry saw for the first time how beautiful and long her eyelashes were.

"Swelling in her hands and feet, or any peeling of her fingers and toes."

They reached the elevator, big enough for all of them and Priscilla's portable bed. "How did this happen? Is it infectious?" Lizbeth looked less pale than she had immediately following Stowe's reveal of Priscilla's condition and had regained her voice.

"We may never know," Burnett explained. "Sometimes it's caused by an infection, other times it can be from exposure to an environmental toxin. It's such a rare disease and often isn't caught early enough because symptoms are missed in combination with the fever. It's good for Priscilla that you're such observant parents."

They reached the fourth floor and emptied the elevator in silence.

"Would one of you like to accompany Priscilla and me?" Dr. Burnett asked as the orderlies waited to wheel Priscilla along the corridor.

"I'll go." Lizbeth was already holding Priscilla's hand.

Caitlin leaned over and kissed Priscilla on the forehead. "Be a brave girl for me, beautiful."

"I will, Mommy. I'm always a brave girl."

Lizbeth and Caitlin kissed and held each other tenderly, their deep and loving connection obvious to all present. "We'll be right back, Cait."

"I know, baby."

The team began to wheel Priscilla away, and Landry felt optimistic already. The girls had acted fast enough to stop anything bad from happening. Priscilla was going to be okay; she could feel it.

"Let me show you to Priscilla's room." Stowe headed off in the opposite direction, with Caitlin and Landry following behind. After she'd given a quick tour of the suite, and Caitlin had sat beside the bed, waiting for her girls' return, Stowe motioned for Landry to join her outside.

"You're not related to any of them, are you?"

Landry grimaced slightly. "How'd you guess?"

"There's no family resemblance at all, to either of the parents." Stowe waited for an explanation.

Landry raised her eyebrow playfully. "Are you gonna throw me out?"

"No. But I was thinking I might *ask* you out."

She thought about Jade, who she'd left behind at the club's bar. Things had been getting hot and heavy, but then they'd gone deeper. They'd started to share their histories. Landry didn't want to ruin the friendship that was building by fucking her. *Seeing the doc might take my mind off her and make it easier to be friends.*

"Just thinking about it?"

Stowe smiled, moved in a little closer to Landry, and rested her fingers on Landry's belt buckle. "Yeah, just thinking. Because you might say no, and I'm not really used to people saying no to me. You know what it's like, a doctor and their God complex."

Landry leaned into Stowe's touch. "You don't strike me as fragile or having a low self-esteem. Or has your power over people's lives corrupted you, Dr. Stowe?" She whispered her words seductively and could see the desire flaming in Stowe's azure blue eyes.

"I do like a woman who knows her psychology."

"And I like a woman who knows what she wants. Especially when that want is directed at me."

"So you'd say yes?"

"If you actually asked instead of just thinking about it, yes. I'd say yes."

Stowe pulled a card from the top pocket of her white coat and slipped it into Landry's inside jacket pocket. "Call me." She let her hand linger on Landry's chest before she exhaled deeply and walked away in the direction of the elevator.

Landry leaned back against the door of Priscilla's room and was about to pull the doc's card out, when her phone buzzed in her jean pocket. The Warriors' yellow and blue team emblem of the Golden Gate Bridge flashed on the screen, and Landry felt like she'd been caught cheating.

"Hey, friend," she said as breezily as she could manage. *If I call her my friend enough times, does it make it so?*

CHAPTER FOURTEEN

December 30, 2075—Pulsus Island

"Tell me what you know and this ends. Right now. No more pain, no more suffering."

"Please, Molina. I don't know how many times I can tell you the same thing. I don't know where he is."

Delaney punched her across the jaw. Bright crimson blood hit the dirty gray concrete floor. She flexed her hand before dipping it in the bowl of glue and broken glass. She's a tough bitch. We've been here for two hours already. She needs to hold out a little longer. Landry's not here yet.

"This is going nowhere. Hook her up to the parrilla. We don't have any more time to play games." His voice was harsh. Impatient. He's dangerous.

She tried to struggle, but the two of them subdued her easily. The woman was in no state to really fight back. They threw her against the vertical metal bed and secured her wrists and ankles to the posts with metal cuffs. He sliced through the woman's tank and tore it off completely. Delaney threw a bucket of water over her.

She wrapped a wire around her neck and switched the control box of the parrilla on dial marker one. Delaney picked up the wooden wand with the bare wire wrapped around its end that made it look like a child-made microphone. She pressed it against her bare, wet nipples, and her body danced violently, uncontrollably.

"Where is Byron Crenshaw?" He was the journalist who intercepted Kissinger's communication to the Argentinean military Junta. The journalist Delaney needed to locate so Landry could save him before this guy can get to him.

The woman looked up and spat at Delaney, who snarled and traced the wand from nipple to nipple and along her stomach. Her muscles convulsed, and she screamed loud enough to stir the dead from their slumber.

"Stop being so gentle, Molina. She's a woman—you know what to do when they won't cooperate."

I know what to do. What I *have* to do. Something I don't want to do.

Delaney turned the control box off. She could see the fear and desperation in her eyes. She knows what I'm about to do, too.

"Please don't. You're a woman. How can you do this?"

Delaney smiled. Her heart broke.

The woman squealed like a dying fox as Delaney pushed the metal tipped wand inside her.

She wanted to close her eyes. Shut off her ears. But any visible sign of sympathy would give her away.

"You fucking bitch."

He grinned. He actually grinned.

Delaney turned the control box on. Dial marker two.

"Tell me where Byron Crenshaw is."

Expletives fountained from the woman's mouth. Screams exploded from her lungs.

Dial marker three.

"Tell me where Byron Crenshaw is."

She shrieked and yelled.

Dial marker four.

"Is he worth this? Would he want you to suffer like this?"

She pleaded and cried.

Dial marker five.

"Make it stop. Tell me where Crenshaw is."

She howled like an animal and sobs wracked her tortured body.

Dial marker six.

"You don't have to take this. Tell me where Crenshaw is."

She yelled more obscenities. Then she wept.

Dial marker seven.

The woman fell unconscious with the shock.

He nodded, and Delaney prepared a needle to shoot her with adrenaline.

Her body jumped back into unwelcome awareness.

Dial marker eight.

Broken.

Delaney jerked back to consciousness, her T-shirt saturated in sweat, and her heart pumping. She looked down at her hands and saw blood. She squeezed her eyes tightly shut and opened them again. This time, she saw just her hands.

Get a grip, Delaney.

Today was a training day, and though she felt rough from spending the weekend with several bottles of Widow Jane, if she missed it, the higher-ups in Pulsus might start to ask questions. She didn't want a personal visit from Lindsay Castillo or a member of her team. Her method of recycling her bourbon bottles by using them as target practice was creating a carpet of glass in her backyard, and she didn't particularly want anyone seeing it.

Delaney tried not to think about Friday's board meeting. It'd already ruined her weekend. Simson came around, but Delaney had been in no mood for company and ignored the door. She needed annihilation and sought to destroy the demons disturbing her by submerging them in alcohol. She'd occasionally drifted to sleep, but grotesque visions of previous missions soon taunted her relentlessly, and sleep eluded her. *This is what their way of doing things means. I've had to do whatever's necessary to get the job done, but they can't fix my head or get rid of what comes home with me. I have to convince Landry my way would work better, and she can convince her mom.*

She didn't have time for this. She had to pull herself together and get to the training station to lead an undercover workshop for the latest new recruits. But Delaney wondered if she told them what they were really letting themselves in for, if they'd turn and run.

She dragged herself from the sofa and took four max strength Tylenol, chasing them down with two bottles of the protein and spinach shake that sought to combat the effects of the bourbon. It immediately began to take the edge off the excruciating pounding in her head, so she went to the bathroom for her first shower in three days to refresh her body. As the cold water needled into her flesh, Delaney thought of her next mission and then back to her last nightmare, the parilla, and the woman. *Becoming a Nazi will probably make that feel like kid's playtime.*

Chapter Fifteen

December 31—Mainland, San Francisco

"The hospital apologized for not taking Priscilla in immediately. It seems they were so concerned they could've been liable for a lawsuit they haven't charged us for any of the treatments. Which was a damn good thing, because our health insurance company had gone bankrupt, but was still taking our payments."

Caitlin was speaking so fast, Landry was concerned she might collapse for lack of oxygen. Still intent on misdirected Cupid duties, Lizbeth had invited Jade to the restaurant for their New Year's Eve celebrations. Landry had decided to let it be. If she and Jade were going to be friends, Lizbeth and Caitlin would be part of Jade's life too, and Landry didn't want to deny Caitlin the opportunity to be closer to one of her favorite players of all time.

Caitlin was eager to regale Jade with the hospital tale. "We could've been left with a huge bill we couldn't afford, or worse yet, they might've refused to treat Priscilla, and she could have developed heart disease if she'd gone on untreated. Oh, hang on, Lizbeth needs me in the kitchen. I'll be right back."

Jade listened, but Landry could see she wasn't convinced. Sometimes she was hard to read; other times Landry had discovered she was an open book. Jade turned to her and raised her eyebrows.

"That's an amazing story, Landry. I can barely believe it."

Landry shrugged. *Busted. You don't believe it for a second.* "Hospitals are more terrified of lawsuits than they are of airborne diseases. They got lucky, I guess."

Jade shook her head, in obvious disbelief. "And that's the story you're sticking to, is it?"

"Don't you believe it?" Landry tried her best to look taken aback.

"Would you be offended if I said no? Do you want to know what I think happened?"

"Sure, I'll humor you. What've you got?" Landry leaned back in the soft armchair and took a sip of the champagne Lizbeth had insisted she drink. Quietly, she was glad for this distraction. Jade had called on Sunday night while Landry was still at the hospital and invited her back to the bar. Landry politely declined and instead opted for having "the talk" over the phone. She knew if she'd gone, the idea of just being friends instead of throwing Jade down on the pool table and fucking her stupid, would've seemed absurd. Landry had gotten as far as saying they should be friends before Jade said she'd prefer to talk about it tonight. So far, with Caitlin and Lizbeth still high from their hospital win, the subject had been avoided.

Jade leaned forward, and her loose Armani top gaped just enough to give Landry a glimpse of the top of her breasts. *God, you're gonna make this hard.*

"I think that you got there and found out what was happening." She poked Landry in the shoulder. "I think you flashed your credit card and somehow convinced them to put Priscilla on the top of their list. Maybe you used your charm, maybe you were a little more forceful, or maybe you had to use both. They did get lucky with a good doctor, but I think that you spun an elaborate yarn to Lizbeth and Caitlin, who were so relieved about their daughter, that they'd believe anything. Even something as farfetched as the tale you told them."

Landry nodded and smiled. "That's a fascinating version, but you should stick with the day job and never go into the P.I. business. You've got an interesting imagination, lady, but I don't know why you'd doubt what Caitlin told you."

"Maybe because you seem to be their knight in shining armor and their fairy godmother, rolled into one amazingly balanced and very sexy package."

"That's very sweet of you to say, but I thought we agreed we weren't going to mention sex." Landry took a bigger gulp of champagne and tried to focus on the bubbly liquid dancing down her throat, anything to distract her from her growing attraction to Jade.

"I don't remember that conversation, but is that because you think we should be best friends instead of red-hot lovers?"

She raised her eyebrows suggestively, and Landry noticed how the restaurant lights sparkled in the translucent banded circles of her eyes. "Exactly."

"But friends compliment each other's finer points, don't they, to buoy each other in times of doubt? At least, I hear that's how it works."

"I don't know. I've not had a real best friend before. Imaginary ones, of course. Hasn't everybody?"

Jade laughed. "You're a psycho. That's why you don't want to sleep with me."

"Yeah, that's it, because I'd have to be crazy not to want to sleep with you." *But I really fucking do want to sleep with you.* "Anyway, as I was saying before you and your canyon sized ego interrupted, I've had regular friends but not a best friend. It's been a vacant position my whole life, and you seem to be exactly the friend I've been looking for." *Because I want you around for longer than one night.*

"You should know then, that flirting isn't really part of a friendship either. You talk about a best friend like the lover you've been waiting for."

"Lovers are easy to come by. A best friend is someone who really understands and gets you. Someone who shares your perspective, your views on life. That's much harder to find. And I don't want to risk ruining that by having sex."

"You know for most people, your lover is supposed to be the one who shares all those things and understands you. Your logic might seem a little twisted to some."

"What about for you? Does it make sense to you?" *Please God, let it make sense to you, because I don't know if my self-control can stand up to your level of flirtation.* "Neither of us can offer the commitment, availability, or time it takes to have a stable relationship, but we can be best friends. We both get someone who's there for us, whenever. We don't have to see each other every day, every week, or even every month. There'd be no expectations, so we can't possibly disappoint each other. I really like you, Jade." Landry shifted in her seat. This whole emotional ejaculate was new and discomforting. Honesty wasn't something her job often necessitated. "I feel like we've made a good connection, and I want you in my life, which is a new thing in itself. I'm learning to want people in my life in general, and it's taking some adjusting. I'm trying to find a balance between my work and home life, but I know it's not possible to have a normal relationship like Lizbeth and Caitlin have. Every time I go away, I know there's a fifty-fifty chance I won't be coming home. Nobody wants a relationship on those terms."

"I hear what you're saying, Landry. My work life isn't in the same realm as yours, but I've been living by the same kind of ethos as you since 'Dildo Gate.'"

Landry spluttered the swig of champagne she was taking back into her glass. "You've got such a beautiful turn of phrase."

"Thank you." She waved her hand like a theatrical actor does when taking a bow. "I'm a sportswoman, and my career is short-term in the scheme of things. My career on the court could be over every time I get injured, and I know I'm not going to be the player I am right now forever."

Landry nudged Jade's high-heeled foot with her boot. "Oh, I don't know. You've got plenty of good years in your sneakers yet."

She smiled, but Landry could see the sadness in it. She could feel Jade's resignation to the right place, wrong time situation they were in.

"Seriously though, I don't know what it is you do, and you've made it clear you're never going to be able to tell me. I respect that, but maybe your career isn't forever too. And if we build a strong friendship, maybe someday we can be more than that. But—"

"But if we fuck now, we could destroy that possibility altogether. Friends with benefits is a myth. Somewhere down the line, someone always gets more involved than they ever meant to, and everyone ends up getting hurt."

Jade nodded. "Let's face it, we're both predators but that could end up being either one of us, no matter what our intentions are, or how much we convince ourselves it's not serious."

"And I love my job. The work we're doing makes a difference, and I know you have to take that on face value, and I expect that's infuriating. If I was a traveling salesman, or an investigative journalist, this whole situation might be different. If I did any other job in the world, it'd be easier, and we could see where this might go. But that's just not an option."

Jade touched Landry's face softly. "I get it. I really do. And I love that we can be this honest with each other. You're right about everything you've said, and I'm good with it. We keep on having fun when we're both in town, okay?"

Jade smiled, and Landry couldn't figure out how genuine it was. She raised her glass to seal the deal. "Sure, let's do it."

She finished the rest of the glass just as she saw Caitlin and Lizbeth heading toward them. This was Landry's first New Year's Eve not working since college, and she was determined to enjoy it, despite the tinge of melancholy that began to edge into her soul. Work took precedence over everything else. She'd learned that from her father, and given her position, there had never been a greater reason for it than Pulsus. But Landry was beginning to wonder if Jade's appearance in her life presented a problem or an opportunity.

CHAPTER SIXTEEN

January 3, 2076—Pulsus Island

"It's great to see you, Landry. How was the mainland?"

Delaney looked like she hadn't slept since Landry saw her just over two weeks ago. Her hair was greasy, her skin looked dry, and her nose was beginning to develop the telltale signs of too much alcohol. She was dressed in clothes that hadn't seen an iron since they came out of their packaging, but it did seem like she'd put on some more muscle.

"It was…interesting. And a little more varied than usual."

"Yeah? Tell me more. Are the tourists getting kinkier?"

"Not the tourists. I met someone, a basketball player for the Warriors. She's…" Landry paused to search her brain for an adequate adjective. "She's different."

"Different, how?"

"In every way." Landry thought about stopping the conversation there. Delaney was her closest friend on the island, and her occasional fuck buddy. Given that she and Jade had agreed to be friends, there was no reason for that to stop with Delaney. She couldn't really cheat on a friend. But Delaney was a jarhead, through and through. *All bravado and muscle, and probably just can't understand what I'm going through. Maybe this is the kind of conversation I'm supposed to have with my mom.*

"You sound soft. Are you sweet on this bitch?"

Landry tensed. The way Delaney called Jade a bitch didn't sit right. It was dismissive, disrespectful. She rolled her head and heard the cracks in her neck. "No, don't be stupid. We're just friends, you know, part of me trying to lead a normal life outside of this fucking circus."

Delaney sneered. "I don't know why you bother. What's the mainland got that this island doesn't have, apart from an unending variety of fresh pussy?"

"Jesus, Dee, that's a short-sighted way of looking at it. Is that what you think I do for two weeks?"

"From the stories you've told me in the past, yeah, that's exactly what I think you do for two weeks. All of a sudden you're all sensitive about it? Have you been boosting on the estrogen while you've been mainland?"

Delaney unexpectedly shoved Landry in the chest, and she fell back against the wall. She gritted her teeth, but smiled over them anyway. "Have you been boosting the steroids while I've been away?"

"What if she has?"

Landry nodded at Simson as she joined them, and noticed the way she put her arm around Delaney. It could've been just a buddy thing, but accompanied with the quick glance she shot Landry's way, Landry could see it was something more. Something possessive, and Landry wondered if Simson was about to cock her leg and mark her territory.

"I'm a big believer in doing things naturally."

"Yeah? Then what are we all doing here, 'cause there's nothing natural about our interfering with the past."

Landry felt her jaw tighten. She'd never much cared for Simson; she was too overzealous in her physical training. Landry pegged her as quite the sadist, given how much pleasure she took in personally teaching the recruits how to take a beating. Landry had always been too good for Simson to overcome, and she had a suspicion that Simson might still begrudge that. "It was a specific reference, Simson, to building muscle, not rebuilding the world."

"I haven't been pumping steroids, Landry. You don't have to worry about that," Delaney said, shrugging Simson's arm from her shoulder.

Simson's eyes narrowed slightly and briefly, but again, Landry could feel the dynamic between the two of them had changed.

"She's been working hard in the gym for two weeks, getting ready for the next mission." Simson squeezed Delaney's bicep. "What've you been up to?"

Landry smiled at the way Simson's tone implied she'd been less productive than Delaney. "It's called a vacation for a reason. The idea is *not* to work."

Simson snorted derisively. "That's a European way of looking at it. We have more vacation time in a year than most people get in half their working lifetime. We don't need it."

"Most people don't do the work we do. And anyway, I disagree with you. If we don't get away from this bubble of existence every time we get the chance, there's a danger we could drift into other, more harmful, ways to cope." Landry looked directly at Delaney as she spoke, suddenly aware that maybe that's exactly what was happening. It wasn't unusual that Delaney didn't leave the island; Landry was the anomaly there. But apart from Simson, it seemed Delaney wasn't engaging with anyone else when she was on vacation, and Landry felt certain Simson couldn't be the best influence for her.

Simson continued to prod. "And fucking hundreds of random women isn't a harmful way of coping, for them, at least?"

It was beginning to feel like whatever had happened between Delaney and Simson while Landry was away had fueled some kind of contempt on Simson's part. "They never seem to complain."

"How would you know? I heard you never hang around to find out."

"Anyway, about this mission…"

Landry was grateful for Delaney's interruption. If Simson continued to push, Landry felt there was a distinct possibility she might have ended up knocking her on her ass. She pushed aside the thought that the reason Simson had angered Landry was that her words hit their intended target. Landry never did stick around after the sex was over. Sure, there were no complaints while it was happening, but she always chose to ignore the wounded and wanting looks she'd seen in the eyes of countless women when she left them alone. It was easy to defend it. She couldn't offer them what they wanted beyond one night of passion, and they were better off not being disappointed when she didn't make any promises. But what of the aftermath she left behind?

"What do we know about it?"

Landry disregarded Simson shaking her head and smiling like she'd won their little battle.

"Not much, yet. I know we're going back to the Second World War, so I've been polishing up on my German."

Landry groaned. With its harsh, angular words and hardening of the final sound of a sentence, it wasn't her favorite language. As operatives and extractors, being multilingual was part of their training, and an ongoing requirement, and for the most part, Landry enjoyed it, but German was just about bottom of the list. She wasn't sure if it was the phonetics of it, or just the association with Hitler and how he manipulated the language.

Pamela Diaz, director of mission operations, entered the room with someone Landry didn't recognize. He was about six feet tall, with blond hair, blue eyes, and an impressive physique. *A prime example of Hitler's master race.* It was easy to see why he'd been chosen for this operation.

She placed her briefcase on the table and sat in the chair at the front of the room. "Good morning, people. How are we all?" She didn't wait for a response. "This is Eugene Griffin. Delaney, Simson, this is his first mission. Teach him well." She motioned for him to join his new team.

Griffin nodded and strode toward them with as much swagger as he could muster. Simson kicked out a chair indicating for him to sit.

"Our target is Bina Chernick, aka Dr. Chaim Galitz. Our research shows her living in Cologne from 1933 to 1939, where she'd secured her residency at University Hospital. Hitler had just come into power, and within months, began reversing the liberation women had experienced under the Weimar Republic. When she realized the only way of continuing in her dream as a doctor was to masquerade as a man, Chernick falsified her paperwork and medical degree, and began living her life as Dr. Chaim Galitz from the age of twenty-seven. She never transitioned, but merely transformed herself every day of her life so that she could fulfill her potential in an adversarial world. Bina was thirty-six years old when she disappeared."

"So the Nazis killed her for being deviant? What does that have to do with us? How has she gotten on our radar?"

"Patience, Delaney, I was getting to that. Her secret life was discovered in 1939, and she was shipped off to the women's concentration camp, Ravensbrück, where they forced her to become part of the experiments that went on there. Soon after, she continued her research into carcinomas, and a friendly female guard, Ilsa Blumstein, smuggled her research journals out of the camp for safekeeping. Chernick wanted them sent to the States, where she believed her work could be followed up. Blumstein was dismissed from the camp in 1943. She was no longer able to cope with the brutalities she was witnessing and refused to be part of them. Unfortunately, she never did get the journals out of the country, but she did keep them safe in her attic for decades. In 2044, Blumstein's great-granddaughter came across the journals and took them to an auction, where Jenkin bought them. It turns out she was definitely on to something, but our scientists haven't been able to pick up the threads, or decipher much of the code she was writing in. We need to extract her from the Nazis and relocate her to the States, so she can continue her research. Given the requisite environment, she should find a cure to eighty-five percent of cancers."

"What if her research doesn't pan out? It seems like a pretty big risk, and it could be a waste of a damn expensive mission. We could rescue her, and she could die of cancer a few years later."

Landry smiled at Delaney's deadpan humor. Maybe she was right. When the board chose these missions, she knew they calculated the risk, but this could be a long shot. "We follow the orders, buddy. Finer minds than ours make decisions based on knowledge we could never hope to have."

"So if the Nazis didn't kill her when they found out she was a woman, what happened to her?" Griffin asked.

"That's where our knowledge ends, I'm afraid. The last entry in Chernick's journal is in July of 1942. They were expecting a visit from Josef Mengele. It is clear that he experimented on her, among the hundreds of others he mutilated in the name of science. There was extensive mention of Chernick in Mengele's diaries that were found in Sao Paulo in 1985. Hitler had given him strict instructions to discover what it was that made Chernick try to live like a man. He wouldn't accept the simple sociological explanation. He believed she was mentally ill, and he was desperate to determine the differences in her brain that made her that way, so that he could keep it from ever happening again. It was part of his plan for the master race."

"Can't we just extract her before she was taken in 1939?"

"I'm afraid not, Donovan. It seems that Chernick didn't get to a key position in her research until she was imprisoned in Ravensbrück. It might be that inspiration struck her during the work she had to complete there. We can't risk extracting her until the last possible moment, to make sure she's where we need her to be in terms of her research."

"Is it a simple raid, or have you got something more elaborate in mind? Like, what year are we going back to?"

Delaney motioned to herself, Simson, and Griffin. Landry could hear something new in her voice. *Tension or nerves?* Operatives spent so much more time in the past than she or her fellow extractors ever had to. *Is this beginning to wear her down?*

Diaz took a deep breath and pulled her sleeves up before answering. That was her tell, and Landry knew it was going to be a long mission for the operatives. "Nineteen thirty-eight. Griffin will infiltrate the SS, and become part of the guard to be assigned to Ravensbrück." She opened her briefcase and removed three slim folders, giving one each to Delaney, Simson, and Griffin. "You and Simson will become workers in the prison service, in workhouses for prostitutes. When Hitler initiated his Action against the Workshy, prostitutes were targeted and taken to the camp. That's when your career path opens up for you both, and you apply for the new jobs at Ravensbrück in 1939. Griffin will be well placed to ensure you're taken on. You have to be embedded in the Nazi party to get this detail, and it will give one or more of you time to establish a trusting relationship with Blumstein. We need to come away with the doctor's diaries as well as the doctor, and Blumstein is the keeper of those journals."

Landry watched Delaney take her file, but she didn't open it. Usually, she was eager to find out who she was going to be. It seemed this was one mission Delaney wasn't looking forward to.

Diaz continued. "The camp is guarded by over eighty personnel. We can't send more than six through the time circle, and it would be too risky to send in such a small team in the hope they could break in, secure the doctor, and exit successfully. This isn't your first rodeo, Delaney. We don't do smash and grabs because we want to minimize disruption."

"So we should avoid starting families while we're there? You know, to minimize disruption?"

Simson's question seemed serious, and Diaz looked exasperated.

She glanced at Landry, perhaps in the hope she might step in and save her.

"I'm sorry, did I take a wrong turn into the amateur department? You know how this works. You've been doing it for three years. Did the previous mission fry your brains, or are you just trying to mess with Griffin?"

Landry held her hand up in apology. "Sorry, Ms. Diaz, they're just being obtuse. If we have to get there before Mengele begins experimenting on Chernick but after she's well into her research, when do I go in, and how?"

"We've calculated that early June 1942 will be sufficient for your entry, Donovan. You'll be a carpenter and plumber by trade but also a habitual criminal."

Landry couldn't withhold a laugh. "And what kind of crime have I habitually committed?"

"We found records of a German version of Bonnie and Clyde who were never caught." Diaz pulled another folder from her briefcase, opened it, and placed it in front of Landry. "Donovan, meet Truda Stark. This is her background and her papers. You're going to borrow her identity for a few weeks. You'll enter and hide the people retrieval unit as usual, then somehow get yourself arrested."

"People retrieval unit?" Griffin interrupted.

"Yes. The PRU for short. It's the unit the extractor uses to bring you all safely back to the future." When Griffin nodded his understanding, she continued. "When the police have finished with their interrogation, they'll send you to Ravensbrück. We've given you that background so you get the green triangle, and Delaney will be able to make you the block guard where Chernick has been placed. You've got the trades so you're useful to them and don't end up in the sand pit."

"The sand pit?" Landry had a vague memory of the term and figured it had to be more sinister than it sounded.

"Yes, where they had the prisoners shoveling sand from one pile to another for no other reason than physical torture, particularly unpleasant in the summer heat. And there are some awful accounts of a sadistic game called *abdecken*. The guards would make prisoners tunnel underneath soil piles until they caved in and buried them alive. If they were lucky, they'd let their friends pull them out."

Landry clenched her fists and shuddered. She'd recalled the course text that was a Longman prize-winning book at college when she studied European history. Focused entirely on Ravensbrück, it was by an excellent female British journalist, but its contents had haunted her for months afterward. It was full of tales of torture, needless degradation, inhumane experimentation, and what seemed to make it worse was that much of it had been carried out by women. It shattered her naïve belief that women were somehow incapable of such barbarity, and taught her that every human being was just as proficient as the next in committing atrocities. Gender was irrelevant.

"You'll need to get close to Chernick and make her your friend… or whatever it takes." Diaz smiled and winked at Landry. "Use your considerable charm."

Simson shook her head and let out a snort of air. "Lucky doctor."

Her tone was recognizably sardonic, and again, Landry chose to ignore her.

"Whatever you do, and however you do it, the four of you need to have the doctor out of that camp soon after the seventh of July. That was the date of her last journal entry. You can't take her before."

"This seems pretty straightforward. I'm assuming we all just need to ensure our German is top drawer and we can get moving. When's the jump date?" Landry much preferred missions like this, with no long, drawn out training programs.

"Yes, that's right, as long as your carpentry and plumbing skills are also exemplary." She focused on the three operatives. "You're all soldiers, so this shouldn't be a hard stretch for you. Professor Castillo has recommended that you all visit her department prior to your jump, and also to check in with the environmental psychology team, so they can prepare you for what you might witness while you're there. You jump Monday."

Landry imagined they'd be made to watch black-and-white videos and photo slideshows of the horrific cruelties that were emblematic of Hitler's reign and the subsequent World War. She remembered the account of one female guard at Ravensbrück, who used the skins of prisoners to make lampshades, and winced. That guard escaped without punishment and lived the rest of her life in Argentina. Landry was concerned for Delaney who didn't seem to be herself. As a guard, Delaney might have to be party to merciless acts of "sadistic pleasure." Landry wondered if any amount of time with Professor Castillo and her team could ever heal those kind of mental wounds.

Chapter Seventeen

January 3, 2076—Pulsus Island

Delaney's whole body was on fire with rage. Was the great bachelor, Landry Donovan, in *love*? It certainly fucking sounded like it. What was so fucking special about this basketball player, anyway? Jade fucking Carter. Who the fuck was she? Running up and down a court shooting hoops for thousands of dollars, while she and Landry risked their lives to make her future better. What the fuck could she offer a woman like Landry? Carter wouldn't have the first clue how to handle her; non-military personnel never really knew how to live with someone in the service. Sure, they tried to understand, but people in the military were a different breed than regular people. *We're made differently.*

Worse still, Landry had seemed a little sentimental, like this hankering for a "normal" life might just have her giving up on Pulsus and settling down with this Carter bitch. As far as Delaney could tell, the utopia Landry was so desperately seeking just didn't exist. They gave up on any semblance of a regular family life when they signed up for the military, and that was only compounded when Pulsus recruited them. Landry couldn't have it both ways, no matter how hard she tried. She'd made her choice, and she should live with it, just like Delaney was trying to.

And she'd been touchy too. Landry had looked almost ready to deck Simson when she prodded her about her exploits with mainland women. *What the hell was that about?* Simson had spent much of the last two years jabbing and digging at Landry, trying to get a rise out of her, but she never took the bait. Delaney had needed to intervene before Landry took a swing at Simson. Which was obviously what she was after. Delaney needed to have a chat with Simson about that. She acted like a petulant high school kid trying to lay claim to her property. Delaney was no one's property, least of all Simson's. *But I want to be Landry's.*

Fuck this love shit; it's making me crazy. Up to today, there'd been no hint of Landry doing something as banal as falling in love with a civvy. Why couldn't she see what was right in front of her? Delaney understood her better than Landry knew, and the sex they had was like nothing Delaney had before. It was raw, base, instinctive, and she never needed the extra stimulation like she did with Simson. She was kidding herself thinking that she could get over Landry by having endless sex with Simson over the past two weeks. There was no getting over Landry. She was perfect. And Delaney was perfect for Landry. All she had to do was convince Landry.

Now though, she had to concentrate on getting through this next mission. She'd calmed down considerably after the board meeting, but was still convinced that Pulsus just needed a push in the right direction to change the way they thought about the missions. She was jumping back to 1938. Did she have time to plot and carry out an assassination of Hitler? She was sure Simson was in tune with her way of thinking, but Griffin was another matter. Was he malleable? He was freshly graduated from the Pulsus training program, and in itself, that was like indoctrination. It might be too soon to turn him, and she wouldn't be able to work on him once they jumped because he'd be following a different path from her and Simson. They wouldn't meet up again until 1939, by which time it would be too late. But if she and Simson could kill Hitler in 1938, the Second World War simply wouldn't happen. They could travel Europe for a few years and return to Ravensbrück when Landry was due to arrive, explain everything, and jump back to 2076. Delaney wondered what the world might look like if it hadn't been subjected to Hitler's demonic Reich. Six million Jews wouldn't die. Nearly sixty million other people wouldn't perish, as soldiers or civilians. Wouldn't she just be doing her duty, not just as a soldier, but a human being?

How easy could it be to get close to Hitler? Delaney realized she might be being too ambitious. If only she had more time to prepare, and to recruit Griffin. If there was a chunk of training time she could use to research Hitler's movements around the time she was being sent back to, then she'd have a chance of doing it right, but she knew she couldn't risk getting herself killed. Delaney wanted to be part of the work she envisioned Pulsus could do, and a suicide mission to assassinate Hitler wasn't part of that plan. Delaney resolved to make Hitler her first target as soon as she could get the Pulsus board to agree to her new approach. She just had to think of a way to get them to give her the go-ahead.

A short rap on the door disrupted her ruminations. Delaney saw it was Landry from a quick glance at her door monitor. She looked around the apartment, assessing whether to invite her in. She decided it was way beyond time to give it a thorough clean. *This can't be a booty call.*

Delaney played it cool. "What can I do for you, Landry?" She blocked the door with her body, so Landry couldn't see inside.

She was obviously puzzled, evidenced by her furrowed brow. "Aren't you going to invite me in?"

"I haven't scrubbed up for a while, so it's pretty fucking messy in here. Do you want to go to Rik's Place instead?"

"I'm not sure going to the bar is a good call…pre-mission."

There was something in Landry's voice she couldn't quite place. She wasn't usually reluctant to share a few drinks, and the jump was two days away. *Are you worried about me?* "We've got a couple of days. What's the harm?"

"Are you gonna let me come in, or not?"

"I told you, it's a dump. It's a warm evening, let's sit outside." Delaney motioned to the rockers on the front deck, and was glad when Landry shrugged and lowered herself into a comfortable old porch chair. "I'll get us some drinks. What do you want?"

"Do you have any Coke?"

"I've got the liquid kind. Do you want it with bourbon?"

"Just ice is fine."

"Suit yourself." Delaney closed the door behind her as she went to get drinks. She didn't want Landry to see her apartment like this.

She hadn't quite realized how badly she'd let it deteriorate, and it stunk of stale cigars and sweat. She sniffed under her armpit as she wandered to the kitchen for drinks, and thought she should probably shower. Instead, she grabbed a fresh sweatshirt from the closet and pulled it on.

Delaney put a few chunks of ice in the last clean glass she had in the house and filled it with soda. She took a fresh bottle of bourbon from the half empty crate on the counter and looked at the mug or shot glass that were her only options. She chose the mug and headed back outside to Landry.

"I saw your mom over Christmas. She wasn't happy that you didn't bother coming back to see the family." Delaney handed the Coke to Landry and sat beside her on another rocking chair. She had a fleeting thought about them both being in their eighties, watching the world go by from their front porch behind a white picket fence, and laughed inwardly at her own absurdity. That was such a normal thing to do, and they'd probably never lead normal lives, even at that age.

"Is that what she told you?"

Delaney knew that would bug Landry. She didn't like her mom talking about them as a family to anyone, even Delaney. "No, but she didn't have to say it. Your mom's an open book."

Landry leaned back in her chair and put her glass on the table beside her. She was acting strangely, edgy almost, like there was something she wanted to say but didn't know how to say it. *That's got to be a first.*

"Did you go see her?"

"We bumped into each other when I was visiting Simson the day after Christmas. I asked her if you'd been back, and she said no. It was easy to see how upset she was about it. I think she'd even been crying."

Landry shook her head. "I doubt that, unless she's getting sentimental to go with her new lesbian persona."

Her aggressive tone surprised Delaney. Pulsus's first mission ensured Landry was given time with her mom, and not only was she not making use of it, she seemed angry too. Delaney would've given anything to have a mom like Landry's. "You've still got a problem with your mom liking the ladies?" Her distraction was working.

"I've got a problem with all of it. Jenkin's first mission was to send me back to rescue my mom, supposedly because they were working on this whole 'fix the world time travel' thing together. Now I'm wondering if it was just so she could seduce her, or even if she sent me back because they were already fucking before mom died, and I was the last one to know."

Delaney filled her mug with the amber liquid and took a long swallow before answering. "They *were* working on it together. Jenkin needed your mom for the regenerative tech. Elena doesn't seem the kind of woman who suddenly decides she's gay. Maybe you just didn't want to see it. And what if you were the last one to know? It's not like you make a huge effort to spend quality mother-daughter time together, is it? You can't have it all ways. Either you want to be part of the family, or you don't."

Landry shook her head and stood. She went over to the deck railing and leaned against it to face Delaney. "I've got two memories of my life, Delaney. It's not as simple as you make it sound."

"Can't you talk to Castillo's team about it?" Delaney had to be careful. Landry seemed to be revealing some inner discord. She always seemed so composed and self-possessed, like nothing could agitate her. If she was feeling like this, maybe she'd be interested in what Delaney was thinking about how Pulsus worked. Maybe Landry was her way to convince the board that her idea was sound.

Landry laughed. "They think they fix you, but they don't. The brain is too complex for them to be able to really help. Sure, they can fix our bodies, but our minds? That's another thing altogether."

Delaney's excitement rose. Landry was even using the same terms Delaney was thinking in. Landry could convince Elena to let them do a trial mission, just the two of them. Maybe not something quite as big as killing Hitler, maybe start a little smaller. Maybe they could do it off books, and when they got back, they could show how positive it was. How much easier it is to kill one bad guy than save one good guy, and how the benefits are even greater than what they already do.

"I know what you're talking about, believe me. I can't get rid of the things I've had to do for some of these missions. I have nightmares, crystal clear visions, and I wake up in cold sweats. Most nights, I just don't want to sleep."

"Is that why you're drinking so much?"

So that's what this is about? "What do you know about my drinking?" She had to play it a little coy, let Landry believe she was coming to Delaney's rescue.

"We've always been honest with each other, yeah?"

No. Otherwise I would've told you that you destroy me every time you leave my bed. "Sure."

"Buddy, you look like hell. Your face telegraphs your drinking habits. You look like you've worn your clothes to sleep in, and Jesus, you stink."

"Maybe honesty isn't the way for us. That was brutal." Delaney raised her mug to drain it, but Landry's raised eyebrow and judgmental glare temporarily stopped her.

"What's going on with you? You're not spending time with anyone other than Simson, and I don't know that she's the perfect companion."

"At least she's around." Delaney immediately wanted to pull the words back into her mouth. Now wasn't the time to be guilt-tripping Landry, not if she wanted to get her on her side. She looked up at Landry, whose body language told Delaney she was about to bolt. "Forget I said that." Delaney saw her relax, and she sat back down beside her. "Simson is easy to be around, and we have great sex. I don't need a huge array of friends, Landry, and I've never been big on socializing. You know that."

"Sure, but the drinking, Dee, and your appearance. I've known you long enough to know when something's bothering you. We've always liked a drink, it takes the edge from what we do, but there's something more. Something deeper. I know you're never going to lay your soul down with one of Castillo's minions, but it looks like you've got stuff to talk about, and it worries me that you might think you can't do it with me."

Delaney sighed. *Here we go.* "Do you ever question what we do?"

Landry's brow furrowed, and she shook her head. "No. What we do works. You're having doubts?"

"No, I know that. And I know we're making a difference." *Easy does it.* "But I don't think we're doing enough. Take our next mission, for example. Why don't they just send us back to assassinate Hitler? The doc we're trying to save will go on with her research, because Nazi Germany will never have existed. Sixty million people died in that war, and the board can't possibly know everything about that lost potential. Who knows how many missions we save ourselves with just one change."

"We can't go back and make wholesale changes that would have such a huge effect on the future, on our past. Any mission like that could have colossal implications that we just couldn't manage. Jenkin has Jewish ancestry—what if her family tree was affected by that genocide? She might end up not being born, Pulsus won't even start, and everything we've already done post-1945 could be undone. We could complete that mission and not even be able to come home. Another despot could rise, and we simply wouldn't be there to help. And it's not just that. Great minds are way ahead of their time. They see things in a way other people can't. Like this doctor. She'd got the way forward for cancer, but it was all in her mind, and no one else thinks that way. That's why even our scientists can't follow her journals. You can't hope to navigate the inside of someone else's brain, especially when they're fucking geniuses."

"There's got to be another way, Landry." *This isn't working. I've got to go deeper.* "I go back, for years sometimes, and I have to live with what I've done between missions. There's no amount of time with Castillo that can take that away. I've racked up over nine decades of mission time, and I'm not sure how much more my brain can take. You kind of know what I'm talking about; you're walking around with two lives in your head." Delaney poured another mug of bourbon and knocked it back.

"Is that what the drinking is about? You're trying to numb yourself?"

"You don't know what I've had to do. And what about this mission, going into the concentration camp? You think I'm gonna be serving those women three course meals and running hot baths for them? Fuck no, I'm going to have to herd people into the gas chamber. I'll have to whip the women who fall down exhausted and starving on their work duty. I'll be choosing candidates for the sick experiments they conducted. You'll come in, rescue the good doctor, and kill a few

Nazis. You're fighting the good fight. You have a clear conscience. All you have to deal with when we get home is assimilating any changes we've effected." Delaney sighed deeply and relaxed back in her chair. She wasn't an emotional person, but it felt good to get out what was bothering her. If anyone would be able to empathize with what she was going through, it was Landry, and if she could get her to empathize, maybe she'd see that Delaney's new protocol was the future of Pulsus.

Landry placed her hand gently on Delaney's forearm and leaned closer. "But changing the way we operate our missions won't take away the memories you already have. I get what you've had to do, and you wouldn't be human if it hadn't affected you. Maybe you need to take a longer break, get off the island, and build some different memories."

"Maybe I just need you." Delaney took Landry's proximity as an indicator, and leaned in to kiss her, but she pulled back.

"That won't solve anything, Dee. We can't fuck your issues away."

"You mean you won't because you're in love with that ball player?" *Fuck, how did we get here? I'm supposed to be getting her on my side, not fucking pushing her away.*

Landry shook her head. "This isn't about Jade. I told you, we're just friends. It's part of keeping sane, which is what I think you need. We both know you're not going to see Castillo or one of her cronies. We're soldiers, and that's not what we do. So get away from this place for a while on an extended vacation. Recharge. You need a different perspective on what you've had to do on missions. You're absolutely right about what I do, and I have no real idea how doing what you do affects you. But what you do matters. It's utterly vital, and we wouldn't be able to achieve anything without you. Dee, you were chosen for the position of operative because you've got the emotional resilience for this kind of work, but you're burned out right now because you've done mission after mission with no real break. But I need you with me, Dee. We're the best team Pulsus has, and I can't do this without you."

Delaney knew she needed to back off if she had any chance of convincing Landry to join her. "You're right. You always are. I'll take a break after this mission, and I'll even give the mainland a try, if you help me set something up."

Landry looked appeased, clamped her hand on Delaney's shoulder, and squeezed. "Of course, buddy, anything you need."

Delaney thought about Landry's words, *I can't do this without you.* She knew she'd made a mistake and come in too heavy, but Landry's words gave her hope. She'd do this mission and work on Landry when they got back. Once she was on board, Elena would follow, and Delaney was sure Jenkin would then do anything to keep her new lover happy. It was going to take a little more time than Delaney anticipated, but it *would* happen. Delaney was sure of that.

CHAPTER EIGHTEEN

January 6, 2076—Pulsus Island

"How's your German?"

"Mein Deutsch ist einfach perfekt. Wie geht's Dir?" Landry delivered the words in an impeccable native accent.

"I'm fine. I would've been better if you'd spent Christmas with us."

Her mom failed to hide the bitterness in her whispered voice. Landry ignored it and shook her head. Her mom knew that maintaining a professional relationship with her was paramount to Landry not losing the respect of her colleagues.

Delaney, Simson, and Griffin stood a few feet away. They were jumping together and were already dressed and styled for the era. Delaney and Simson both wore high-waisted wool trousers with one-inch turn-ups with a thin belt, simple three-quarter-length sleeve linen blouses, and boots with a stubby heel. They'd both had their hair lengthened with extensions to suit the period, and were styled with smooth sweptback rolls. It suited Delaney, but made Simson's face look even harder. Landry had a suspicion she'd fit in well, even enjoy herself, at Ravensbrück.

Griffin had the best deal, sporting a horsehide motorbike jacket Landry immediately coveted. He had gray wool trousers, held up with suspenders, and a simple cream linen shirt, hugging the contours of his Adonis body. His hair had been styled with a Wehrmacht cut, shaved to the skin two inches above his ears, and the remaining blond tuft on the top of his head was parted on the right.

"That blouse really sets off your green eyes, Delaney."

She punched Landry on the shoulder. "Fuck you. You got lucky getting to butch out in your carpenter-cum-cargo pants and man shirt. You're gonna get a rough ride when you land in our KZ."

Landry didn't miss the smirk that Simson quickly tried to hide. *She's counting on giving me a hard time.* "You're just jealous, *Sieglinde*." Landry hooked her thumbs onto the three-inch-wide leather belt holding up her masculine pants.

"You'll need to forget you know that name or you'll blow her cover," Simson said as she adjusted her belt.

"Really, *Johanna*, is that how this works? Now I know where I've been going wrong with the past twelve missions." Landry pulled in a deep breath and rolled her shoulders, the cracking of tortured muscle was audible. "Is there anything else you want to teach me?"

The challenge was clear, and Delaney stepped in front of the advancing Simson and pushed her back. "Leave it, Simms. She's just fucking with me."

"That's exactly what I have a problem with," she muttered quietly.

Landry heard, but was sure she wasn't supposed to. It explained why Simson was being more confrontational than usual, and why Delaney had been spending so much time with her. Simson had nothing to be jealous of. She had no claim on Delaney, and she didn't want one. *Especially now that everything is more complicated.*

"T minus ten minutes. Time for you three to go down to the jump platform." Elena motioned to the door. Simson shot a glare at Landry before heading out, closely followed by Griffin.

"Stay safe." Landry grabbed Delaney's forearm and pulled her into a tight hug.

"I'll be fine. You watch your step. This mission ain't no walk in the park."

"I'll see you at the camp in four years."

Delaney smiled, but there was no hint of it in her eyes. "I'll see you back here in four and a half months."

"It'll fly by, Dee. Then we hit the mainland and get your head cleared."

"Sure."

Delaney said the right thing, but Landry didn't feel it resonate. She just hoped it wouldn't be too late.

❖

"Please be extra careful with this mission, Landry. You can't afford any mistakes before you enter the camp."

"Thanks for the vote of confidence, Mom," Landry replied, gently laughing.

"You know what I mean, pumpkin. This is the not the kind of time you can, well, be you."

She put her hands on Landry's shoulders, and Landry put her own hand over one of her mom's to reassure her. She was glad they were in the debrief room, and that nobody could hear them. She'd never live that nickname down. Her mom's use of such an endearing term made her discomfited and yet comfortable at the same time.

"Keep digging that hole. I'll be fine. I know what I need to do, and I know when I need to tone *me* down."

"I know, baby, but you seem…distracted. Usually, you're so focused pre-jump, but I noticed that Simson managed to irritate you. She often tries, but I've never seen her succeed, until today." Her mom pulled a swivel chair and sat directly in front of Landry. "Is there something you want to talk about?"

Is there? Is Mom who I talk to about Jade? "I don't know…you think I'm distracted? Can anyone else see that?"

"Of course not. You wear a great mask for everyone else, but I'm your mom, and I can tell when something's bothering you. I'm not quite good enough to figure out what it is without you talking to me, but I can feel you're not quite right."

Landry broke the intense stare and looked at her feet. "I think I'm developing feelings for someone. Beyond the usual, beyond sex…" She let the words sink in, not for her mom, but because she was admitting it to herself.

"Jacqulyn?"

"God, no. We're just—" Landry stopped herself. *I'm not saying "fuck buddies" to you, no matter how close a relationship we're trying to develop.*

"Friends with benefits?"

"Friends."

"Who fuck."

"Mom!"

"What? I can't say fuck?"

"Not about me, no."

"So if it's not Jacqulyn, who is it? Have you taken a liking to a new recruit?"

Landry exhaled a deep breath, preparing herself for her mom's reaction. "Her name's Jade Carter. She's a basketball player for the Warriors." Landry saw something in her mom's eyes, but it was too fleeting to name. Fading hope? Disappointment? Resignation?

"Baby, you know I support your choice to have a life outside of the organization, but can't you fall for someone in Pulsus? Wouldn't that be easier?"

"Because I have a choice? Did you have a choice when you fell for Jenkin?" Landry didn't hide the contempt in her voice, but the look on her mom's face made her wish that she had.

"Is that why you didn't come back for Christmas?"

"We haven't got time for this, Mom. I need to get my head straight for the jump." Landry started to rise from her chair, but her mom pulled her back down.

"We're making time. That's what we do here. Sit."

Landry sighed but did as she was told. *This mom-daughter thing can be a pain in the ass.*

"Is my relationship with JJ the reason you didn't come home for Christmas?"

She took issue with her mom's wording. "This isn't home."

"Stop being pedantic and answer the question. Is it?"

"It wasn't the only reason, but yeah, it was part of it. I need my space from the island, and you know that." She said the words, but as soon as they were out of her mouth, she knew she was sounding like a spoiled child.

"But this is the first Christmas you've been around for three years. It would've been nice for us to spend it together."

"Nice for you maybe, but not for me. What is it with families that there's so much pressure to do what makes other people feel better instead of what you really want to do? Did you enjoy it? Was it everything you'd hoped it would be?"

"Don't do that. Don't get angry and turn this on me. Why is it so hard for you to be part of our family? Your brother and his family made—"

"He's not my brother, and he never will be."

"Are you still angry about me remarrying?"

"Dad was barely lukewarm in his grave."

Her mom got up from her chair and headed for the door. She had a hold of the handle and opened it before she turned around and looked at Landry. Her stare was cold and hard.

"You have no idea who, or what, your father really was."

The door slammed behind her, and Elena's words slammed hard into Landry's consciousness.

"Donovan, please report to the jump site. T minus twenty minutes to activation."

The speakers reverberated in the darkened, sparse debriefing room.

Her mom's words echoed in Landry's head. When they'd gone into the room to talk, it was two hours before she needed to be ready for the jump, to give them time to recalibrate the jump machine, and refresh the consumables required for time travel. She estimated their mom-daughter chat had taken less than fifteen minutes, so she'd sat there in the dark for over an hour, in some kind of shock. She'd believed her parents' relationship was perfect, and neither of them had ever said otherwise. Sure, he wasn't there a lot because of his job, but her mom had never complained. *What the hell does she mean?*

There was a sharp knock at the door before it was pushed open and one of the jump team peered around the corner, somewhat gingerly.

"Landry?"

She stood and stepped toward her. "*Ich komme*...I'm coming." For now, she needed to push her mom's cryptic claim aside and focus on the job, which was already proving difficult with thoughts of Jade swimming around her mind.

"This is a tough mission, Landry. Good luck."

Landry thanked Micky and walked beside her toward the operations landing.

"This one's personal. There are a lot of us Jews around this place. I wonder if we could do more."

That's what Delaney thinks too. She put her hand on Micky's shoulder to stop her before they entered the jump room. "We do what we can, Mick. We can't make wholesale changes when we have no idea what the consequences will be. You're a techy. You know that better than any of us."

"I guess. Just be careful, Landry. You're our best extractor. You lead the way for many of us, and we can't lose you. It feels like there's a lot more riding on this one." Micky didn't wait for another response, but opened the door and motioned for Landry to go in.

She looked up and saw her mom on the operations platform but didn't acknowledge her. Micky handed her the PRU, and Landry tucked it into the inside pocket of her leather flight jacket. She climbed the short ladder to the jump platform and waited for the countdown.

"T minus thirty seconds."

Landry wanted to look back at her mom, but restrained herself. Micky's worry about her not returning had made her a little uneasy. *What if I don't come back this time?* Every mission was a risk. There was always a strong chance of failure if something went wrong on the other side. It hadn't bothered her until now.

But now, there's Jade.

Chapter Nineteen

November 9, 1938—Berlin, Germany

Looking around, Delaney found it hard to believe the country was less than a year away from invading Poland and setting in motion the world's most lethal military conflict to date. They'd jumped to Grunewald Forest in West Berlin, far enough away from the city that their time entry wouldn't be detected, but close enough to make their first journey relatively easy. They were surrounded by conifers, birch trees, and shrubs, and had entered on the edge of the Havel River. She took a deep breath of the fresh, natural air. It was peaceful and beautiful, a far cry from where they'd all be tonight, taking part in *Kristallnacht*, the night of broken glass, to announce their allegiance to the Führer. Griffin would head to the Fasanenstrasse Synagogue to carry out Joseph Goebbels's destructive orders, justified by the assassination of Hitler's ambassador to France, by a seventeen-year-old German Jew. Delaney and Simson would join the general populace on the streets, raiding homes and destroying shops. The air she'd be breathing tonight would be full of smoke and fire.

For now, she tried to distract herself from the impending pogrom. "I'm glad they always get the dimension calculations right. I'd hate to ruin my only outfit by getting it wet."

Delaney had emerged from the jump spot a few minutes before Griffin, who was closely followed by Simson. It was something to do with her height to weight ratio, and being the lightest, Delaney moved through time slightly faster than the other two. It seemed like it should be that heavier things dropped faster, but she didn't grasp the science of it, she didn't need to, so she didn't think about it all that much. Just as she never liked to dwell on the knowledge that unless the extractor showed up, there'd be no way of getting home.

"Didn't they tell you not to eat before a jump?" Simson laughed while Griffin continued to cough up what seemed like the entire contents of his stomach, and its lining, into the river.

"The first jump is always the worst. The speed and bright lights mess with your eyes," Delaney offered to comfort him. "It gets easier."

"Butch up, Griff." Simson showed little sympathy.

"Don't you mean, 'man up'?" Griffin asked, spitting out the last chunk of his breakfast.

"No." Simson spat the word like a shotgun. "I said what I meant."

Griffin moved farther along the river, away from his vomit, to rinse his mouth. "If it feels like that every time, I'm not sure I want to go back." He wiped away the excess water with the sleeve of his jacket. "So we go our separate ways now?"

Delaney laid out a map on the floor. "You do. We're heading for the train lines. We're about six clicks west of platform seventeen. We'll catch the train to Berlin, and you get to walk. Head north-northeast for five clicks, and you'll hit the B2. Stick to that road all the way into the city, for another ten clicks. It's thirty degrees, so keep a swift pace, and you'll be in Berlin in less than three hours." She folded the map and handed it to him.

"I guess I'll see you in a year or so then?" He took the map and a step back, but seemed slightly hesitant to leave them.

"If we don't bump into you tonight and everything else goes according to plan, that's the idea. Are we good?" Delaney could see a hint of anxiety in his eyes. It had been so long, almost a century in real terms. It was hard to remember how she'd felt the first time she jumped for a mission.

"He'll be fine." Simson ate up the ground between them with three large strides, and whacked him hard across his back. "Won't you, *Christoph*? This is what you've been training for, what you joined us for. There's nothing more thrilling than going it alone on the first mission, trust me." She shoved him hard in the chest. "Now get moving. We can't risk being seen together. Go make some nice Nazi friends, drink lots of German beer, and try not to get killed."

Delaney watched him turn and walk away, without a second glance. "Your methods of motivation are questionable."

Simson laughed. "But they work, so who really gives a shit? He's ready, or he wouldn't be here. This'd be a tough mission for a novice, but he's ex-CIA. Deep cover like this is a walk in the park."

"Time to go catch a train then, sister."

"Sister. Dumb fucking luck. Next time we mission together, I want input on our cover story. How are we supposed to fuck without getting accused of incest?"

Laughing, Delaney shook her head. "We're not gonna be fucking. You'll just have to satisfy yourself for the next four years."

"You know that's not happening. If you're gonna ration me, I'll just have to find myself a nice plaything at the Magic Flute Dance Palace, and then a hefty little guard to occupy myself with when we get to the camp."

She knew Simson was trying to make her jealous, but she didn't have it in her to feel that emotion when it came to Simson. *But when Landry gets here, that'll be another thing.* "It's comforting that you've researched the important things about Nazi Germany. I'm glad that the mission won't get in the way of your raging libido."

"We're gonna be here for four years, Delaney. I'll bet you a thousand dollars you take a few lovers."

Delaney tilted her head, conceding Simson's point. Four years was a long time not to have sex with anyone but herself, and their "sister" cover story meant Simson was off-limits, no matter how desperate either of them were. At least lesbians weren't persecuted like gay men. The Third Reich decided it was too difficult to differentiate between social affection and true lesbianism, and regardless of sexuality, all women could still do their Nazi duty by giving birth to more Aryan babies. Not being physically able to carry a child was the only thing she could be thankful to her father for.

She pushed thoughts of her father as far from her conscious mind as possible. "I'm not taking that bet; the odds are slim."

Simson nodded and laughed lasciviously. "That's the Delaney I know."

"So, *Johanna*, my much heavier and uglier sister, let's go find lodgings in Berlin and employment at the workhouse. Maybe that's where you'll find your first sex toy of this mission, a prostitute."

"I've never had to pay for it, and I'm not about to start, *Sieglinde*."

"Then it'll be the best place for you. That's the reason these women are there, so you can teach them how to give up sex for free."

"Suddenly, the next four years are starting to look a little brighter."

Delaney's mind flashed to the images she'd seen and the texts she'd read in preparation for this mission. Once they hit Ravensbrück, bright wouldn't be part of their vocabulary. Part of their job was to look after the doctor, which would mean being stationed in the medical facility, selecting prisoners for experimentation and shipping out body parts to the Race Hygiene and People's Biology Research Institute.

Delaney could only hope that Landry's cover held up to scrutiny, and she didn't end up being one of the guinea pigs. Delaney knew if it was a choice between the mission and Landry's well-being, she'd choose to save Landry every time.

Chapter Twenty

June 2, 1942—Tollensesee, Neubrandenburg

Landry knelt in the sand and leaned against the trunk of the impressive tree that stretched itself fifteen meters over the Tollensesee, before its end branch dipped delicately into the water. The effect of the faint clouds veiled thinly over the rising sun and the still lake created a perfectly lit reflection silhouette. It would've made a beautiful canvas against the stark brick wall of her lounge, maybe opposite the pool table...*where I'd like to lay Jade.*

She pushed the distracting image away and focused on finding the perfect place to hide the PRU while they completed their mission. Once they left the camp, they'd have to come back here before heading for America to safely deposit the good doctor at the New York University Hospital. Safely there, the doctor would be able to continue her research, and when the team jumped back to 2076, there'd be no more cancer. This time, the effects of her mission would be seen close to home. Caitlin's first partner, Theresa, died of cancer, and Landry was concerned she'd get home to a completely different scenario in the unit beneath her apartment. With Theresa never getting cancer, would she be Caitlin's wife, or were Lizbeth and Caitlin fated to spend their lives together? Priscilla was Lizbeth's biological daughter, but would she have had a baby without Caitlin, and would she still have gambled on the restaurant business? The thought of not having that family in her life was physically painful, but it was an absolute possibility. Every mission she or the other extractors completed would change aspects of their lives in the future. It was yet another reason she couldn't get involved with Jade. Landry could jump back to 2076, and Jade might not have ever existed.

Landry knocked her head gently against the tree trunk. *Jesus Christ, if I don't concentrate, I'll end up dead.* She stood up, glad the slight nausea from the jump had worn off. That was something that just didn't stop, no matter how many times she did it. She slipped the small black rubberized unit into its watertight housing and climbed the tree until she was over halfway along it. It bowed slightly under her weight, and its dipping end branch formed ever-increasing circles in the water. Landry stuck three fingers into the tree hollow she'd spotted from the lakeside and dug out the fungi, careful not to let any drop into the water. She took the waterproof bag holding their passports and other mission papers from her pocket and placed them into the hole. She put the PRU after them and pushed them deep enough into the hole so that she could just reach it with her index and middle finger, before replacing the fungi and patting it back down. Confident it looked as though she'd never been there, she retreated along the trunk to the shore.

She took one last look at the age-old tree to ensure it was imprinted on her memory, and began her five-kilometer trek along the path toward Neubrandenburg.

Just over an hour later, Landry was circling the outside of the city walls, looking for a place where she could be discovered. She'd read about this perimeter, and seen photographs of its four Brick Gothic city gates, which still stood in 2076. She was glad it survived the assault by the Red Army that would take place in three years, at the end of this deadly war. The timbered Wiek houses built into the wall reminded her of Stratford, England, a place she'd visited after she finished college. She couldn't help being typically American that way, in her love and envy of British history. In her time, the houses had been converted and were restaurants, museums, and wineries. Now, people loved them as their homes.

As the sun rose and the temperature hit the sixties, she stowed her leather jacket over the satchel she was carrying. Her shirt had followed, and she'd stripped to her tank top halfway through the trek. A woman hanging her washing eyed Landry suspiciously from one of the house gardens outside the perimeter wall, and she became slightly conscious of her conspicuous appearance. She pulled her shirt on, but left it open and tucked it into her carpenter pants. The heat was stifling, and she needed water. Given that the woman was airing only dresses, Landry calculated she must live alone, or her husband had joined the army. Either way, she was probably lonely and Landry could exploit that loneliness. The three-story house looked run-down and in need of a coat of paint. The garden was overgrown and clearly hadn't been tended in a while. She smiled at the woman and strode toward her, stopping at the closed gate.

"Could I trouble you for some water?" Landry asked in German. A few silent moments passed while the woman took her time looking Landry over. She said nothing, but went inside and emerged with a glass of a murky looking liquid.

"Come inside," she said finally, stepping a little closer.

Landry smiled and did as she was told, closing the gate carefully behind her. She took the proffered glass and knocked it back. "Thank you."

"Why have you come here?"

No small talk, then. "I'm looking for work." A simple response. No need to complicate things.

"What kind of work?" The woman retrieved her glass, and her fingers brushed lightly over Landry's hand.

"Anything physical. I'm a carpenter. And a plumber. Do you have work for me?"

The woman's eyes darted to the left and right, before she smiled. "I can't pay you, but I can give you lodgings. No doubt you need a place to stay."

No, Landry didn't need a place to stay. She needed a place where she could draw attention to herself and get arrested. A garden on the outskirts of this town fit that bill, and a Nazi patrol was sure to pass by soon enough, on the lookout for anything out of the ordinary.

"For a few days, perhaps. What work do you have?"

"I'm told it is man's work, but there are no men around anymore. They've all gone to join Hitler."

She extended her right arm in the air, but her "Sieg Heil" lacked passion and commitment. Landry frowned, fully aware the straight-arm salute had been appropriated from the USA's early pledge of allegiance to the flag, enforced in schools when racism and segregation were rife.

"I can do just about anything a man can do."

The woman looked Landry over once more, a little slower and perhaps more appreciatively than the first time, before a smile began to form on her lips. "My name is Margret."

"Truda." Landry offered her hand. "What can I do to help?"

"Truda." Margret shook Landry's hand as she rolled her name around her mouth as if she were tasting a fine wine. "You can start by rebuilding that wall. You will find everything you need over there." She pointed to a dilapidated building beside the house. "I'll make lunch in a few hours. You might want to avoid the midday troop unit by busying yourself in the shed. If there is trouble, you are on your own."

Landry nodded her understanding and thanked her again before turning to gather some tools. The wall was close enough to the main road for her to be noticed without making an obvious scene.

All she had to do now was wait.

Chapter Twenty-one

December 13, 1940—Ravensbrück

A hundred yards outside the camp walls, in a perversely idyllic setting amidst pine trees, Delaney sat on the edge of Ilsa Blumstein's bed in their shared villa. Through the window, she could see the moon bouncing off the still waters of the Schwedtsee Lake, and it cast a soft light into the room. Were it not for the grotesquely fresh memory of transporting ten dead, but still warm, bodies of women to the ovens of the Fürstenberg crematorium a few miles from the camp, Delaney might have thought she were on vacation in a national park. The prisoners she'd helped to move brought the death toll to just under forty for the year. In her first year there, just four women died, all from relatively natural causes. If she didn't know exactly how this camp panned out, and that 90,000 women and children would be killed here over the next five years, she might have thought the place wasn't so bad. But Hitler and his Jewish Solution was just beginning, and her job here was only going to get worse, starting next year, when the mass murders would begin.

For now though, the camp was just a prison, and Delaney was working her way into Dr. Chernick's small inner circle of four trusted prisoners…and this female guard. She pulled the thin cotton sheet back to uncover Ilsa, and caressed the curves of her breasts with her fingertips. She smiled as Ilsa raised her body from the bed, urging her to explore further.

"Please…"

Softly spoken as she was, Ilsa made the German language seem almost romantic. Delaney was glad Ilsa turned out to be gay. It made getting close to her easier. She suspected it was the reason Ilsa had ended up smuggling Dr. Chernick's research journals, fueled by the sisterly connection of sexuality.

"Aren't you worried you might be caught?" Delaney needed Ilsa to be concerned for her own safety so she'd accept help. When Landry came to complete the operation, it was important for Chernick to know that Delaney was on her side. Ilsa was her way in.

"It's just research. Bina tells me she's working on a cure for cancer. If she's on to something…if she never gets out of here… Maybe someone can continue with her work if I can get them to the right person." Ilsa wrapped her hand around Delaney's neck and pulled her down to kiss her. "You can help me. You can protect me, my strong guardian angel." Her other hand gripped Delaney's bicep, barely wrapping even halfway around.

"Protect you with these?" Delaney flexed, and Ilsa moaned appreciatively. "We'll have to be careful. How many journals do you have already, and where are you hiding them?" Delaney moved from Ilsa's mouth to her nipple, and sucked one between her lips.

"I have just one so far. And I'm not hiding it. It's in plain sight on the bookcase in the reading room." She gasped as Delaney nibbled lightly with her teeth. "They have no reason to search our living quarters. I provide her with the same journals I buy from Fürstenberg, so they blend in with my own."

"Such a clever girl." Delaney continued downward, kissing Ilsa's ribs and stomach. She made a mental note to buy some identical journals, so she could replace Chernick's. When Landry got here, and they began the doctor's extraction, Delaney would need to have secured the books to take with them to the States. Getting Chernick out was only half the problem. Getting her halfway around the world to her university hospital was the truly dangerous part of the mission. At least in that part, Delaney would only have to kill the bad guys.

"I'm wasted here, but my law degree means nothing in Hitler's world."

Delaney sighed, glad she hadn't been born into this time, this place. Women had been blamed for taking "men's jobs" and corrupting the morals of the country. As soon as Hitler had taken power in 1933, women were fired or barred from most jobs, and access to universities was restricted. It made her rethink her strategy. She and Simson had been present at the failed assassination attempt on November 8, 1939, in Munich. She could've helped them succeed. She could've put an end to all of this, and women could've continued to follow a more liberal path. Ilsa could still be a practicing lawyer.

Delaney brought herself back into the moment. "I'm sorry, Ilsa." Her words were genuine, even though her interest in Ilsa wasn't. She pushed Ilsa's thighs apart and settled between them. She lightly blew hot breath onto her swollen lips, and Ilsa raised her hips to meet Delaney's mouth.

"Don't be. I'm not. I would never have met you if I was still a lawyer in Berlin, would I?" She placed her hand on Delaney's head and gently pressed her down. "Enough talking, sweet Sieglinde. Please make me come...again."

She smiled, and the desperate need in her eyes was clear. Delaney began with soft kisses and ran her tongue along from the tip of Ilsa's clit to the hot, wet hole that was dripping with desire. She pushed her tongue deep inside, and Ilsa moaned as she tenderly wrapped her fingers in Delaney's hair. Ilsa's delicate touch was something Delaney simply wasn't used to. With Landry and Simson, the sex was hard, fast, and hot. It delivered much but promised little. Without saying a word, Ilsa was demanding that Delaney make love to her. It almost felt like a welcome change to be wanted this way. The problem was, Ilsa wanted Sieglinde Thalberg. She had no idea who Jacqulyn Delaney was, and if she did, she'd probably want nothing to do with her.

Delaney took a deep breath and centered her concentration. Ilsa had to feel her there, physically and emotionally. Even though they'd only been having sex for three weeks, Ilsa knew when Delaney's mind wandered. And it wandered often. But Ilsa would stop whatever they were doing, look into Delaney's eyes, and ask "Where are you?" It was more than a little unnerving, and Delaney was finding that the only way to stop it from happening was to be fully present.

She grasped Ilsa's thighs and pulled her deeper. She circled her clit soft and slow, just the way Ilsa had taught her that she loved. Ilsa reached down, took one of Delaney's hands, and pressed it over her breast. She knew what she wanted. Delaney really liked that about her. So much better than a woman who would just lie there, uncommunicative, expecting Delaney to guess what turned her on, then blame her for not being telepathic. That kind of woman was infuriating.

Delaney ran her finger over Ilsa's nipple, mirroring the movements of her tongue. Ilsa groaned and began to raise and dip her ass as she approached her orgasm. Delaney felt the throbbing in Ilsa's pussy increase, pulsing her pleasure. She gripped Delaney's hair just a little tighter as her grinding became more frantic. Delaney kept the rhythm of her tongue and finger in strict synchronicity, knowing that the combination would soon have Ilsa riding out her release, and yelling into a pillow to subdue her animalistic cries.

"Perfect...please...don't stop."

Delaney couldn't resist a smile. "Don't stop" was a plea she liked most. So much more than "please stop." She squeezed her eyes shut tightly and refocused again. Now wasn't the time to be thinking about her missions.

Ilsa's climax was fast approaching. She let go of Delaney's hair and took hold of the headboard, gripping it so tightly Delaney could see her knuckles whiten. Her thighs held Delaney in place, though she had no intention of moving. Ilsa pushed her hips up hard, thrusting herself into Delaney's mouth. She turned her face into her pillow and suffocated her scream, desperate not to wake her sleeping colleagues in neighboring villas.

She remained in place until the throbbing subsided, and Ilsa's thighs released her. She took her place beside Ilsa and pulled her into her arms, covering her with the sheet to keep her warm. Ilsa nestled her face into Delaney's neck and murmured her gratitude before quickly falling asleep.

Delaney looked up at the ceiling. She tried to fix her attention on the uneven brushstrokes and count them. Maybe that would help her fall into an uninterrupted sleep. She was kidding herself. All she could really see were the prisoners in the crematorium, sweeping out the remains of their friends from the ovens. They'd only been here just over a year. It was another eighteen months before Landry would show, rescue Chernick, and take them on the final part of the mission to deliver the doctor to the States. Delaney took a deep breath and let it out slowly, cooling the sweat on her body. *How many more innocent people do I have to kill in that time?*

CHAPTER TWENTY-TWO

June 2, 1942—Neubrandenburg

Landry only had to work three hours before two gray-green uniformed police officers strolled into view. The heat of the noon sun, coupled with the strenuous work of wall building meant she'd stripped down to her tank, so she knew she'd attract their attention without really having to try. A woman with her physique wasn't inconspicuous in this time, and in a town this small, she expected the police knew everyone by name.

"Where is Margret?"

Landry could tell from his fancy plaited epaulettes he was a major, while his colleague was merely a sergeant. "I believe she's inside, Major. Do you want me to get her for you?"

"I will see for myself." They came through the gate and marched to the door, their eyes narrowed and questioning. The major didn't knock, but merely stepped inside the house while his sergeant stood guard, watching Landry as she continued to build the wall.

In her peripheral vision, she saw him light a thin cigarette before he sat down on a metal garden chair with a clear view of Landry. He tried his best to look menacing as he took slow, deliberate draws of his smoke, but Landry simply smiled to herself and carried on with her work.

Margret appeared in the doorway with the major, just as the sergeant finished his cigarette and flicked it Landry's way. She could clearly see her looking panicked and terrified. Her blouse was torn, and her hair and makeup disheveled. Landry tossed the stone she was moving to the ground and advanced toward them.

"What happened, Margret?"

"Your papers. Show them to me." The major stepped in front of Margret and held out his hand. His sergeant stood at attention, obviously anticipating trouble.

"Why?" *Game on.*

He laughed and flicked a backhanded slap at Landry's face. She saw it coming in super slow motion, much like a fly sees any human movement, but she didn't move to avoid it or block it. She let his leather clad hand connect with her cheek and lip, and her head snapped to the right.

"I don't need a reason, bitch."

The sergeant pulled his Browning GP-35 from his hip holster and leveled it at Landry's face as she turned back to them. She spat out blood at the major's feet and smiled. "Auditioning for the SS?" Landry briefly saw the shock on Margret's face, before the major struck her again.

The sergeant grabbed Landry by her neck and shoved her into the wall of the house. The rough brick grazed her face as his gun pressed into her temple, and his stale breath invaded her nostrils.

"Margret. Her bag."

Landry blinked, trying to signal to Margret that it was okay and she should do as he asked. She hesitated for a moment before disappearing from Landry's view to retrieve her satchel. The sergeant spun Landry around and forced her into the seat he'd previously occupied. His sweaty hand gripped her neck and his gun still nestled at her temple. The major snatched Landry's bag from Margret and tossed it on the table in front of her.

"Is there anything in here you shouldn't have?"

The sergeant cuffed Landry's head hard with the butt of his gun when she failed to answer, and she closed her eyes to fight off a threatening lack of consciousness.

"Depends. I'm sure you'll find something you think I shouldn't have."

The major smiled widely, revealing yellow, tobacco stained teeth. "Spoken like a true criminal. What is your name?" He opened Landry's bag, turned it upside down, and emptied the contents across the table.

"You don't want to ruin the surprise."

He nodded to his sergeant, who slammed Landry's head against the table. She saw stars, and a growing blackness seeped into the outer edges of her eyes. When he pulled her back up with a handful of her hair, the major had found what he was searching for, and opened up her papers to inspect them.

"Truda Stark. I see. I think you will join us at the station to see if there are any notices for a Truda Stark. Perhaps there we will persuade you to be more forthcoming."

He nodded again to his lackey, and the sergeant quickly secured Landry in metal handcuffs. He pulled her from the chair by her neck and shoved her forward toward the gate, while the major quickly refilled Landry's bag with her few belongings, mostly collected from empty houses and cars on the way from her jump site.

"Margret."

"Yes, Major Oster?"

Landry heard the fear in her voice.

"How long have you been harboring this…woman?"

"She stopped by here this morning, looking for work. With Dierk away, I needed some help. She said she could fix the wall."

Oster caught Landry by the shoulder. "Is that right, Stark? Did you offer to do the work of this woman's husband?"

"I did. She doesn't know me, and I don't know her. I'm just passing through."

Oster smiled as he picked up her leather jacket from the half-repaired wall. "Not any more. You'll be staying while I get to know you, and that could take some time."

Days passed. Nights dragged. In the dark, concrete cell, the screams of fellow inmates echoed around the walls and filled her ears. When it was her turn, Landry was hauled from the floor, stripped down, and beaten with rubber clubs until her consciousness crumbled. Ice-cold water pulled her back to a vague awareness of her surroundings, only for them to begin again. They never asked a single question.

Oster had visited daily, after each session of abuse, to ask if she was ready to give up the location of her "husband." Landry knew they'd never find him, and she had no information to help them in her search. And since the real Truda Stark was holed up with her husband somewhere, she had to hope history didn't change because of her presence.

On what was maybe her sixth or seventh day in his prison, Oster entered Landry's cell, dragged her to the door, and knelt beside her. She could hear the distinctive sound of multiple, synchronized gunshots. *The firing squad.*

"Your days as a criminal are over, Stark. It would be better for you to tell us where he is. Then we can pack you off to a comfortable women's prison, and you will serve your time. We have no more time for your resolve. Talk to me now, or…"

He looked outside and Landry looked away. "I don't know where he is. We were in Hamburg three weeks ago after a job went wrong, and I woke to find him gone. I can't help you." Landry turned to face Oster, careful to portray the fear he wanted to see in her eyes. "If I knew anything, I would've told you. I don't owe him anything, least of all this." She motioned to her bruised and battered body.

"I want to believe you, Truda, I do. But you've been nothing but obstinate since you crossed my path."

"I was angry. My husband had just left me, and I was… frightened." Landry could see him processing, and his grip on her arm loosened slightly. "If I knew where he was, I'd tell you. I can't take this anymore."

He released his hold on her completely and stood up. "Richter, Scherer."

The two guards appeared around the edge of the cell door. "Sir?"

"Prepare Stark for transport."

One of them looked down at her with what looked like concern. "To where?"

"Ravensbrück. Gather her things. Get her jacket."

Score. "Thank you, Major Oster. For sparing me, thank you."

He smiled, smug and self-congratulating. "I'm sure they will find good use for you there, Truda. Perhaps you might emerge a reformed woman."

Landry nodded, looking as contrite as she could manage. Internally, she was pleased with getting to Ravensbrück in less than a week. *Phase one complete.*

Chapter Twenty-three

September 23, 1941—Ravensbrück

A new intake was about to arrive at the small railway station in Fürstenberg. Over five hundred Polish women packed on a train, some from the infamous Lublin Castle, with no idea where they might end up. Delaney bet they were thinking that no matter where they were traveling to, it couldn't be any worse than where they'd already been held and tortured. *You couldn't be more wrong.*

Delaney had volunteered to head up the team collecting the women. She needed a break from the invasive viciousness of the camp. She and Simson had just returned from a recovery party for an escapee, a Romany woman called Katharina, for whom the four-meter walls of this hellish prison were too much to bear. She'd managed to scale them, avoiding electrocution by virtue of an ingenious use of her raggedy, threadbare bed blanket. It was the second time she'd escaped, and the camp commandant, Strauss, took it as a personal affront to his authority. She'd been in the punishment block, so he chained her fellow prisoners together and made them stand in their cells, without food or water. He ordered the rest of the prisoners to stand in the grounds of the camp indefinitely, or until the gypsy woman had been captured. They finally found her living up a tree in the Müritz national park, and returned triumphant on the fourth consecutive day. Strauss had spent that time deciding on her punishment, and gathered the whole camp to watch as the starved and delirious prisoners were directed to beat Katharina to death with the legs of their cell chairs.

Delaney had tried to look beyond the slaughter. The stench of vomit from the prisoners as her cellmates continued to pound Katharina's limp, bloodied body into the mud, temporarily replaced the smoky soot of freshly cremated bodies. She saw Ilsa slip away from the edge of a group of prisoners, her hand clamped over her mouth in an obvious attempt to stop being sick herself. Simson seemed to look on dispassionately, and Delaney wondered if any of this affected her, or if she managed to stay completely remote and removed from it. If she did, Delaney needed some tips on how to do exactly the same. There was another ten months of this before they would bust out with the doc. The nightmares were getting worse. She felt like the violence was conquering her.

The smoke from the train was visible before the train appeared. Vogt smacked her across the shoulder forcefully.

"I bet these bitches think they're coming to a vacation camp. We'll show them, Thalberg."

Delaney nodded and smiled with enough sadistic enthusiasm to satisfy the camp's most notorious female guard. There'd been a rumor she'd used the skin of a prisoner she particularly liked to make a lampshade. When she and a select few guards were invited to Vogt's villa for dinner, there was a lamp matching its description standing proudly in her living room. Ilsa wouldn't sit anywhere near it, particularly after Simson asked Vogt outright if the rumor was true. Vogt had smiled broadly and wiggled her eyebrows playfully, her lack of respect for human life blatant. "*Of course it is, Johanna. What is the point in having a reputation if you do not deserve it?*" She was referring to her unofficial moniker of the Angel of Death, a title she clearly appreciated, and one she worked hard to maintain, abusing prisoners at any and every opportunity.

As the train slowed, Delaney took the opportunity to study the twenty-year-old Erika Vogt. The soft waves of her hair fell onto her shoulders lightly, 1940s movie star-style, but that was in complete contradiction to her hardened face and her brown eyes…Delaney wasn't a religious person, but it was easy to say there was evil in those eyes. Unadulterated, pure, deep evil. And it was being allowed unchecked access to vulnerable souls, allowing her to play out any sick and twisted fantasy she so desired. In her knee-high socks, checked shirt, and sweater vest, she could've been mistaken for a school matron. But what the prisoners saw was a tyrannical beast, and to say that the ones about to disembark were in for a shock would've been the understatement of every century Delaney had operated in.

The train doors were pulled open, and women of all shapes, sizes, and ages tentatively emerged. Vogt moved forward, yelling orders in German, ordering the prisoners to line up in rows of five. Her Alsatian, Buster, costumed in his dog jacket replete with the SS logo, strained at the leash, and echoed her orders with deep throated barks. She and other guards struck out at the stragglers with plaited whips and threatened to flog their breasts if they didn't get in line fast enough. Delaney saw Ilsa helping the older prisoners from the train and onto the platform, gently organizing them into the group. Her compassion and care was so utterly outweighed by the other guards' wretched behavior.

Delaney would be sorry to leave her behind, but was marginally comforted with the knowledge that she would be dismissed from the camp the following year, unable to cope with the deteriorating treatment of the prisoners, and unwilling to participate in the ever increasing brutalities. She would miss the worst of it, but Delaney decided that when they jumped home, she'd find out what happened to Ilsa Blumstein after 1943. If she were in charge of this operation, maybe she'd just take her home with them. Maybe Ilsa was the antidote to Landry, and if she took her back to 2076, they could have a life together and Ilsa wouldn't have to witness any more of this.

Delaney pulled her attention away from Ilsa and watched as, bewildered and confused, the prisoners quickly did as they were instructed, and Vogt soon had her one hundred lines of women ready to march. *To their death.* Delaney tempered the thought that it wasn't necessarily true. They had a one in three chance of not being exterminated or dying from disease or exhaustion, and surviving until they would be liberated in three years' time, only to be raped by their own soldiers.

Delaney looked along the mass of women, some in rags, some in finer clothes, and others with bags of their own possessions, ignorant to the fact they would be stripped of them once they were within the cold, callous walls of Ravensbrück. An uneasy hush overtook the cacophony of barking, shouting, and crying as Vogt began to lead the prisoners on the one-mile march to their new home. Delaney slowed her pace so she could walk alongside Ilsa. She was becoming reliant on Ilsa's softness to balance the pitiless cruelty she had to exhibit and live with on a daily basis.

"That woman makes my skin crawl," Ilsa whispered quietly. "How can one so young be so vile?"

"Maybe she had a tough childhood and this is her way of working through that."

"Don't joke, Sigi. Your childhood was tough, and you're not being a sadistic monster to these poor women."

Delaney bit her lip. In building her cover story with Ilsa, she'd told her way too much of her real life. There was something so ingenuous about Ilsa that Delaney found it hard to lie to her, any more than was absolutely necessary.

"Things are changing around here, Ilsa. Maybe this isn't the place for you anymore." Ilsa had served her purpose in the mission. Getting close to her had resulted in Chernick trusting Delaney. She now had access to Chernick's journals, and had already smuggled two out of the camp and into her villa. Delaney couldn't see what the harm might be if Ilsa got out of here earlier, with a little more of her innocence intact. *But it'd make this mission a whole lot lonelier*.

Ilsa grimaced and shook her head. "Do you want rid of me so you can move on to that new guard, Jennell Decker?"

Delaney cocked her head and smiled, recalling the pleasant image of Decker. She was typically Aryan—crystal blue eyes, hair as blond as sunshine, legs up to her ass and beyond. Even if Delaney wasn't otherwise busy with Ilsa though, Simson had already decided she was having the first shot at bedding her.

"Of course not. I know I've got the most beautiful woman in here. I'm worried about your state of mind. This place…it'll infect you. It could taint you for life. I don't want to see this place dull your spirit."

"You're sweet, but I have no intention of leaving you here on your own. You're not immune to the effects of this place, no matter how tough you are."

Delaney didn't respond. She *had* no response. Ilsa had more of a grasp of Delaney in three years than most people had in a lifetime.

She might know Delaney under a different name, but there was no denying, she did know her. "I'm going to circle around the back and make sure there're no stragglers. I don't want to see another Katharina incident."

Ilsa took a deep breath, as though she might be stopping herself from being sick again. "That was..."

Delaney put her hand on Ilsa's shoulder. "Don't think about it."

Thankfully, the rest of the march was uneventful, and there were no attempts to escape the throng. Most of these women were political prisoners, and Delaney could see the resolute determination in some of them. She hoped they held on to it, and expected that the ones who did would be the ones to beat the odds and survive this place.

They passed the welcoming sight of well-kept flowerbeds in front of the SS headquarters, as the gates were being opened. They seemed so out of place, vibrant and colorful in a place that sought to draw the life and individuality from all of these women. Vogt and her posse herded the new prisoners into the yard, and it was made clear they should remain still while they waited to be passed through administration. Delaney saw the attempts at communication between existing and new prisoners, and ignored them. Other guards did no such thing, and a few strategically placed strikes of their whips put an end to it.

Four lines of five were called forward to enter the bathhouse. As they did so, they were robbed of their possessions. They were tossed dismissively into a pile on the floor. Moments later, existing prisoners would retrieve armfuls of goods and head to the clothes store to number and file everything. It was all such a waste of time. Most of these women would never see their things again, and most of them would simply die here with nothing but a prison-issue uniform, an arbitrary number, and a triangle of colored felt. Delaney escorted them into the bathhouse and ordered them to strip. The male SS officers stood languidly against the wall, watching and laughing amongst themselves. Delaney recognized it for the sick power play that it was. She knew they had no sexual interest in the women; they saw them as filthy and beneath them, but their polished performances were meant to increase the inescapable feelings of vulnerability and helplessness. They invariably succeeded.

After the women stripped, the bathhouse guards took over, forcing them into chairs and shaving their heads. It reminded Delaney of being a grunt in the army, the first stage initiation process of leaving your vanity behind and becoming part of a team, of something bigger than yourself. But this was about dehumanization and uniformity, destroying individuality, and the first step in breaking the women's spirits. Delaney found the next stop in the production line particularly unpleasant, but if she were seen to not be taking an active part assisting the bathhouse guards, she knew her cover would be jeopardized. So she forced them to stand with their legs apart while they were inspected and shaved. In years to come, women would do this as a choice, but all Delaney could see were rows of naked women looking strangely prepubescent. The sight sickened her, but she looked on as impassively as she could manage.

Simson strode purposefully toward her, and Delaney was glad of the acceptable distraction. It was the first time they'd been able to speak since they'd returned from finding Katharina. *Katharina.* Simson had told her she'd be better off referring to the prisoners by their last name, or better yet, just their number. Delaney believed otherwise. Katharina would be a name and an experience she'd never forget. She knew her mind would never relinquish the graphic images of Katharina's death, even if she ever wanted it to.

"How was the march in?"

"Same as usual, nothing special."

"It was probably a good thing you got that detail. I ended up supervising the disposal of fourteen seventy-six. That was some messy, fucked up shit." Even with the German accent, Simson still managed to sound as American as apple pie when she spoke to Delaney.

"I think the commandant succeeded with his message. I can't see anyone trying to escape after that." Delaney blinked away the visceral images of the half-crazed inmates clubbing Katharina into a bloody mess, venting their anger, frustration, and fear.

"I saw your girl disappear around the medical block during the punishment. It's no wonder she ends up being dumped from this place. She's not got the stomach for it."

"She shouldn't have to have the stomach for it. I've told her she should consider leaving."

Simson raised her eyebrows. "Are you trying to convince her to leave before history says she's supposed to? What about her part in the mission?"

"She's served her purpose." Delaney tried hard to sound dispassionate about Ilsa but wasn't sure if she succeeded. "Chernick trusts me now, and I've got the journals in my villa."

"The villa you share with Blumstein. What if she takes them all with her, like she does when she's supposed to leave in forty-three?"

"Then I'd convince her to leave them with me so I can keep them all together. I'd handle it."

"I'm not doubting your ability to handle anything. I'm just wondering if this is you starting to work in your new way. As opposed to the way Pulsus wants us to work?"

"And if it is?" Delaney didn't mind Simson questioning her motives. It would serve to clarify where Simson stood, and if Delaney would be able to count on her.

"If it is, then you know I'm with you. You know I think you've got it right, and if they'd let you handle this mission the way you wanted to, I wouldn't have had to watch a hundred pounds of female flesh stuffed into three refuse sacks and thrown into a Dumpster like it was leftovers from a frat party."

Delaney balked at both the image and the metaphor, but was pleased Simson had pledged her allegiance. When they jumped home, she'd do as Landry had asked and find a vacation place on the mainland. She'd play along, but ultimately, her goal was to secure Landry's buy-in. Together, they'd reform Pulsus and get it working how it should be. These kinds of small-scale missions wouldn't be part of that future, and maybe, just maybe, Delaney would finally get to sleep peacefully again.

Chapter Twenty-four

June 6, 1942—Ravensbrück

Landry had been transported with six other prisoners from Neubrandenburg in the back of an army truck. She'd managed a whispered conversation with a British woman called Adelita, who'd told her she was suspected of being a Special Operations Executive. Landry knew better than to ask her to confirm their suspicion, particularly with the two male guards itching to pounce on any crumb of information they might be able to take back to Major Oster.

As soon as they were pulled off the truck and into the camp square, a female guard singled out Adelita, and Landry saw Griffin, disturbingly striking in his SS uniform, march toward them. She quickly scanned for Delaney and Simson, but they found her with Simson appearing beside her silently. She said nothing, but Landry followed the line of her gaze to see Delaney standing next to the woman she recognized as Ilsa Blumstein. It looked like their part of the mission was proceeding as planned.

"Adelita Lake, meet Erika Vogt."

Griffin's perfect German accent was impressive. Four years of going native had improved it immensely. He blended in perfectly.

Vogt thrust the handle of her whip into Adelita's stomach. She doubled over, and Vogt struck her across the back, knocking Adelita to her knees in the mud. She tossed a piece of chocolate onto the ground.

"Like a dog, scum."

Landry stepped forward, but Simson pushed her forearm across her chest, blocking her path. "Stay put or you'll end up in the ovens. There's no place for your heroics here."

Landry unfurled her clenched fists and went to turn away. If she couldn't help, she wasn't going to give Vogt the satisfaction of an audience.

Simson stopped her again and whispered quietly, "I told you, stay exactly where you are. There's no version of this that ends well for you if you do anything other than stay put."

The guard placed her boot on Adelita's back and pushed her toward the candy. Adelita reached to retrieve it, but the guard kicked her hand away. "Like a dog."

Landry clenched her teeth, knowing exactly what the guard wanted Adelita to do. Adelita looked to Landry, her eyes wet with tears and shame. She turned back to the chocolate and picked it up with her mouth.

"Filthy Juden-lover." Vogt laughed and motioned for Griffin to help her up.

Adelita stood, and Landry hoped her little show had convinced Vogt she was no threat, let alone a spy.

"Why are you in my country?"

Adelita looked puzzled, and Vogt backhanded her. She fell against Griffin, and he held her in place with his hands wrapped around her upper arms.

"Why are you in my country?" Vogt repeated.

"I do not understand," Adelita said quietly, in a perfect Berliner accent. "I was born here."

Vogt snarled, and Landry could see she was a barely controlled dog herself. She slapped Adelita three times, and Griffin's grip stopped her from falling to the floor with the force of the blows.

Landry moved against Simson's arm, intent on intervening, but Simson shook her head.

"She's not the mission."

Landry took a deep breath. Inaction wasn't something she was comfortable with, especially when she could do something to stop it.

"Are you or are you not a British spy?"

Adelita shook her head slowly. "No. I'm a proud German. I don't know why this is happening to me."

Vogt stepped to Adelita's side and hit her in the stomach four times with the whip handle. She crumpled to her knees, but Griffin pulled her back up to face Vogt.

"This is happening because you are a British spy, and we've caught you because you're stupid enough to think you can outsmart us." Vogt nodded to the ground, and Griffin kicked Adelita to her knees. He pulled out his pistol and pressed the barrel against her neck.

Landry closed her eyes. There was only one ending to this scenario, and she couldn't do a damn thing about it.

"Confess, and I'll spare you."

Adelita shook her head. "I'm not who you think I am."

Vogt smiled. "I was hoping you'd say that."

She walked behind Adelita, wrapped her hand around Griffin's, and her index finger caressed his trigger finger as though she were caressing a lover. Landry wondered how far he'd had to go to be accepted as an SS officer.

"I will ask you one more time, for the sake of leniency. Are you a British spy?"

Landry saw Vogt's other hand rest on Griffin's bare neck and watched the two exchange a quick glance that only lovers would share. Adelita took a final look Landry's way and gave her a slight smile. *Good-bye.*

"I am not."

Landry saw Vogt's smile, sadistic and satisfied, as she squeezed Griffin's trigger finger. The bullet tore through Adelita's neck and throat and hit the ground before she did. Death was instant. Three of the women beside Landry vomited at the sight of sinew and blood. Their political activism clearly hadn't prepared them for this.

"What about the rest of you? Are there any spies among you?"

Landry clenched her teeth. She wanted to rip this woman's throat out with her bare hands and wipe the blood and flesh on her uniform. Vogt came into Landry's eye line and stopped directly in front of her.

"Stark. A career criminal. You've misplaced your husband? How careless." She snickered, humoring herself and Griffin. "I'm sure he'll turn up somewhere—probably on the end of a German bayonet."

Landry said nothing and kept her expression blank. She couldn't give this bitch anything to go on. She was nothing more than a power crazed thug, and Landry couldn't risk the mission by engaging with her now. *She lives through this*. Landry recalled the files. She escaped the camp before the Red Army got there and lived as a fugitive in Argentina until she was in her sixties. *Every mission has collateral damage*. They did their best to minimize the impact of their presence, but sometimes, some people just had to die.

"I've read you're a carpenter and a plumber. They're not usual trades for a woman."

It was tempting not to respond again. There was no question, after all, but it obviously wouldn't take much to make Vogt strike out. "I wanted to make sure I could take care of myself if there was no man around."

Vogt nodded and looked slightly impressed. "We can make use of your talents here, you can be sure of that." She placed her whip handle under Landry's chin and forced her head up slightly. "No use wasting someone like you on the road gang, shifting soil and sand for no good reason."

She and Griffin laughed again, and Landry couldn't miss the sexual undertones of Vogt's statement, nor the lustful look in her eyes. The Angel of Death chose her partners from both sexes, even having sex with some prisoners before sending them to the crematorium. Landry hoped she could keep her at bay. She'd had to do some unsavory things with some unpleasant people, but she wasn't sure if she could be the plaything of this twisted bitch. An image of Jade surfaced involuntarily. She wasn't sure if she could be anybody's plaything anymore.

"I'd be happy to do whatever you need." The words burned her lips as they escaped her mouth. *Please, God, don't let it be me that you need.* It'd take gargantuan control to keep from wrapping her hands around Vogt's throat and squeezing the sadistic life out of her.

"Thalberg, take our new inmates to the bathhouse and get them more appropriately dressed."

Simson nodded. "Yes, ma'am." She grasped Landry's elbow and pulled her away. "Looks like you got away with the shit duty," Simson whispered when they were a few steps in front of the following prisoners. "Bet you were hoping to keep your pants. It's gonna be hard to keep a straight face with you wearing a dress."

"You're wrong if you think you're rocking that skirt and sleeveless sweater look yourself."

Simson shoved Landry into the bathhouse. "Have fun."

She was quickly relieved of her leather jacket and the rest of her clothes. They were tagged and bagged with the same prisoner number they gave her, and Landry would insist Griffin make sure she got those back for the rest of the mission once they had the doc and were on their way out. There was no way she was going outside of these gates in a dress.

Having her head shaved didn't bother Landry. It was just like being back in the Seals. When they roughly shaved between her legs, she remembered the time when her dad had brought back crabs from a tour of duty, and everyone in the house had to lose their pubic hair. Landry had been mortified, because at ten, she'd only just started to cultivate a little bush that made her feel more grown-up. She'd overheard an argument, and her mom accused her father of sleeping around. Her father was adamant he'd caught it by having to share towels with the guys in his company. Landry had always assumed his innocence, but after what her mom had said before the jump, she wasn't so sure of anything to do with her father.

She was handed a dress with a green triangle, the code for habitual criminal, while the others who'd come with her received either red or black. Ravensbrück was originally built for the political opponents of the Nazi regime and so-called asocials, such as beggars, lesbians, and prostitutes. Landry didn't know what made Hitler decide to destroy thousands of women, but how well he succeeded was something she really couldn't get a handle on. Most of the guards in this place claimed to just follow orders, but were personally responsible for ending the lives of thousands of women. Maybe Delaney did have the right idea. If the mission had been to assassinate Hitler, none of these women she stood with now would be in this place, let alone die before their time.

Landry's thoughts were interrupted and she was pulled back into the moment as a fellow prisoner handed her a blanket. It was topped with a set of crockery and basic cutlery, a toothbrush and paste, a chunk of soap, and a towel that would barely qualify as a washcloth, another element of the camp to further humiliate the women. She was ordered to wait while the rest of the women were given their rations before being led to their block.

Inside the block were rows of three tiered wooden bunk beds, and each unit was approximately four feet long. When the camp was built, they were meant to sleep one woman. Now each housed four. As she filed down the narrow corridor between the beds to her bunk, she tried to make eye contact with every woman. Hundreds of shaved heads, sunken faces, and starved bodies melded into a vision of one woman. Malnutrition, disease, and overwork. Landry was suddenly grateful for her position as extractor. She only had to be here for a month, *and* she was comforted with the knowledge that if all went according to plan, they'd escape. She wondered how these women, who looked at her now with compassion and sympathy, held on to those sharp shards of desperate hope. She wondered how they could continue to believe in good being triumphant over evil, when they could hear the screams of their tortured friends all day long.

And what of Delaney? She'd made a promise to Landry to seek help after this mission, but what if that turned out to be too late? What if the atrocities she not only saw, but also had to perpetrate here, left scars that could never heal? Landry berated herself for not bringing Delaney's mental health to the board. The mission could've been delayed, or Delaney could've been replaced while they helped her. The realization hit Landry that she was responsible for Delaney. She was an integral part of Landry's team, and Landry had failed her.

She placed her blanket on the cot and stacked her stuff on the tiny empty shelf built inside the beds. A gaunt woman looked up from the bed she would be sharing with Landry and two of the other new prisoners. There was hope in her eyes, and Landry found herself wanting to feel that same hope, more than ever before.

CHAPTER TWENTY-FIVE

June 16, 1942—Ravensbrück

Vogt had given Delaney the gruesome duty of selecting "guinea pigs" for the next round of experiments the camp doctor had planned. Among the more sadistic guards in the camp, it was considered a much sought after detail. Delaney would've happily swapped it with any one of them, Simson included, because she seemed to be handling this mission far better than Delaney was.

The dreams that haunted her in 2076 were competing for show times with new visions of the vile acts she'd been involved in over the past three years. For appearances and the sake of formality, Ilsa kept her own room in their shared villa, but each evening Ilsa would unmake her own bed before joining Delaney for the night. And each night, Delaney woke with her tank soaked in sweat, shouting and shaking. Ilsa would wipe away the sweat from her face with a washcloth and hold her tight, whispering that everything would be okay.

But everything wasn't going to be okay, and Delaney was fast losing any residual faith that it might, not unless she did what she felt she had to do. She didn't doubt they would complete this mission, and she tried hard to settle her disquiet by counting down the days to the seventh of July. Twenty-two days until the team left this shit-pit of a prison and began their trek back home. Part of her was looking forward to seeing what New York looked like in 1942. It had always been one of her favorite places to visit during vacation time from the army. She could blend in, be invisible, and navigate the city unnoticed. But she was also impatient to get back to 2076, to put her plans into action and start concentrating on how much more good Pulsus would be able to do when they did it her way. *With me at the helm*. That was it. It would have to be that way. The board lacked imagination, ambition, vision. Mission by consensus was ineffective. Pulsus needed a strong leader, someone able to make the tough decisions, and Delaney now saw she was the person they needed.

It was only 6 a.m. when she entered Block F. At this hour, and flanked by two female guards, the prisoners knew why Delaney was there. Most of the women refused to look at her, but others, mainly the prisoners with the red triangle, would meet her gaze and stare straight through her. Delaney took it to mean that she meant nothing to them. That she, or any other guard here, could commit any number of egregious misdeeds against them, and they would never break.

Who would Vogt choose? She'd asked Simson the question after being told she'd be doing this job the next day. *Pick numbers, like an unlucky lottery, but don't look at faces. This would happen anyway. Don't think you're changing history, because you're not. You're just doing your job*. But she had to look like she'd put some thought into it, like she was exercising her power, and perhaps even punishing prisoners who'd broken rules. It was like a warning system—mess up and you'll end up a being a rabbit for the doctors here. Doing less could mean blowing her cover, and if she ended up a prisoner instead of a guard, it would make the mission far harder to complete.

Vogt had given her instructions to meet specific parameters. Older than twenty and younger than forty. Not fat, but not skinny. Healthy, but not the healthiest, otherwise there'd be no one left to do the hard work around the camp. There was no easy way out; she'd have to choose. Choose five women to undergo excruciating operations with no anesthesia. She reminded herself that this was the easiest, and least conspicuous, way of getting to Chernick. And she was the mission. Delaney strode alongside the beds and pointed at five women who matched Vogt's exacting requirements. In the end, she tried not to think too much about it. She couldn't use the lottery method Simson had suggested, so she tried to see the characteristics rather than the woman, and she convinced herself that would work.

Delaney and the two other guards escorted the women to the medical block. They shuffled behind her, their ungainly wooden clogs clomping noisily on the pathway. The sun had been rising for more than an hour, and it cast a beautiful light across the lake. Surrounding them with beauty was another pitiless way of penalizing the prisoners, sitting them so close to such natural splendor without providing access, but Delaney hoped that it kept the women's hope alive, that they might one day get to swim in that lake. Delaney shook off the romantic notion and refocused to prepare herself for entry into the medical block.

Chernick greeted the prisoners, and Delaney all but saw the unspoken words exchanged in their looks.

"Thank you, Fraulein Thalberg. The doctor has asked for your assistance to restrain the…test subjects."

Delaney could see how hard it was for Chernick to use the terminology she'd been instructed to use. The word practically formed a wooden chunk in her throat and stuck behind her teeth.

"Just me?" Delaney motioned to the guards with her.

"Just you, Fraulein."

"Have fun, Sigi," one of them said, laughing as they exited the building. Delaney couldn't decide if they were serious or joking. As more time passed within these high concrete walls, the fewer guards like Ilsa remained.

"The doctor would like you to strap down the…subjects, to those tables."

In the next whitewashed room, Delaney saw five medical gurneys, replete with ankle, wrist, and neck cuffs. She saw Drescher, the camp "doctor," preparing his tools, humming a jolly tune as he did so. Delaney motioned for the prisoners to go into the room, and they did, quietly and calmly, as if they were going to see their own doctor for a routine checkup.

"Select a table and get up on it."

Again, they did as they were instructed. Delaney started at the one closest to Drescher.

"Good morning, Sieglinde." His tone was light and breezy, apparently devoid of any misgivings he might have about what he was about to do, if, in fact, he had any.

"Morning, Doctor. How are you?" Delaney matched his tone, and hated herself for doing so.

"Marvelous, actually. I feel at my most inspired at this time in the morning. I have a feeling we're going to have a breakthrough with this batch."

He nodded in the direction of the prisoners, and Delaney fought the urge to react against his use of dismissive language toward the women. "I'm glad to hear that. At least they're useful for something." Delaney swallowed hard and avoided the stare she could feel from Chernick.

"Absolutely. I tried to join the army, but my eyes aren't up to scratch." He tapped the glass on his gold-rimmed spectacles. "At least this way, I get to help them in the field."

"What are you doing differently this time around?" Delaney had seen the large open wounds inflicted on previous subjects in the camp. She didn't want to hear it, but she had to seem intrigued.

"You saw the previous experiments, yes?"

Delaney nodded.

"Follow me."

Drescher led her to a smaller room and approached a three-foot by six-foot wooden tub. As Delaney drew closer, she could see it was filled with female limbs floating in God knows what. All of them had wounds between six and ten inches long, and one to two inches wide. Delaney wondered if Chernick had been forced to separate the limbs from the rest of the victims' bodies.

"These are some of the last batch. We tried to simulate lacerations similar to those sustained by our boys, from bayonets and bombs, but they were too clean. You can see that even now the flesh hasn't putrefied, although the formalin has helped in that respect." He used a pair of long tongs to prod one or two of the gashes to illustrate his point. Drescher walked back to the table he'd been preparing, and as she followed, Delaney sighed deeply. The new women lay there, perfectly still, making no attempt to communicate with each other or with Chernick. She wondered what would happen if the fifty thousand women currently in the camp rose up and rioted. Some would die, of course, but there weren't enough guards or bullets to kill them all. *Why didn't they?* The question never stopped bothering her.

"This is what I'm going to do differently, Sieglinde."

He slipped a latex glove on, carefully picked up a shard of glass from a small pot on the table, and offered it to Delaney for inspection. Similar pots contained collections of dirt, sawdust, splinters of wood, and rusty nails.

"You're going to…?" She played along, but Delaney knew exactly what Drescher had in store for these poor women.

"I'm going to slice them open and introduce each of these into a deep incision—to mimic the environmental situation of our soldiers. Very rarely are the medics seeing clean wounds. It seems they always have some foreign body or other in there. This way, we can let the injuries fester for a suitable amount of time before beginning treatment, as so often happens in the field, to our brave soldiers. That's why I need them secured to the tables. They're to stay there for the duration of the experiments."

Delaney nodded, feigning interest and admiration. "That's impressive, Doctor. How will you keep them alive if they're not to move from the tables, to empty their bladders and feed them, etcetera?"

"That's where she comes in." He gestured dismissively at Chernick. "She'll fit the bags for nature's call." He nudged Delaney in an attempt at playfulness. "And empty them, of course! I couldn't have you or other guards doing that. She'll also feed and water them."

He smiled brightly and Delaney returned it with jaded enthusiasm. He spoke about the women like they were plants, not human beings. Drescher would be hung for all of this in 1946, but Delaney wasn't sure that was enough punishment for all the suffering he caused.

"Then I'll get on so you can begin." She turned away and returned to the gurneys, one by one, securing their ankles wide apart, and their wrists and necks so they could barely move. Putting the neck cuff on was the hardest. All of them stared at Delaney, as if they were looking deep into her soul for some shred of decency, something that would stop her from doing this, and release them. She could only hope that they could see the truth behind her dispassionate gaze, but knew it was impossible. She pushed the coarse blue-and-white striped dress up from the ankle of the final woman as Chernick appeared beside her.

"I have to perform a laparotomy. I'll need your help." Chernick took a pair of scissors from an adjacent table. "Alicja...be brave."

She quickly cut through Alicja's dress from the hem to the collar and laid it open. She'd only been in the camp a week so her body was still in good condition, and she was yet to take on the uniform appearance of the longer-term prisoners, emaciated, gaunt, and skeletal. She cut off another piece of the dress, balled it up, and offered it to Alicja to bite down on. Drescher wouldn't "waste" anesthesia on these women. She opened her mouth cautiously, and fear flashed across her eyes. It was only when Chernick gently touched Delaney's wrist that she realized she had gripped the table so hard, she was beginning to bend it.

"You'll need to hold her shoulders down while I make the incision."

Delaney moved to the top of the gurney and placed her hands over Alicja's bare shoulders. Now she had a name. Now she was no longer just seventy-five thirty-three, like Simson had told her to focus on.

Chernick placed her left hand on Alicja's stomach. "Ready?"

Delaney nodded. Alicja shook her head. Chernick drew her scalpel down to create a long incision across her waistline. Alicja did her best to thrash and escape what must have been excruciating pain, but the combination of the restraints and Delaney's grip held her in place. Chernick placed her scalpel aside, and pushed a clamp into the incision to stretch out the skin at about the same time as Alicja passed out in agony. She slipped her scalpel into the cavity, sliced through a section of Alicja's colon, and pulled one end of it out. She began to sew the stoma to Alicja's skin, and Delaney was glad she'd spent years with a mom obsessed with medical TV dramas. Even so, she felt the acid burning at the back of her throat, threatening to make her vomit. Alicja stirred a little, and Delaney hoped she wouldn't wake. There was good reason this was a procedure usually done with unconscious and anesthetized patients.

Chernick fixed a stoma bag in place, changed her gloves, and moved on to the catheter insertion. Delaney took a breath and looked around. Four pairs of eyes, wide with terror were fixed on the horrific scene, but still they didn't move an inch in their bindings.

Delaney helped Chernick with the other four prisoners, and they were finished by 10 a.m. Drescher instructed Chernick to furnish Delaney with some paperwork to take to the commandant, so she followed her back into the front area of the med block. Chernick gathered the required paperwork and slid a tan leather journal amidst the stack of folders.

Aware they were out of Drescher's earshot, Chernick asked, "You are keeping them safe, yes?"

"Of course. And when you get out of here, you'll be able to continue your research, maybe even in America." She couldn't risk giving Chernick a hint of their rescue, but Delaney wanted to give her something.

She smiled wryly. "There is no escape from this place. I will die here."

"You don't know that for sure."

"It's only a matter of time before Mengele comes for me. I lived a strange version of a life before they caught me and put me in here. I'll soon be on one of those tables, with my scalp removed and quacks poking around in my gray matter. And you will hold my only legacy."

Her prophetic words stopped Delaney from responding. That had been Chernick's fate before Pulsus discovered her journals, one of which Delaney had in her hands right now. Delaney gave Chernick a look that she hoped might convey a message of hope. It didn't really matter what Chernick believed. This operation would rescue her from that fate and set her on a path to rid the world of cancer. *If only you knew how important you're about to become.*

Chapter Twenty-six

June 18, 1942—Ravensbrück

They'd just returned from the morning count, and Landry was polishing off her daily bread and coffee ration. It wasn't Starbucks, but at least it was hot and full of caffeine. The women who would spend the day working the sandpit needed all the energy they could get.

Landry saw Simson enter the block and watched as the women hurried to get out of her way. Landry had soon discovered she'd established quite the reputation around the prison, not in the same league as the Angel of Death, but she certainly wasn't known for her compassion like Ilsa Blumstein. Despite Vogt's apparent intention to have Delaney as her lieutenant, she was still known to be firm but fair. Landry hoped Delaney was managing to stay away from the truly dark dealings of the camp, but she'd also been involved over in the medical block, so God knows what she saw there. Landry was marking the days to their escape from this place, for Delaney's mental health as much as Dr. Chernick's.

"Stark. Vogt wants you in her office. Follow me."

Landry pushed the last piece of stale bread into her mouth and washed it down with the thick black liquid. One of the first things she wanted when they jumped back would be a chai latte, to wash away this particular taste memory. She was using things at home to focus on to help navigate this mission in a way she'd never done before. Jade was a constant visitor in her dreams.

She stood and adjusted her dress. Landry missed her jeans. Not only did she feel near-naked and incredibly vulnerable, the dress was proving impractical for the work she was doing. Her knees were skinned and bruised, and she felt the constant need to tuck the dress under her ass when she bent over. The only thing that made her feel a little normal was the hefty leather tool belt she collected when she was given her work duties each day. It looked a little incongruous around the waist of her dress, but its weight was somehow grounding.

Landry followed Simson silently out of the block. When they were on the path toward the main admin building, with no one around, Simson gave Landry a quick rundown of where she and Delaney were with their part of the mission, including the journals and the doctor.

"How's Griffin? It seemed a little like that execution was run-of-the-mill stuff for him."

Simson shook her head. "He's doing fine. Vogt's taken a shine to him, and he's having to fuck her when she's not busy fucking the prisoners. He's worried his dick might fall off because she's so fucking toxic, but he's handling it. He's doing his job well, if you've got concerns about him disappearing into his cover."

"It's his first job, and we'll be relying on him to get the weapons we need for the rest of the mission."

"It's his first job with Pulsus. He's not a wet behind the ears raw recruit, he's ex-CIA. Don't forget he was in deep cover with the Villanueva gang for six years, *and* developed a drug habit to cement his place with them. Griffin is solid. You've got no worries there."

"I'm assuming they're not sharing a villa, so getting out on the night of the seventh won't be a problem?"

"The duty rosters are set for a month in advance, and Griffin and I are already on night watch. Delaney won't have any trouble getting away from Blumstein; she often takes late night walks."

When she can't sleep because of the nightmares? "Will you be able to get hold of my clothes?"

Simson chuckled. "We don't think so. Everything's labeled and itemized, but getting it from the store to our villas would be too difficult. Delaney's secured some clothes. She's confident she knows your size."

Landry glanced at Simson and saw her jaw clench. She had no reason to be jealous of her, but it was clear she wasn't happy with their friendship.

"As long as I don't have to stay in this getup a minute longer than necessary, I don't care if it's all three sizes too big. Does Griffin have access to the transport keys yet?"

"He does. He'll grab the keys to a Kübelwagen before we go on shift at ten p.m."

"You'll feign illness and Griffin will take you to the medical block. I'll already be there, and that's when we swap you for Chernick. Griffin drives her out of here, picks up Delaney, and the journals, and drives up to the rendezvous point on the map Delaney slipped me. You and I escape over the far wall, trek through the forest, and meet them at the rendezvous point."

"Sounds nice and easy when you say it fast like that."

Landry nodded. "It'll be like clockwork."

Simson opened the front door to the admin block, and followed Landry up the stairs to Vogt's first floor office. She knocked and waited to be invited in, with Simson at her side.

"Stark, I have a job for you. Sit."

Simson shoved Landry forward and pressed her into the wooden seat in front of Vogt's desk. She stood, came around her desk, and sat on it so her crotch was in Landry's eye line.

"You may go about your duties, Thalberg."

"Yes, ma'am."

Simson left, closing the door behind her, and Landry felt an unpleasant mix of unease and aggression sweep over her.

"Some glass needs to be replaced in the medical block."

Vogt opened her legs, and Landry was reminded of the old nineties movie with the murderous blond female lead who did the same thing in a police interview room. *Difference is, that woman was sexy as hell…and not a real-life psychopath.*

"No problem. Do you have the supplies, or is that why you wanted me, to get a list of what I'd need?" Landry had become just as much of an expert in fending off unwanted attention as she had in faking interest in women for the sake of a mission. The problem here was Landry knew that if it came down to it, and Vogt had decided that's what she wanted, Landry wouldn't be able to do a damn thing about it. Not without jeopardizing the entire mission. This was a woman who had sex with prisoners one moment, and sent them to their death in the next. Thoughts of Jade raided her mind. *What would she think if I didn't come back from this mission?* They'd agreed to have fun whenever they were in town, but what if she never saw her again? Up to now, Landry only had to concern herself with her own well-being, and she lived by the philosophy that if her time was up, so be it. She hadn't been reckless with her life, but now that she'd met Jade, a latent motivation to cheat death had surfaced. Landry had to make that work for her, rather than making her less effective and too cautious. Maybe it could turn out to be a new strength.

"We have what you need." Vogt pushed herself from the desk and circled behind Landry, putting her hands on Landry's shoulders. "But you have something I need."

Landry took a deep breath and tried to relax every muscle that had contracted in revulsion the second Vogt touched her body. "And what might that be?"

"I need your carpentry skills. I want you to build a bookcase in my villa. It looks like I'll be here for a while, so I want to be comfortable. I want this to feel like home. And what is a home without books?"

Landry's relief bled from her pores, though she'd never figured Vogt as a reader. She imagined she'd be making room for the complete works of the Marquis de Sade. "A poorer home," Landry responded as cheerily as she could. "When would you like me to start?"

"I'd like to see some designs first." Vogt walked back around to her desk, relaxed back into her chair, and pulled out some loose-leaf papers from a top drawer. "Here are the measurements for the wall I'd like it to cover. I want it to feel like a grand library, with wall-to-wall books." She handed Landry the papers and two pencils. "Come back to my office when you need to sharpen them."

Landry took the proffered items and smiled, feeling like this was an out of place business meeting. "Will I be working on this during the day?"

"No, this is extracurricular. When I'm happy with the designs, you can let me know what supplies I need. When I have them, you'll be working at my villa every evening until the job is satisfactorily complete."

Vogt smiled widely, and there was a flicker of flirtation in her eyes that made Landry think she might not be safe from her desires after all. If she dragged out the design process long enough, and if the supplies took enough time to be sourced, maybe they'd be gone before she had to step inside Vogt's lair. "Then I should get on with the glass job?"

"Yes, you're free to go."

Landry nodded, folded the papers in half, and put them in the front pocket of her dress before getting out of the chair.

"Thank you, Fraulein Vogt." Landry retreated from the office and closed the door behind her.

Outside, she took a deep breath of fresh air. Vogt's office had been stifling, and it smelled of something that caught in Landry's throat. *Death?* She remembered reading about Vogt and her lampshades made of prisoners' skins. She closed her eyes and mentally scanned the inside of the office. Yep, in the corner of the office as she'd turned to leave, next to the wingback chair beside the small bookcase. A lampshade made of human skin.

Landry shuddered and went to collect her belt and tools. Being assigned a job in the medical block was fortuitous. She'd managed a few conversations with Chernick, but this would be the perfect opportunity to get closer. Landry needed to know whether she'd cooperate when the rescue took place, or if she was going to complicate matters by not coming willingly. She couldn't fathom why Chernick might want to stay, but it was a possibility she had to eliminate or identify.

Ilsa Blumstein called Landry forward to skip the line. She walked past the long line of women waiting to collect shovels to shift soil and sand all day, and was glad Pulsus had given her this cover. It would've been hard to establish any kind of relationship with Chernick if she'd been working outside the camp gates every day.

Blumstein handed her tool belt over, along with the putty, nails, and three panes of glass. "Do you need help taking that to the medical block?"

Landry smiled. Blumstein's softness was apparent in her demeanor and the gentle way she addressed the prisoners. Landry was surprised she lasted as long as she did, but was grateful she had. Without Blumstein, this mission simply wouldn't be.

"I'll be okay, but thank you." Landry picked up her supplies and turned away. It was almost unkind that Blumstein would never know that she'd already made a unique contribution to the development of a cancer cure.

❖

"Ah, our new handyman. Or should I say, handywoman?"

Landry put the glazing panels down and extended her hand. "I've been called both, so it doesn't matter which you choose. My name's Truda Stark though, Doc." Chernick seemed to smile at Landry's formal address. They had yet to speak of Chernick spending six years living as a man, so Landry figured using that angle might speed up the friendship process.

Chernick shook Landry's hand firmly. "I saw you when you came in. It looked like you might've been living like I once did."

Landry feigned surprise. "What do you mean?" She took a quick look around and figured Chernick was speaking so freely because Drescher was nowhere to be seen.

"It's the reason I'm in here. Not because I'm a lesbian, but because I pretended to be a man."

Landry appreciated the way she was so matter-of-fact about it, and that the topic had been raised so quickly. "Really? For how long?"

"Six years. When Hitler came to power, he made it clear the only position women should be in was beneath a man on a bed. It was obvious I wouldn't be able to pursue my career as things stood, so I falsified my papers and secured a seven-year residency at UHC in 1933. I was so close to finishing it, too."

She looked almost wistful.

"How was your secret discovered?"

"Listen to you, with all the questions. What about you? How did you end up here?"

"I'm sorry, I didn't mean to pry. I was arrested in Neubrandenburg flying solo after my husband left me in the middle of the night."

"Oh. I'm sorry. I assumed…"

"That I was a lesbian?"

Chernick looked guilty and chastised at the same time. "Yes. Now it's my turn to apologize for being stereotypical."

Landry laughed and shook her head. "No need to apologize. You're right. We all have to do things to make our life easier."

"Indeed, and speaking of which, perhaps you should start on your work before Drescher returns."

"Sure. So where are the broken ones?" Landry didn't need to push it. She'd already got further with Chernick than she expected in a short space of time. She could make the window job last the better part of the morning if need be.

"The first one is in here. You should prepare yourself for what you'll see."

Landry nodded and followed her. She knew that nothing, no amount of words or photos she'd already seen, could prepare her for what she was about to see in this room.

"I need to quickly give them these injections before Drescher comes back." Chernick lifted a hypodermic syringe and a bottle of yellow liquid.

"What is it?"

"Homemade anesthesia. These women need something to ease their suffering. Can you imagine being opened up like this without being numbed?"

Landry looked at each of the women, and they stared back, glassy-eyed and hopeless. The open wounds all over their bodies, the foreign objects forced into them, the infections clearly present, and the colostomy bags and catheters. She'd been tortured numerous times, both before Pulsus and on their missions, but Landry couldn't begin to imagine what this felt like.

"You're taking a risk, aren't you? What if Drescher discovers what you're doing?"

"I don't care. I have to do something to help."

Chernick began to address the full colostomy bag situation, so Landry began her own job.

Drescher arrived and prodded and poked the women while Landry worked on two of the three windows. She hadn't managed to renew her conversation with Chernick, so she'd slowed down to an amateur degree, hoping he'd break for lunch and leave them alone again.

"Chernick, photograph and catalogue the wounds, then extract the infection seepage and add it to each subject's tube. I'm going for lunch. Enjoy your bread."

"Yes, Doctor."

He picked up a journal that looked similar to the photos she'd seen of Chernick's, and quickly left the building.

"Join me for lunch?" Chernick offered up a chunk of bread, her own rations for the day.

"I'll join you to chat, but I won't take your food. I've already eaten mine."

"You must share. I get double rations for working in here. Please…"

Landry smiled and accepted the torn off bread. "So what made you do it?" Landry really wanted to know. If she'd been a Jew in Germany when Hitler took power and his genocide began, she would have been one of the first out of the country. "You could've sought refuge in Britain, or America even, and continued to practice as a doctor there. Why stay here and risk…everything?"

Chernick smiled. "A strange mix of a stubborn streak and a desire for freedom, I suppose. No tiny man with a bad haircut and a penchant for shouting hateful rhetoric was going to stop me from pursuing the career I'd worked so hard for. And being a man gives you a freedom you simply can't experience as a woman. And I'm patriotic. I love my country, despite its recent history and current leadership. We can be a great country, a supportive one, helping others. We'll make up for this historic hiccup in years to come."

Landry nodded, knowing Germany would do exactly that, particularly in the first half of the twentieth century. "I like your passion and commitment. There's talk of the research you're doing here, and that you've got two guards helping you. Do you think they could help you escape?"

"Then people should stop talking, or I might end up dead. But escape? Absolutely not. The last escape attempt was last year, and the camp commandant let her fellow solitary confinement prisoners beat her to death. That's not an ending I'm prepared to face. And anyway, who would look after these women if I left here? I wouldn't escape even if it *was* an option, which it's not." Chernick leaned forward and placed her hand on Landry's knee, her eyes full of concern. "You should think very carefully if that is your goal, Truda. Very carefully indeed."

Chernick's response complicated the rescue. They'd have to sedate her for the swap with Simson if she refused to come willingly. That would mean somehow having to drag her unconscious from her block. "But what about your research? Don't you want to complete it?"

"Of course I would, but I've left clues for others to follow. Another doctor would be able to pick up the threads, and continue… wherever it is I leave it."

Landry picked up on the hint of melancholy in her voice that meant she was having second thoughts. "What if they can't? I hear you're looking at a cure for cancer. Scientists and doctors have tried for decades for breakthroughs and have gotten nowhere." *And we're still no closer a hundred and thirty years later.* "Don't you owe it to the world to complete your research, if you were given that opportunity? You're helping a few women here, sure, but cure breast cancer and you help millions, not just now, but in the future." *The future I'm from, so I know what I'm talking about.*

Chernick had been slowly nodding as Landry spoke. "You make a salient point, and very eloquently for a career criminal."

"There's more to me than what I'm in here for, Doc." *And you'll soon find out how much more when we bust you out of this hellhole.*

Chernick smiled. "Charm and intelligence being just two of those things. I'm sure you were a hit with the ladies before you were married."

"My husband and I had an agreement, so I've always done okay. Our marriage was one of convenience for both of us. Which reminds me, you never answered my question about how you ended up in here."

Chernick's expression darkened. "There was a nurse. She was such a pretty little thing, all bouncy brunette curls and brown eyes. I'd been so careful to that point, going out of town to discreet lesbian bars to get what I needed. She flirted with me mercilessly, and I thought maybe I could get away with it. If we only ever had sex in the dark. If I never let her touch me. If I never fell asleep afterward, and always went home alone. And it worked, for a little while. But we ended up in her apartment after I'd pulled a triple shift. I was exhausted, but she wasn't taking no for an answer." She balled her hands together tightly and rested her chin on them. "I'm sure you can guess. I fell asleep and she woke before me. I'll never forget that look of disgust and disappointment."

Landry reached over and put her hand on Chernick's shoulder firmly. "She reported you?"

"Yes. I tried to explain, but she wouldn't listen. She kept repeating that I'd lied to her, that I'd betrayed her and she'd be tarnished for life because of what I'd done. I bolted from her apartment to my house and tried to gather a few things in an attempt to run. The SS arrested me at the train station—stupidly, I had no women's clothes as a disguise, well, to reverse my disguise. I was here within the week, after a short and terrifying spell of senseless torture at the local Gestapo office." Chernick's hand went to her ribs, and she held herself for comfort. "That left more than physical scars."

Landry nodded. "Torture always takes away a little piece of you, and you have to fight to get it back. Maybe surviving this place and continuing your research can be your way of doing that."

"Yes, Truda. Perhaps you're right."

Landry smiled and moved closer to hug her. *In your case, I'm definitely right.*

Chapter Twenty-seven

July 7, 1942—Ravensbrück

"Is this a special occasion I don't know about?" Delaney asked as she stood in the kitchen doorway and watched Ilsa slicing a loaf of bread. She'd come home from her afternoon shift to find the table set, replete with candles, fancy napkins, and wine glasses.

Ilsa had insisted on turning the second reception area into a dining room, so that she could entertain her colleagues, but she soon found there were few of them she wanted to spend any more time with than was absolutely necessary. Apart from Delaney. It seemed she wanted to spend every spare moment with her, and though it had taken some getting used to, to be wanted that much, Delaney found it easier to handle than she expected.

"It's been eighteen months since we first slept together." Ilsa stopped slicing and pointed her knife in Delaney's direction. "I think that's worth celebrating, don't you?"

Delaney held her hands up in mock surrender. "If I don't say yes, are you going to chop me up with that knife?"

Ilsa laughed. "No, silly, I'm teasing. Would you open the wine?"

Delaney approached Ilsa from behind, moved the hair from her neck, and kissed her bare skin. "Can I do this first?" She slipped her arms around Ilsa's waist and pulled her body closer to hers.

"You want to skip dinner and move straight to dessert?"

Ilsa's hushed voice dialed the atmosphere up a notch and almost made Delaney forget this was their last night together. *Does it have to be our last night together?* She wanted to convince Landry that it was a good idea to take Ilsa back with them, but knew there was no way Landry would allow it.

"You know I'd take three courses of you over food any day of the week."

"You're such a charmer, but dinner's up first. There's something I want to talk about with you and see what you think."

Something akin to anxiety gripped Delaney by the throat and squeezed. She was hoping to get through tonight without any deep conversation. She wanted to spend the evening being as real as she possibly could. She pulled away and tapped Ilsa on the ass before picking up the wine bottle and opener and going into the dining room.

Ilsa called out to her. "How was your day?"

Delaney smiled at such an ordinary question. *Is this what Landry is always talking about? The normal she strives to hold on to?* "I saw Chernick, and she gave me another journal, and I managed to avoid Vogt all day. That's always a good thing." She pulled the cork, poured two glasses, and took them back into the kitchen. "She's decided my sister is a better bet for her lieutenant, and I think she's on to something. Johanna's not been the same for a few weeks now. I feel like I don't know her anymore."

"What do you mean?"

Delaney took a sip of wine before answering. She had to set this up perfectly, because her plan for keeping Ilsa safe after the escape would partly depend on it. "She's acting strange and spending a lot of time at the medical block. She talks to that handywoman all the time too, but I'm not sure if that's because Vogt has a thing for her. I heard she's designing some bookcases for Vogt's villa, and I reckon her carpentry skills aren't all that she's after."

Ilsa prepared their plates and gestured to the dining room for Delaney to follow.

"So what do you think's going on? Does she know about the journals we're smuggling out for Bina?" Ilsa's brow furrowed in worry.

"No, I haven't told her about those. It's best if you and I keep that between us." Delaney sighed. "Something's going on, I'm sure, but I can't figure it out right now."

Ilsa speared a potato, dipped it in the white sauce on the steak, and chewed it slowly. It was something she did when she was figuring out how to say something. She was so innocent and transparent, Delaney found her easy to read.

"So, you've got something you want to talk about?" Delaney asked before popping a piece of steak in her mouth.

"Do you love your sister?"

"She's my sister. I don't really have a choice. What are you asking?"

"You came to the camp together. Have you always been close, and done everything together?"

Delaney laughed and shook her head. She wasn't sure where Ilsa's line of questioning was going, but it was feeding nicely into her plan. "God, no, that was a coincidence. We answered the same ad without even talking to each other about it. We barely saw each other before this camp."

"So, if she…or you, left the camp, it wouldn't have to be together?"

"No. We've always led very separate lives. We wouldn't really miss each other. Still, I don't get what you're asking."

Ilsa took a big gulp of her wine like she was hoping it might give her some Dutch courage.

"I've been thinking about what you said to me a couple of weeks ago, about this place infecting me, and breaking my spirit. I think you're right." She reached for Delaney's hand and tenderly stroked each finger in turn. "I want to be someone, do something. I don't want to change like you're saying your sister has changed. I don't want to keep seeing the awful things going on around here and accept that it's okay. It's not okay. What they're doing to the women in that lab is not okay. And I can't do anything about it other than hope we lose the war soon and someone else stops it from happening."

"And you're thinking of leaving?" Delaney withdrew her hand and continued eating. Had she misjudged their relationship? Did Ilsa feel nothing for her?

"I don't want to go alone…I want us to leave together before we both become tainted by what's happening here."

Ilsa took Delaney's hands in hers and squeezed them gently. She looked deep into Delaney's eyes, and Delaney could see the longing and the love.

"Will you come with me so we can start a new life together?"

Briefly, Delaney considered the proposition. It wouldn't be hard to stay here tonight. The team would only wait at the rendezvous point for thirty minutes. Protocol would see them leaving her behind, with the assumption that something bad must've happened. They couldn't come back for her, so they'd be none the wiser. She dismissed it almost as quickly as she considered it. *This isn't good-bye. This isn't forever*. She'd already decided to come back once she'd taken control of Pulsus. She'd figured she'd come back on this exact night, one hour after the rendezvous time with the team. That way, she wouldn't be jeopardizing this mission, and it would still go as planned. Ilsa would never know the difference. She'd come back with a couple more years on the clock, but it probably wouldn't be noticeable. If she went with Ilsa now, they'd have maybe thirty good years together. If she stuck with her own plan, with the regenerative technology, they'd both be all but immortal. Ilsa wanted to do something special with her life, and Delaney could give her that. She'd even be able to tell Ilsa that she'd played a part in ridding the world of cancer.

"What about Chernick and the journals?"

"We take the five we have and give them to scientists in England. We can use them as a bargaining tool to get into the country. Or maybe America, I've always wanted to see Hollywood. We can't do any more for Bina. There's a rumor that Mengele is visiting the camp later this month. They say he's coming for her because of how she lived before she was arrested. So how much more research will she do in the next two weeks?"

She'd obviously spent a lot of time thinking about it, and Delaney mentally kicked herself for sowing the initial seed in her head. *No, I'm thinking about this all wrong.* If Delaney played this right, when she returned after the mission, Ilsa would have her bags packed and be ready to go. "Are you sure that's what you want?"

"I'm positive. And I'm positive I want you to do it with me. I love you, Sieglinde. I started to fall the moment I first saw you, and you sealed it when we had sex for the first time."

Her eyes twinkled mischievously, and Delaney felt caught up in Ilsa's enthusiasm and emotions. "Then I guess we'd better start making plans."

Ilsa grinned widely, pushed out her chair, and embraced Delaney hard. "Is that a yes? That's a yes, isn't it? Oh, I'm so excited, Sigi. I can't wait to get out of here and start anew."

Delaney pulled Ilsa into her lap and kissed her hard. She looked so beautiful and full of verve that it made Delaney even more determined to pull this off. She needed to be inside her, and all over her. She wanted to possess and be possessed by her. In the eighteen months they'd been together, Ilsa had made her see that she could be happy without Landry. She knew she was still in love with Landry too, and she somehow needed to stop herself from being in that place. She still had to rid herself of those feelings, but Ilsa gave her the strength to do that. She was so completely different from Landry that Delaney almost couldn't believe what she felt for Ilsa.

"I have to make love to you." Delaney checked the wall clock. It was after eight already, and Landry's plan would be put into motion at ten thirty. She needed to be at the rendezvous point by midnight, and she had to travel by foot. She also had to finish up her plan to keep Ilsa safe by eleven to make it in time. That only gave her two more hours with Ilsa before she had to leave her behind. *Until I come back.* Delaney thought about her plan, the casualty of which was already in the woods.

She'd realized some weeks ago that she'd put Ilsa in danger, and had to do something to make sure she wasn't implicated in the escape. It didn't take her long to come up with a plan that even Landry would've been proud of. Landry often spoke of the collateral damage their missions incurred, and Delaney had to frame her plan within those terms. She'd taken a trip to Berlin two days ago and visited the underground lesbian bar, the Blue Lounge. There was plenty of interest in her, but she was looking for something very specific, someone who had a similar build and look to her. When a woman came in who fit the bill, Delaney didn't ask her name, and she didn't engage in the usual small talk and flirtation. She just took her outside to her car in the alley, and they drove out to Grunewald.

It wasn't the first time Delaney had strangled someone. It wouldn't be the last. But it was the first time she'd killed an innocent for her own purposes. Not for a mission, or to maintain her cover, but so she could protect Ilsa.

When the escape had been discovered, they would find a body matching their missing guard, in Delaney's clothes and with her ID and papers. She'd be just off the main road, and her face would be unrecognizable. The large rock the escapees used to bludgeon her to death would be in the dirt alongside the body.

No one would question Ilsa about anything, and if they did, she'd tell them exactly what Delaney had told her tonight. She'd tell them that Sigi said something wasn't right about her sister, and that she'd been spending time with Chernick and Landry. She'd tell them they weren't close and give them the old cliché that there was no love lost between them. She'd be left alone, safe, and that was worth murdering the innocent lesbian and transporting her body back to the villa in the trunk of Delaney's car. Luckily, they hadn't used the car since, so the naked body wrapped in the newly invented duck tape and garbage sacks lay undisturbed, until Delaney had moved the body last night.

"So take me to bed."

Ilsa's words were like gasoline on the smoldering fire of Delaney's need for her. She slipped one arm beneath Ilsa's knees, one behind her back, pushed her chair a little farther back, and stood.

"Your strength does so impress me," Ilsa whispered in Delaney's ear.

"Then this will really impress you." Delaney walked up the staircase with Ilsa in her arms. This was good-bye sex for Delaney, but Ilsa had no idea. If everything went well, in Ilsa's reality, she'd only be without Delaney for an hour. But for Delaney, this encounter would have to sustain her for months, possibly even a year.

Delaney let Ilsa slide from her grip to stand beside the bed. She slowly undid the front buttons of her dress from top to bottom and slid it from her shoulders to the floor. She stepped back and admired the view before quickly taking off her own clothes and discarding them in the chair beside the bed.

"You are so undeniably beautiful."

Ilsa smiled shyly and looked away. "No one's ever called me beautiful before."

"Then no one really ever saw you before."

Ilsa lay down on the bed, and Delaney joined her, eager to get as much of her as possible before she had to leave. "I love you, Ilsa

Blumstein," she whispered, as she lowered her mouth onto Ilsa's swollen clit.

❖

Delaney took one final look at Ilsa after she'd slipped into a satisfied post-orgasmic sleep. Delaney wanted to be sure she'd memorized every contour and every freckle. She had a photo of the two of them together, but it was in black-and-white, and Delaney wanted to remember Ilsa in bright, vibrant colors.

Delaney kissed her soft lips one last time before grabbing the clothes she'd tossed aside, and going downstairs to dress and retrieve Chernick's journals. Delaney grabbed the bag of clothes she'd left at the foot of the basement steps and set off to place the body before meeting up with Griffin and the doc at the agreed rendezvous point. She jogged to the place she'd left the body covered with forest debris and was relieved to find it still there. She hefted it over her shoulder and began the half-mile trek through the trees to the roadside.

Five minutes later, Delaney dropped the body onto the ground. She sliced through the tape and plastic, before pulling off her shirt and putting it on the body. It was a warm night, but Delaney didn't want to be fully naked in the middle of the woods, so she retrieved a new shirt from her backpack and put it on. Her boots and the rest of her clothes followed, and she was glad she'd taken the time to tie the limbs down and together. She didn't want the body's cadaveric spasms to shoot an arm in the air before rigor mortis began to set in.

By the time she'd finished dressing the corpse, Delaney was sweating hard from shifting and dressing the body. She stuffed the plastic and tape into her backpack and shoved her papers and ID into the shirt pocket. She made the short trip to the roadside for one of the rocks that lined the crude walkway and picked one up without putting too much thought into it.

This'll be the hard part. Strangling someone was relatively easy. Delaney thought about it as putting someone to sleep. *A permanent sleep.* But picking up a twenty-pound rock and dropping it onto someone's face was a different prospect. Delaney straddled the body, took a deep breath, and raised the rock over her head. She was about to drop it when she considered splatter. The impact from this height would explode the skull, and flesh and blood would fly everywhere, including all over Delaney's clean trousers. She knelt down, one knee on each side of the corpse, and held the rock at chest height. She closed her eyes and saw Ilsa. *Protecting her is why I've got to do this.* The thought gave her fortitude, and she slammed the rock down. The crunching and cracking of bone sounded desperately loud in the still of the night, and Delaney paused to look around. The only sound she could hear was the gentle deep two-tone hooting of an eagle owl.

Though she knew she'd have to in order to check that the ruse would work, Delaney didn't look beneath the rock as she lifted it and brought it down on the corpse's head three more times. She could feel sticky moisture on her fingers and was glad it wasn't warm, so it didn't feel quite as real. An image of the woman climbing into her car, to her death, came to Delaney's mind. She saw the look of expectancy and saw it turn to terror and fear less than thirty minutes later when Delaney fixed her hands around the woman's throat and began to choke the life out of her. Delaney squeezed her eyes shut to force the image away and tried to replace it with one of Ilsa. She hauled up the rock and saw that she'd pulverized the face beyond recognition. Teeth were smashed and embedded in parts of the face they shouldn't be, and Delaney couldn't even see where the eyes were. She wiped her bloodied hands on the body's shirt and stood. Her surroundings went a little woozy, and her vision blurred. She stumbled backward and was grateful for the solidity of a tree behind her. *Take a breath. I had to do it.*

Delaney steadied herself and did one last check of the scene to make sure the setup was perfect. Satisfied the body she'd left would serve its purpose and protect Ilsa from any undue SS attention, Delaney continued through the woods to the rendezvous point. She allowed herself one last thought of Ilsa and how soft and peaceful she looked when she'd left her asleep. Delaney felt confident that Ilsa would be safe until she was able to return. Now, she had added motivation to take control of Pulsus.

CHAPTER TWENTY-EIGHT

July 7, 1942—Ravensbrück

Landry lay fully clothed in the bunk she shared with three other prisoners and waited. She gripped the pocket watch Delaney had hidden in her tool belt earlier that day. She experienced an unexpected moment of melancholy when she realized it was Adelita Lake's, the British spy she'd come into the camp with. The inscription on the rear of the black copper casing read *Yeshuat Hashem k'heref ayin*. Landry had no time for faith or religion, and this quote likened the salvation of God to the blink of an eye. Still, she liked the sentiment that no matter how dire the situation, redemption or rescue could be in the next moment—always have hope. Landry had always loved pocket watches. Her father had a small collection from his worldly travels, which she treasured but never used. *You have no idea who, or what, your father really was*. Her mom's words were like an infected splinter in her finger, and she resolved to challenge her when she got home. She couldn't just say something like that and expect Landry to accept it without question. There was a depth of anger and bitterness Landry had never seen in her mother before, and Landry had to know where that was coming from.

She stared at the second hand on its never-ending circular journey around the intricate clock face and decided she'd keep the watch. Usually, she worked hard so that missions didn't stay with her, but this one was different. It wasn't the end result that was making her feel this way, though being part of a team that purged the world of cancer was going to be a damn good feeling. It was about having been part of a history that should never be forgotten, and she wanted it to live and breathe inside her. She wanted it to remind her of how appallingly the human race could behave when given half a chance, and how resilient the human spirit could be.

Ten fifteen p.m. Time to roll. Landry slipped out of her bunk and headed to the toilets at the end of the block, muttering something about a painful stomach. She was confident her bunkmates wouldn't raise the alarm when she didn't return, and had to hope they wouldn't be punished, but that's all she could do. The mission was the doctor, not the rest of the women, and she again thought of Delaney's idea about making bigger incisions in the past for bigger outcomes. *Maybe it's a goal we should be working toward.*

Landry propped the two-foot square window open with a torn off piece of her dress and climbed out to drop silently six feet onto the ground below. She stayed close to the block wall, quietly making her way along the grim "shooting alley" to the medical block where she'd have five minutes to explain the plan to Chernick before Griffin arrived with Simson. There were no watchtowers or gun emplacements, making Landry glad the Nazis had figured the women were no threat. Once she was safely at the medical block, Landry removed the glazing panel of the window she'd deliberately not fixed in properly and climbed through the wooden opening. As she slid down the wall, her dress snagged on the window fastening and tore it all the way to her ass. *I fucking hate dresses.*

"Truda—what are you doing here? You'll get us both shot."

Landry took Chernick by the shoulders, guided her to the nearest chair, and gently pressed her into it. "You need to listen to me." She pulled out her pocket watch and checked the time. "In approximately eight minutes, the man you know as SS Officer Christoph Mahler will come in here, propping up the guard you think of as Johanna Thalberg. He'll leave her here and go to get a Kübelwagen, which he'll tell the gate guards he needs so he can take Thalberg to the hospital."

"What are you—"

Landry pressed her finger firmly to Chernick's lips. "Quiet and listen. When they get here, you and Thalberg will exchange clothes, and you'll be the one Mahler takes in the Kübel out of the camp. Are you with me so far?"

Chernick shook her head vigorously. "You're talking about an escape. Are you out of your mind? It'll never work."

"It'll work. We've done this plenty of times before."

"Done what? Broken out of Nazi concentration camps?"

"All sorts of prisons. That's not important right now. What's important is that you understand the plan and are ready to go."

"Who are you…really?"

Landry glanced at the watch again. "We're US Special Forces." Chernick would only discover Landry's lie in about a decade, when the Green Berets were really introduced in the States. Right now, it was the easiest explanation. "We know you're working on a cure for cancer, and we're going to get you out of here. Mahler and Thalberg are actually Griffin and Simson, and my name's Donovan. Okay?" Landry allowed Chernick a moment to absorb the information.

Chernick gasped and grabbed a handful of Landry's dress. "My research—the other Thalberg and Blumstein have my journals. Are they in on this?"

Landry tilted her head slightly. "Sieglinde is, but Blumstein has no idea. They're not sisters, and her name is Delaney. She'll meet you at a rendezvous point, and she'll have your journals with her."

Chernick suddenly looked distracted and turned away. Landry followed the direction of her gaze to see the five women still strapped in place on the metal tables. She reached down and gently brought Chernick back around to face her.

"We can't save them, and neither can you. You're going to save millions, possibly billions of lives. We need to get you out of here."

"The greater good?"

Landry nodded. "Exactly. You're an important woman, Bina. So important, the US government has sent my team to rescue you and take you to New York so you can continue your research there." Landry could see Chernick was torn between her current duties and the thought of what her research might be able to achieve. "The journal you're working in right now, is it here?"

"Yes, I've just finished making an entry."

Landry smiled. "Good timing then."

The main door swung open, and Griffin walked in, with Simson draped around his shoulder. She looked up and grinned. "Get your clothes off, Doc."

Griffin walked over to a filing cabinet, opened the bottom drawer, and pulled the files to the front. He reached toward the back, pulled out a sack, and threw it to Simson before waving his radio and walking through to the back room to report Simson's life-threatening illness.

Simson took out a set of clothes before passing the bag to Landry. "I don't expect a kiss for that. Getting you out of a dress and back into trousers will be payment enough. Your calves are way too muscular to pull off that look without six-inch heels and a wig. Even then you might end up looking like a drag queen."

Chernick looked puzzled as they exchanged clothes.

"Fair point, Simson. Do you speak English, Bina?" Landry asked, still in German.

"Not enough to understand when someone speaks that fast." She seemed reluctant to admit it.

"Then we'll stick to German when it's important, but the rest of the time, we'll speak English so you can start improving yours. By the time we get to New York, you'll be talking like a native."

Chernick nodded, and as she pulled on Simson's sweater vest, Landry was once again struck by how skinny she'd become compared to her original photos. It must've come across on her face, because Chernick met her gaze and indicated toward her own body.

"I'm looking forward to eating a few of your famous hamburgers and hotdogs."

Landry laughed, slightly embarrassed at being so obvious. "Wait until you taste a Philly cheesesteak." She checked the pocket watch again and nodded at Griffin. "Griff will take you outside, help you into the backseat, and cover most of you with a blanket. He's already raised the alarm, so they're expecting you both at the gate. Don't panic if they look in on you, just groan and cough—possible communicable diseases usually deter thorough inspections."

"I hope so. I don't want to end up like Katharina."

Me either. Landry hadn't been around when that escape and subsequent capture had happened, but she'd read all the gruesome details. "We've got this, don't worry." She grasped Chernick by the shoulders. "Go."

Griffin took her by the shoulder but she spun around suddenly. "My journal."

She went back to her desk and picked up the leather book. Griffin took it and stuffed it down the back of his trousers.

"See you soon."

Landry and Simson watched as they got into the Type 82 and drove away. They saw the gates open moments later, and the lights dimmed as they made their escape. She fastened her thick belt around the slightly baggy trousers and tugged her shirt out of the waistband a little. "Let's get the fuck out of this death camp."

"Copy that, Donovan."

Simson grabbed the sack, which now only held blankets, and Landry led the way to the exit window. They climbed out and made their way toward the back wall and electric perimeter.

"You first, Simson."

Simson looked quizzical. "Are you sure?"

"I don't leave any of my team behind. I want to make sure I'm the last one to leave this place."

Simson titled her head in acknowledgement. "You're the extractor."

She quickly turned and scaled the two-meter high wall with exceptional agility, considering her bulk. Landry pitched the bag to her and watched as she covered a good section of the electric wire with the blankets. Landry was glad they were the soldiers' blankets, which were far thicker than the threadbare pieces of material they issued the prisoners.

"See you on the other side," Simson said before dropping out of view.

Landry turned to take one last look at the camp, and her face met with the handle end of a whip. She dropped to the ground, and a boot connected with the pit of her stomach, sending her slamming against the wall. She managed to identify the distinctive features of Erika Vogt in the moonlight before her boot smashed across her face. Landry's head connected with the concrete wall. Black edges appeared around her vision, closing in, and threatening her consciousness. She felt Vogt's boot several more times in her gut as she battled with her own body to stay awake.

Vogt crouched down, put her knee on Landry's chest, and fixed one hand around her throat. "Where do you think you're going,

Stark?" She connected a punch across Landry's jaw. "I heard the alarm raise for my friend, Thalberg, so I came to visit the doctor to see what had happened."

Another strike, and Landry tasted her own blood.

"Imagine my surprise when I find there's no sign of the doctor in the medical block, and I see two shadows dashing across the camp."

She tightened her grip, and Landry grabbed at Vogt's hand to loosen it so she could breathe. Vogt lifted her knee slightly before slamming it back down onto Landry's chest, knocking the air from her lungs.

"You don't get to leave here, Stark. Not until I've finished with you."

Landry summoned her strength from the memories of what Vogt had done, not just to Adelita, but also to the thousands of women before her. She thrust her hips and swung her legs into the air, scissoring Vogt's neck between them. Landry pulled her backward, and Vogt lost her grip on Landry's throat as she fell to the ground. Landry sat up and delivered three solid punches to Vogt's gut, as she pressed her thighs closer together around Vogt's throat. She struggled and thrashed, her hands clawing at Landry as the breath escaped her. Landry knew it only took ten seconds to fall unconscious from being strangled, and only a few extra minutes were required to make their lack of consciousness permanent.

"Please…"

Landry clenched her teeth. Vogt wasn't the mission. If she killed her, it wouldn't be collateral damage, though she could easily explain it as such. *It'd be murder*. But if she didn't kill Vogt now, she'd be able to raise the alarm when she regained consciousness. Landry had nothing to tie her up with. Vogt wasn't wearing a belt, and if Landry parted with hers, her trousers would soon follow.

She looked into Vogt's eyes as she began to lose the fight for her consciousness, and they began to close. *What am I looking for?* She looked up to the wall where Simson had gone over. She was nowhere to be seen. Landry took a deep breath, emptied the emotion from the situation, and focused on the options. If she left Vogt alive, she would regain consciousness in less time than it took Landry to scale the wall. Vogt would raise the alarm, and the mission would be compromised.

There'd be no way she and Simson could get to the rendezvous point. Delaney and Griffin could still succeed in getting Chernick to New York, but they'd be stuck in 1942 and unable to jump home.

If she killed her, Landry could conceal the body against the wall, and she wouldn't be found until the morning. Hell, they might even think she was part of the escape until they discovered her.

Vogt's grip on Landry's legs softened, and she stopped resisting. *It's for the good of the mission.* Decision made.

Landry raised her left leg from the floor, leaving her foot dug into the ground. *Deep breath.* She slammed both legs down, twisting her right one across and beyond the left, snapping Vogt's neck. She got up and pushed Vogt away from her.

"What the hell is going on?" Simson whispered loudly.

Landry looked up to see her peering over the electric fence. "Slight complication. I'll be with you in two minutes." Landry pulled Vogt's body to the wall and laid some loose branches over her, before scrambling up the wall. She carefully crawled over the electric fence then pulled the blankets over with her as she dropped to the ground on the other side.

"What happened?" Simson grabbed the blankets and quickly concealed them in forest debris.

"Vogt blindsided me. Took me a moment to put her down."

"Couldn't happen soon enough. You've done the world a favor."

Landry nodded. *It was justice. There was easy escape to Argentina for Vogt now*. She took another look at her pocket watch. "We've got three clicks to cover, and this terrain is hilly. Let's hit it."

Chapter Twenty-nine

July 7, 1942—Neustrelitz

"Good to have the team back together."

"And even better to be out of a dress." Landry grabbed Delaney's hand and pulled her in for a hard embrace. "I've missed you. Are you doing okay?"

"Not now, Landry. Let's talk later."

Landry tilted her head and looked at Chernick. "How are you, Doc?"

"Better than your face, it seems. Let me look at that."

She stopped Chernick's reaching hand mid-air and winced slightly as she did. "My face is fine."

"Yeah, Doc, a bit of swelling should improve it."

Simson nudged Griffin, and he laughed briefly before he met Landry's glare. "She can get away with that because we've been working together for a while. You should keep your mouth shut."

"And what about your ribs? You're bleeding."

Landry looked down to Chernick's pointing finger. When she and Simson were racing through the hilly woods, she'd felt no pain, but now she could see the left side of her shirt was wet with ruby red blood. She lifted her shirt and saw a fracture in one of her lower ribs.

Chernick pressed her fingers to the area below, and Landry took a sharp intake of breath. "No wonder it's pierced the skin, there's nothing here to protect them. What's the point of having all that muscle if it doesn't protect what's underneath? There's severe bruising here too. What happened?"

"Vogt delayed my exit from the camp."

Chernick leaned back on the hood of the bucket wagon, and Landry swore all the color drained from her skin in seconds. Landry let her shirt fall back into place.

"That woman…is pure evil. She's responsible for the deaths of so many of my friends."

Landry placed her hand on Chernick's shoulder. "She won't be hurting anyone else."

She looked up, relief and gratitude apparent in her face.

"She is dead?"

Landry looked at Delaney and saw something she couldn't define. "Yes. She's dead."

Chernick turned to Delaney. "And what of Ilsa? Won't your disappearance mean trouble for her? Why didn't you bring her out with you? She should not stay at such a place. She's too soft for it."

Delaney smiled, and Landry waited for an explanation for her apparent good humor. Ilsa was an angle she'd had no choice but to leave to chance.

"They won't touch Ilsa. She's got nothing to worry about."

"Did you get her out, Delaney?"

Chernick clearly wasn't satisfied with Delaney's answer, and neither was Landry, but they needed to get on the road. "We've got to go. We've got a six-hour head start before the morning head count, and Bremen is nearly three hundred miles away with the detour for our US papers." *And the PRU.* "With any luck, we can be in the air before they even figure out we're missing." She pointed to the bucket wagon. "Load up."

"I need to treat your ribs." Chernick stood directly in front of Landry.

"Then you can do it while we drive. Griffin, take the first hundred miles. Simson, ride shotgun. Delaney, you're going to have to squeeze in the luggage rack."

They all climbed onboard. Griffin fired up the engine, and Landry was glad of its reliable VW engine. The Germans knew how to build a car almost as well as they knew how to start a world war.

After Chernick had managed to patch Landry up as best she could on the move, in the dark, and along bumpy, windy roads, Landry turned to Delaney.

"Tell me more about Ilsa. How did you manage to protect her?" She wished the moon cast a better light inside the moving vehicle so she could see Delaney's face better. She was easier to read than a children's book.

"I took care of it. I don't have to run every element of my behavior by you. I made a judgment call, and I'm happy with it."

"If you don't tell me, you'll end up telling it in debrief when we get home." Landry was careful not to use any jump terminology when the doc was so close and could hear them. As far as Chernick was concerned, the team was of this time. She had no reason to suspect anything else, and it was imperative they kept it that way.

Delaney sighed loudly. "I had to do something for her, Landry. We shared a villa, and some people knew we were sharing more than that. She would've been the first person they dragged in to interrogate once they discovered the escape involved me and Simson."

"So what *did* you do?"

"I went to Berlin and picked up a woman with a similar look and build to me. I killed her, brought her back to Furstenberg, and left the body, dressed in my clothes and with my papers in her shirt, by the roadside a half mile from the camp."

"Fuck, Delaney, what about the possible consequences of that?" Landry was frustrated she couldn't discuss the issue properly. She'd need more details when they were on the plane, and out of earshot, so she could get a handle on what Delaney had done. "Unless she was a dead ringer, they'll figure out it wasn't you, and Ilsa will still be in danger."

"No, they won't, not after the way I left her."

Delaney looked away, and Landry knew Delaney had done something she wasn't comfortable with. "Explain."

"There was no face left to recognize."

Chernick put her hand to her mouth and gasped.

"Jesus, Delaney. That was some fucking risk. What if you were arrested in Berlin? What if they found the body before we escaped? Did you think about any of those eventualities?"

Delaney smashed her hand against the truck side. "Damn it, Landry, I loved her. But you don't know a single fucking thing about that, do you?"

Landry didn't reply for a moment. Delaney was right. She didn't know anything about love and she didn't try to. She'd never let anyone in, and she really had no intention to, until Jade. *What would I do to protect her, and I don't even love her?* Landry was always trying to convince Delaney she needed something other than Pulsus, a normal life outside of the missions, but she'd applied that advice in the wrong place, and the wrong time. Ilsa was clearly a lovely woman, so *normal*, and caring, so massively different from her soldier buddies. It was little wonder, as vulnerable as Delaney was right now, that she'd fallen for Ilsa in the eighteen months they'd been together. Landry couldn't drop the nagging thoughts that she'd failed Delaney. She should never have allowed her to come on this mission, but she had to admit she'd been distracted by Jade's appearance in her life, and that had impacted negatively on her mission decisions. *How can I sit here and lecture Delaney when it's my fault that I didn't protect her from this mission in the first place?*

"None of us have the time for love, Delaney," Simson yelled from the front.

Delaney lightly scoffed. "I had nothing but time."

Landry stayed silent and focused on the darkness of the road before them, Delaney's last words echoing in her head. Time worked with them *and* against them on missions, just as it did in real life. *Real life. Am I even letting myself have one of those, or am I just playing at it?* She resolved to spend some time with Jade, and the girls, to figure that out. *If the girls are even there.* Caitlin's lover would live because of this mission, and it was possible that everything could be different when she returned to her San Francisco haven. *And what of Jade?* What if there was some history in her family that might mean she wasn't born because of the changes they were making? Suddenly, this time travel shit seemed like more of a head fuck than it usually did. As the road lay stretched ahead of them, Landry had one thought about the future from which she couldn't escape—she had to have Jade in hers.

CHAPTER THIRTY

July 8, 1942—On the road to Bremen

After the detour to the Tollensesee for Landry to collect the PRU and their US papers, Delaney insisted on taking the driving duty from Griffin. She needed something to focus on other than the heavy silence between her and Landry. She hadn't wanted to declare her love for Ilsa to everyone in the truck. She regretted the words the moment they left her mouth. It was unprofessional and weak. It was Griffin's first mission with Pulsus, and the last thing Delaney wanted to do was blow up like she had in front of a rookie. She needed him to keep his mouth shut in the debrief, so she'd asked him to ride shotgun when she took the truck keys.

"So what's your take on the first part of the mission? Did you enjoy it?" Delaney whispered her question so Chernick didn't hear them over the road and engine noise.

"I don't know that enjoy is the right word. Having to fuck that Vogt woman was harder than shooting heroin for the first time, *and* it never got any easier."

Delaney laughed quietly. "Yeah, we have to do some crazy shit."

"How many missions have you completed?"

Delaney tilted her head, as if that would help her bring them to mind. "This one's unlucky thirteen, if you believe in that kind of shit." *Or lucky thirteen. I found Ilsa on this one.*

"How many years have you lived in those missions?"

"This makes it ninety-five." Her answer was instant. She knew exactly how many years, months, and days she'd spent in other pasts.

"You're looking good for your age. You don't look a day over fifty."

His ribbing was clearly good-natured. Delaney liked him and would happily work with him on more missions. She wondered if he'd be interested in her version of Pulsus, or if he'd be a casualty who fell by the wayside. "Watch it, grunt. I can kick you out of this truck right now and leave you here to play with Nazi girls for another three years."

"God, no. I need some hot piece of tight boy ass when we get home." Griffin practically shouted his exclamation.

Chernick leaned forward and asked, "You're gay, and in the army?"

Delaney and Griffin exchanged a knowing look. Chernick was operating on out-of-date principles, and was from a time where homosexuality was an offense punishable by death. Although Hitler wasn't the only one who had that idea, and it would be another sixty-three years before the last country fell in line with the rest of the world.

"America's a very different place than Germany, Doc."

Chernick shrugged and nodded before leaning back into her own seat. They resumed their conversation in their previous hushed tones.

"What's the regeneration like? It must be strange to keep getting older and then be reversed. All the years you've lived, you must feel immortal."

"It's a little painful, even with the anesthetic. You can't be fully dosed up or it interferes with the cell reversal process. It's worth it."

"What's the worst injury you've had fixed? That shit amazes me."

"I've been lucky and have always come back in one piece. Landry's the one with all those stories if you're after gruesome. She came back from the last mission with a punctured lung, three cracked ribs, and a broken nose. But they still can't fix malignant cells. Once the body goes bad, they can't save you." *Just like the mind.*

"Which is why we go on missions like this. It's really something to know that my first mission was helping cure cancer."

"Which in turn makes it easier to reconcile doing things like the British spy."

Griffin didn't respond immediately and shifted in his seat, pretending to flick off some imaginary dirt from his jacket. "I guess that'll be something for me to discuss with Castillo's team."

"Anything else you'll be mentioning?" Delaney decided it was time to stop pussyfooting around Griffin and ask the question.

"If you're worried about me saying anything about the Blumstein situation, don't. I had enough backbiting, with agents trying to crawl over the dead bodies of other agents to advance their career in the CIA. I'm just a grunt here, and I like it that way. I got your back. You need to concentrate on the extractor." He put his hand on her shoulder and gave her a comforting squeeze. "But you two go way back, so that shouldn't be a problem, huh?"

Delaney eyed the rearview mirror to glance at Landry and met her gaze. *That'd be a conversation for the long flight to New York.* And she needed to play it perfectly or Landry would never agree to her Pulsus plan. She turned her wrist to check the time. Ilsa wouldn't wake until mid-morning because of the sleeping pill concoction Delaney laced her wine with. She couldn't risk her raising the alarm when Delaney didn't come back after her regular late night walk. It was strange knowing Ilsa would grieve for her, feel anger at whoever she suspected of killing her, and yet, if all went according to plan, Delaney would be back there only an hour after she left last night. Ilsa would wake and look at Delaney as if she hadn't seen her for an hour. Delaney would take the time to drink her in all over again, because she wouldn't have seen or touched Ilsa for months. She'd finally found someone she could imagine spending her life with, but to be with her, Delaney would have to turn her own life upside down.

CHAPTER THIRTY-ONE

July 8, 1942—Bremen

Griffin had acquired male SS uniforms for Delaney and Simson, and a Luftwaffe flight uniform for Landry, so the four of them could enter the Focke-Wulf aircraft plant and "acquire" an FW 200 Condor. Chernick remained in her slightly oversized guard uniform, and she was to act as their accompanying physician. They were counting on taking advantage of the chaos of the recent RAF thousand-bomber raid that had taken place just over a week prior to their arrival. Under the guise that the constant targeting was causing Hitler to consider shifting aircraft production to East Germany and Poland, Griffin would provide the order to fly the plane to Warsaw, to see if the evacuation of the plant was feasible.

"You all make very handsome men," Chernick said as they got ready a few miles from the base.

"And convincing, we hope."

"Oh, yes, Donovan. You all look the part."

They climbed back into the bucket wagon and drove to the base entrance. The sight of the trio in their SS uniforms elicited the prescribed response of terror and fear in the regular soldiers guarding the base entry, and they were all quick to display their Heil Hitler salutes.

Griffin introduced them all before ordering the cadet to take them to the officer in charge. Griffin's clipped tones were disturbingly menacing. Landry wouldn't have been surprised if the soldier peed a little when faced by the three SS officers in the truck with her and Chernick.

"Yes, sir, follow me." He told the other guard where he was going, before mounting a BMW R75 motorbike and heading into the camp. Delaney drove close behind.

"This is terrifying."

"I know, Doc. Just try to stay calm. Stay in the wagon and don't speak unless one of them asks you a direct question. That shouldn't happen unless they suspect something—it'd be a blunt challenge to their authority." Landry motioned to their SS triumvirate. "We've done our homework, this plan will work, and we'll be on that plane and on our way to New York."

They followed the bike through to the main hangar. The cadet got off and came back to the truck to open the doors for everyone to climb out. He waited while they straightened their uniforms and carefully placed their hats, then motioned for them to follow him again. Chernick remained in the truck.

"Oberleutnant Barth, this is Oberführer Eichman, Sturmbahnführers Seiler and Faber, and Major Adler."

Landry was glad their intel was correct, and each one of them outranked Barth. He dutifully saluted each of them.

"What can I do for you, officers? I was not expecting such esteemed visitors."

Griffin handed him folded papers, lovingly crafted by the reproduction team at Pulsus.

"These are orders from Major General Conrad Hamfeld of Luftkreis III, Berlin. We're here to take possession of a fully equipped FW-200, fully fueled, and battle-ready."

Barth opened the papers and quickly scanned them, before folding them and handing them back to Griffin. "I can have one fully fueled and ready to go in three hours. Perhaps you might travel back into town and have lunch, or would you prefer to wait here in the officers' mess?"

"Major Adler will stay here and oversee preparations, but a local lunch for us will be marvelous. Do you have a recommendation?"

"That would be the Bremer Ratskeller by the market. It has a five-hundred-year history and is the oldest wine cellar in Germany.

I can send a cadet ahead to book you a prioelken; they are a lovely, intimate area of the restaurant."

"That would be perfect, Oberleutnant."

"Of course, anything for our fine SS officers." He saluted again and ordered the cadet on the motorbike to do as he'd promised. "Enjoy your meals. I will see you in a few hours."

❖

"Would you like to follow me, Major Adler?"

Landry nodded and followed Barth into the hangar. Toward the far end of it, sat a pristine FW-200 Condor, an all metal, four-engine monoplane. Once the war had started, the plane was prepared for military service, with front, aft, and dorsal gun positions added. As the main pilot, Landry had been briefed about the history of this plane, and had yet to share with the rest of the team that because of the hurried changes, it tended to break up on landing. It was a problem they never really solved, and Pulsus knew they were taking a calculated risk, but Landry was an excellent pilot. As was her copilot, Delaney. They'd both landed several planes in extreme situations, so it didn't worry her. As long as they dumped all but their necessary fuel prior to attempted landing, she was sure they'd be fine.

She grabbed a nearby flight ladder and pushed it up to the cockpit, while Barth instructed several of his staff to prepare the aircraft. She was hoping to avoid any further face time with Barth or his staff. She pulled out her pocket watch and flipped it over to read the inscription again. They needed hope and a shit-ton of luck to pull this part of the mission off. Barth had barely read the orders Griffin had given him, which she was hoping was a good sign, and that they'd been convincing enough. It made sense, and the orders were actually an exact copy of orders that would come to Barth in around ten months' time. She wondered if he'd recall this day and have a strange sense of déjà-vu, or whether he'd question those orders and get himself demoted, or worse, by audaciously questioning the validity of SS officers.

Landry pulled out the Luger P08 pistol from its holster on her hip and quickly checked it over. She slipped it back into the holster and felt reassured. She was used to operating solo on missions, but with so many of the enemy around her, she felt a little uneasy. She moved through the aircraft to check that everything was where it should be. She climbed the ladders to the front and aft gun positions, where Griffin and Simson would spend the majority of the twenty-five-hour journey to US soil, just in case. Their flight plan took them the path of least resistance, given the capabilities of the aircraft, and avoided all dangerous airspace, aside from when they approached New York. The papers they had would hold up to inspection though, and Nelson and Williams, the operatives they'd sent back to 1935 to infiltrate the FBI, would smooth their way through the military hoopla to place Chernick in a university for five years before placing her at the Brookhaven Research facility on Long Island in 1947. A different extractor would come back to retrieve them, once Chernick had a research team of her own in place, and Pulsus had determined it was a success. Extracting Nelson and Williams would be the next mission once Landry and her team jumped back.

Landry yawned, a jaw-breaking kind of yawn that only comes from extreme tiredness. She checked her pocket watch and saw she had another two and a half hours to wait. She walked back to the cockpit and quickly changed into a flight suit before settling into her chair. She took her Luger from its holster and placed it in the well to her left, keeping her hand on it, just in case. Landry closed her eyes and drifted into a much needed sleep.

CHAPTER THIRTY-TWO

July 8, 1942—Bremen

Delaney touched Landry gently on the shoulder. She saw her holster was empty, and could see her left hand was out of sight. She knew Landry would have a tight grip on her pistol, even when sound asleep, and she didn't want her face blown off this close to the end of the mission. She didn't want her face blown off at all.

"Major Adler," Delaney said, gently bringing Landry back into their current situation. Landry stirred, and Delaney reached over and pushed down on her left bicep to keep her in place. "Everyone's on the plane and ready to fly to Warsaw."

Landry's eyes flicked open, and Delaney smiled when she saw a moment of confusion.

"Seiler. It's time? All on board and accounted for?"

Delaney grabbed their leather flight helmet and comms, tossed Landry hers, and they pulled them on. "Yes, Major Adler, everyone's here. We're ready to complete the mission. Time for you to take us home."

Delaney peered out the cockpit window and signaled to Barth to take away the chocks, before sitting in her co-pilot seat and fixing her harness. Landry hit the brake and locked the tail, before selecting and starting the engines in order. Delaney put the flaps in starting position and opened the cowlings.

"Prop pitch to full."

Delaney nodded confirmation. Landry hit the brake again and started to push the throttle up to full position. She eased it up to full takeoff speed, and the nose inclined until all they could see was sky. Landry confirmed all was well with the ground crew, and Delaney raised the wheels.

They were at cruising altitude before Landry pulled off her headset.

"So you love her?"

Delaney grimaced. *We're going there already?* She was hoping they'd put a few hundred miles behind them before this conversation. "Honestly, I don't know. I lived with Ilsa for nearly two years, Landry, and slept with her for eighteen months. Sometimes you have to feel things on these missions to get through them in one piece, and she made me feel something different. You don't know what it's like to spend so much time being someone else, acting in ways we swore allegiance to the flag not to act." Delaney unclipped her harness and turned to Landry. "You're always talking about having a normal life outside of Pulsus, and my time with Ilsa, away from the camp, felt like that. And I liked it. I started to understand what you've been yammering on about for the past three years. I know you've not been talking about love, but I couldn't stop it. The relationship developed for the good of the mission, and now the mission's almost over."

"You risked everything, Delaney. Your life. The mission. The doc. Hell, you put the life of this woman above the lives of billions of people the world over, for centuries to come."

Delaney slammed her hand against the cockpit window. "Don't you think I know that? We all make mistakes on a mission, Landry… your last one nearly cost you your life."

"That's a low blow."

"Is it? Seems to me like it's exactly the same thing. You felt compassion for someone, and that same person nearly killed you. I felt love for Ilsa and had to kill *for* her."

There was a short cough before Chernick appeared in the cockpit.

"I bought you some cheese and biscuits, Donovan. I thought you'd be hungry." She placed a folded up napkin of food on the floor between the two pilot seats. "And I need to check your rib dressing to make sure the wound hasn't gotten infected."

Landry sighed deeply and picked up the food. "Thanks, Doc."

She unzipped her flight suit and pulled up her tank top. Chernick leaned over and slowly removed the wet bandage.

"It looks okay from this angle, but I need to put a clean dressing on. I found a first aid kit back here." She brandished the box in the air. "It will only take a few moments."

Delaney was glad of the respite, however brief it might be, as Landry unclipped her harness and climbed out of her seat.

"You take your doctoring very seriously. It's just a broken rib."

Landry was all charm, even for Chernick. Delaney wondered if she ever turned it off to have a normal conversation with anyone other than her.

"It's the least I can do since you saved my life…and I'm sure I don't want to die in a plane crash because one of the pilots passed out from septicemia."

Delaney laughed. "The doc has a point, Landry."

"Landry. That's unusual. Is that your first name?"

Jesus, Doc, why don't you just get down on the floor and kiss her feet?

"Yeah, it is. You like it?"

Being grilled by Landry is better than listening to Chernick hit on her. What does she think? That they'll be able to hook up once they hit New York? "Fix her up quick, Doc. I need her back in the chair."

Chernick did as instructed and retreated from the cockpit area. Landry retook her seat and munched on the food Chernick had delivered.

"Nothing like being served tasteless shit for a month to make you appreciate real food."

"I need to know you're going to cover for me in the debrief."

"Is that what you're worried about?"

"I can't be suspended from action, Landry. I'll go crazy."

"That's just the problem, Delaney. I feel like I should've done something before we even came on this mission. I feel like you weren't fit for duty."

Delaney smashed her fist onto the yoke. "Fuck that, Landry, and fuck you. You can't believe that."

"I let you down, Delaney. You told me you were struggling, and I let you come to one of the most heinous places in the history of the world. You might have made the bad decision with Ilsa, but I failed you."

"Jesus, Landry, I think you've been spending too much time with the head shrinks, or maybe the mainland is making you soft. I didn't tell you I was having issues so you could cut me from the team. I told you so you could help me with them when we get back." *And so you'll eventually see my plans for Pulsus are the way forward.*

Simson was the next interloper in the cockpit.

"You might want to keep it down. The doc is getting jumpy. She's a clever woman, but I'm not sure she'll cope with finding out we're time travelers. You don't want to be responsible for sending the woman who could've cured cancer, crazy, do you?"

Landry waved her back. "Take her to the far end of the plane where it's noisiest, and make sure she doesn't hear anything, Simson. Play cards, go to sleep, whatever you need to do to calm her down."

Simson shrugged. She turned, mumbling as she left the cockpit. "You quarrel worse than any lovers I've ever known. Both of you need to get over it."

"What the fuck does that mean?" Landry asked Simson as she disappeared into the back of the plane, where she'd probably claim she never heard her commanding officer's question. "What the fuck does that mean?" She directed her question to Delaney.

It means she knows I'm in love with you. "I don't know. When does she ever make sense?"

Landry took a deep breath, and Delaney could feel her stare boring into the side of her head.

"I'll cover for you, just like you did for me after our last mission. But we need to look at what's going on with you, with or without the head doctors. I still think it would've been better if you hadn't come on this mission, but I guess we'll see what damage that's done."

Don't worry, Landry. We're going to fix all of it, together. And just maybe I get the other girl, if I can't get you.

Chapter Thirty-three

July 10, 1942—New York

"Identify yourself."

Given the aircraft they were in, the controller at La Guardia Field airport had every right to sound agitated as they entered American airspace.

"This is Special Agent Donovan with the FBI. I've got Special Agents Delaney, Simson, and Griffin. We're carrying a high value rescue, Dr. Bina Chernick. Please confirm Special Agents Nelson or Williams are present."

"Please confirm the landing code, Agent Donovan."

Landry could hear the mistrust in her voice. She hoped at least one of them had made it through their part of the mission. Williams was Nelson's understudy, just in case anything untoward happened to him, but she expected it would turn out to be an unnecessary precaution. There was no real danger to their placement, only sheer bad luck would have had any impact on their time in the past, and they'd been immunized against all the possible diseases they might have picked up. All they had to do was infiltrate and wait.

"Papa uniform Lima, Sierra uniform Sierra, two zero, seventy-six."

Delaney smiled widely as Landry relayed the code. The tech guys at Pulsus had an interesting sense of humor.

"Affirmative, Special Agent Donovan, you're cleared to land. Special Agent Williams is waiting in the hangar you'll be directed to."

"Thank you, ground control. Reducing speed on approach. These German built planes may be built to cross the Atlantic, but they're not built to land so well. Do you have a ground crew standing by?"

"Confirm. Ground crew is standing by."

Landry closed off her mic and called to the rear of the plane. "Simson, make sure everyone's strapped in for landing. This is going to be rough. And be ready for immediate evac once we hit the ground. Put your masks on too."

"You got it."

"Would it be ironic if the doc ended up dying in a plane crash after a daring rescue, rather than in a concentration camp?"

Landry smiled at the soldier humor in Delaney's question. "That wouldn't be irony; that would be shit luck. Buckle up, buddy. This is going to be the kind of rough you don't get off on."

Delaney extended her middle finger. "Fuck you, vanilla girl."

Landry centered the plane on the runway approach and slowed to landing speed. She engaged the landing gear.

"That didn't sound healthy." Chernick shouted over the din of the engine noise.

"Don't worry, Doc. We didn't rescue you only to let you die on a United States runway. No one's ever died on our missions."

Delaney shot her a sideways glance, and Landry tilted her head. "We've never lost a mission target." Landry rephrased quietly, knowing Delaney was referring to an operative they lost on their second mission. Someone Pulsus had made a mistake in recruiting, a hotshot sniper with an unwarranted sense of overconfidence and invincibility. His drunken challenge to a far more talented shooter resulted in a bullet to the back of his head, and a seriously compromised mission. The recruitment process tightened up considerably after that mission.

Landry slowed the plane to just above stalling speed in an effort to combat the compromised weight distribution caused by the plane's militarization. They hit the runway and bounced. Chernick screamed. There was a loud crack, as the plane began to break in two, just behind the wings.

"What's happening?" Chernick shouted, her voice panicked and high-pitched.

"The plane's going to break in two," Delaney shouted back. "You'll be fine. That's why you're at the back of it."

Landry couldn't help but laugh. "That's so comforting. I'm sure she'll be really calm now." She called out to the back, "We're going to be fine, Doc. We're almost there."

Landry pulled back on the yoke, keeping the plane as balanced as she could, considering it was about to break in two because of the poor weight distribution. At least this way, the rear part of the plane would be easily accessed by the ground crew, and the doc would be the first one out of the plane.

They slid past the ground crew as the plane slowed, and as it stopped completely, it broke in two and the rear part of the plane fell the remaining few feet to the ground. As Landry and Delaney scrambled out of the cockpit, Simson and Griffin were carrying out an unconscious Chernick.

"What happened?"

"The excitement was too much, and she passed out. It stopped her screaming, which was better than the thing I was considering doing to stop her."

Griffin opened the side door, and Landry saw Chernick being laid on a stretcher. She and Delaney headed back to the top exit. They climbed down onto the wings and dropped onto the ground.

"Nice flying, Special Agent Donovan."

Landry greeted Williams with a strong handshake. "Thanks, Williams. It's good to see you." She pulled him away from the ground crew and the rest of her team. "Where's Nelson?"

Williams shook his head and sighed. "He was coming out of his hotel on West Fifty-sixth Street, walked into the road, and a checker cab plowed straight into him. He's at the New York Presbyterian Hospital all busted up with a broken leg. But he's going to be okay."

"Jesus. I guess placing two of you on this mission turned out to be a damned good idea, then." Landry shuddered to think of what might have happened if Pulsus had sent just one of them. She would have ended up nominating two of the operatives to stay a lot longer than anticipated, to build Chernick's life for her, while Landry returned to Pulsus. She wouldn't have wanted to leave Simson with Chernick, but she was desperate to get Delaney back to 2076. She didn't want to see her suffer any more than she already had. "Is everything in place for Dr. Chernick?"

"Yes. She's got a teaching position at Columbia, as planned. Everyone's prepared to support a new line of research into cancer. Nelson and I have been assigned to the New York office to make sure Chernick is kept safe. I guess you'll know before we do when the mission is complete so we can come home."

Landry gripped his shoulder. "Just remember why you're doing this." It seemed like he needed some reassurance. Though they knew Chernick had the knowledge and was going the right way to discover the cure for cancer, they had no idea how long it might take her, so Williams and Nelson wouldn't be jumping home with the rest of the team. They had to stay in New York to keep Chernick on the right track. When they got back to Pulsus, the next mission would be to recover Williams and Nelson, but there was no telling whether that would be in 1947 or 1967. It was another aspect of the operatives' job that made Landry glad she was an extractor. She hated uncertainty, and besides, she really wanted to see Jade. *If she's still around.* She realized there wasn't just uncertainty here, it was in every aspect of her life following some missions. And this one threatened to have up close and personal consequences. She thought about the girls and Priscilla. Letting them into her life, and the way they'd pulled her into theirs, had been so easy and so natural. Landry wasn't sure how she'd cope if she got home to new tenants in her building.

"What's the doc like?"

"She's a good woman." Landry thought about what Chernick had been through and the difference she'd tried to make to the poor women chosen for the experiments. "Make sure you look after her."

"Landry?" Delaney beckoned her over with a tilt of her chin. "The doc wants to speak to you."

"Give me a minute." Landry jogged over to Chernick. She was conscious and sitting up on the gurney. "What's up, Doc?" Landry smiled as she said it, quickly realizing Chernick probably had yet to see the iconic animated cartoon character.

"Will you tell these people I'm all right, and I don't need to go to the hospital?"

"Are you sure you don't need to be checked out?"

She shook her head. "I'm certain I'm fine, Landry, though I appreciate your concern. I'd rather just get on with…my new life."

Landry saw the tears slowly forming in Chernick's eyes. "Is the magnitude of what's happening starting to hit home, Doc?" It was something they hadn't talked about or considered. Chernick had been plucked from three years of captivity and cruelty, and was suddenly a free woman in a new country. The only expectation placed on her was that she continue her research, which was a scientist's dream scenario, but maybe she wanted more.

"I believe it might well be. Could we go for a meal somewhere, perhaps for one of those famous American burgers you told me about?"

Delaney shook her head and glared at her. She obviously wanted to jump home as soon as possible. So did Landry. The anticipation of knowing if Jade and the girls would be around was eating at her, but Chernick clearly needed someone to speak to. She shrugged apologetically to Delaney.

"Sure, I've got some time."

The look on Chernick's face when she took a bite of the jumbo burger at Ken's Restaurant made Landry smile. "It's a good thing we didn't get home earlier this week. I hear this place is participating in the rations for victory meatless Tuesdays."

Chernick put her burger down, and a look of melancholy passed over her eyes.

"Home," she repeated deliberately slowly. "I suppose I'll be making this my home, since I'll never be able to go back to Germany."

"You don't know that for sure, Bina. This war won't last much longer." Landry took a big bite of her own burger and savored it almost as much as the full bottle of beer she'd knocked back as soon as the waitress set it on their table. "Maybe when you've cured the world of cancer, you'll go back there."

"I do like your confidence in me, Landry. I'm not sure anyone has ever believed in me like you do." Chernick reached over and placed her hand over Landry's. "Will you be staying in New York?"

Oh shit. Landry put her food down and gently put her other hand over Chernick's. "Lots of people believe in you, Bina. That's why they sent us to rescue you." She slowly pulled her hands away and took a quick swallow of her second beer. "But I won't be staying here. I have to go home…to my family." *To the girls. To Jade? God, this friendship thing is confusing.*

"Of course. Of course you'd have someone waiting for you at home."

Chernick smiled, and her face flushed with what Landry took to be embarrassment for the gentle knock-back.

Her statement made Landry smart a little. There was no one waiting for her at home, and that's the way it had always been. That's the way she liked it. *But the closer it gets to the possibility of seeing Jade…*

"In other circumstances, I would've liked to have stayed." Landry delivered the line with as much sincerity as she could muster. There was no way she could've entertained Chernick sexually. Landry mostly liked her women traditionally feminine, and Chernick was anything but.

Chernick smiled tightly at the platitude, and they ate for a while in silence.

"I'm scared." Chernick popped a gherkin in her mouth and let the statement hang in the air.

"I can't even begin to imagine how you must feel. Being taken away from what you know and brought to an unfamiliar country thousands of miles from home. Do you have any family we could try to bring over?" Landry knew the answer, or she couldn't have asked the question.

"No. I'm the only Chernick left, I'm afraid. My hometown was 'cleansed' of Jews a month before I was imprisoned. The whole village was shot or burned to death."

"I'm so sorry."

"Are any of your team staying here, or do you all live in other parts of the country?"

"We're all from the West Coast. Year-round sunshine."

"And will any of you be back this way any time?"

Landry could feel Chernick's enveloping loneliness. She'd escaped a death camp, and unimaginable pain at the hands of Mengele, but it seemed that her main concern was her impending solitude. "I shouldn't think so. You're the first non-American rescue mission, and I'm pretty sure you're going to be the last."

"Landry, I was alone for the majority of the time I was in Cologne. I had hard and fast one-night stands every now and then, but until the nurse, I'd been desperately lonely. I'm done being lonely, Landry. I want something…someone, else."

"New York is a great place to be a lesbian. If you manage to tear yourself away from your microscope every now and then, you never know who you'll find." Landry decided she'd look Chernick up when she got back to the island. She found herself rooting for the doc to find some sort of true love. *Even if I don't believe in it? Will I want it in a few years?*

"And until that time, I'll have my research."

"Exactly. You're going to change the world, Bina. That's an elite club."

Chernick smiled and raised her glass. "To changing the world."

Landry clinked her bottle to Chernick's toast and thought about her own words. She was part of changing the world too. She knew she was fighting the good fight and making a difference. *Have I gotten so carried away with that, that I don't even realize I might be lonely too?*

CHAPTER THIRTY-FOUR

July 11, 1942—New York

Landry woke in unfamiliar surroundings to an insistent knocking on her door. She stirred in her semi-comfortable bed and vaguely recognized the background noise of New York City. It was a far more pleasant environment than the past month in the camp, but it'd felt strange not falling asleep to the sounds of six hundred other women. She wondered how Chernick had found her first night out of the camp. She expected she'd be happy enough given what had happened after the restaurant.

Pulsus didn't want to take any chances on Chernick being distracted from her research, so in addition to Nelson and Williams, they'd sent Lucy Jackson, a cute little brunette operative who matched Chernick's predilections perfectly. After Chernick had made her play for Landry, she pulled that part of the plan forward, and took the doc to Ginger's Bar to meet the orchestrated love of her life on her first night on American soil. Chernick was immediately smitten with Lucy, who fawned suitably when Chernick told her she was a doctor, and they left together shortly after. Landry had to fend off the attentions of several stunning femmes to keep up the charade of her family on the West Coast. There was a niggling feeling in Landry's subconscious, however, that it wasn't just the pretense that was stopping her, and even if she *had* stayed once Chernick had left, she doubted she would've connected with anyone. Landry was trying hard to convince herself that she and Jade could simply be friends, and that she didn't have to act on her every sexual impulse just because Jade was quite possibly the most beautiful and interesting woman she'd ever come across. Even at Ravensbrück, Landry had been unable to stop thoughts of Jade from invading her mind. Now that she was so close to seeing her again, she could barely concentrate on anything else. Always a glass half-full kind of woman, Landry had decided Jade and the girls would be exactly where she'd left them, a hundred and thirty-four years in the future.

"Landry, are you in there?"

The knocking was even louder this time, and it reminded her she'd had a few too many drinks trying to numb her feelings for Jade.

"Give me a minute." She climbed out of bed and half-stumbled into the bathroom, her eyes struggling to adjust to the bright light through the threadbare curtains. Williams didn't have a big budget for their last-minute hotel bookings, and the place he'd put them all in was quite the fleapit. Landry turned on the tap, cupped her hands full of dirty brown water, and splashed it on her face. She wiped away the sleepy crud from the corners of her eyes and ran her hands over the half-inch of stubble all over her head. It reminded her of her grunt days as a Seal, but she wasn't sure if Jade would like the look. A month without her proper nutrition regime, protein shakes, brown rice, and water had made her somewhat gaunt too. Nothing like the average Ravensbrück prisoner, but maybe more like a cancer patient in the early stages of chemo. She was glad the regenerative tech could grow her hair as well as fix her aging.

Landry was pale against the white ribbed tank she wore. *I need some sun.* She ran her fingers over her forearm and smiled. She'd be glad to have her tattoo and some color back. She flexed her arms and shoulder muscles, feeling the need to get back to the gym to bulk up again. She winced a little at the pain in her ribs and was again glad for the tech to fix that when she got home. Between her home setup and the Rogue Gym on Mission Street, she'd soon be back to baseballs in her biceps.

"Christ, how long are your fucking minutes, Landry?"

Delaney's raised voice reminded Landry she was at the door waiting.

"Sorry, buddy."

Landry walked back through and let Delaney in. She held a tray of coffees aloft and wafted a brown bag in Landry's face. Landry noticed the old sailor bag slung over her back and hoped she'd brought what she'd asked Williams for.

"Hungry, stud? Where are you hiding her…them?"

"I'm alone." Landry snatched the bag from Delaney's hand and pulled out a cream cheese bagel. "Ah, yes, my favorite. What would I do without you?"

Delaney huffed. "So we didn't delay the jump for your booty call, then? Or did you kick her out before you went to sleep?"

Landry detected a hint of anger in Delaney's tone and put it down to her having to defer the jump until today. Coming from anyone else, it would've sounded like jealousy, but she wasn't egotistical enough to think that of Delaney. "Sorry to disappoint you, but I have nothing to report in that department. You'd have to talk to the doc if you're after that."

"You spent all night in a New York nightclub after a month without sex, and you're telling me you came back to the hotel alone?"

"That is indeed what I'm telling you. The doc came on to me, so I had to spin her a tale about having a family back home, and fast-forward the hookup with Lucy. I couldn't very well go sucking on someone's face after telling her that, could I?"

"No surprise there. I saw that coming a mile off. But if the doc left with Lucy, how come you didn't stay and find some action for yourself? Or are you saving yourself for your superstar baller?"

Landry shook her head and washed a mouthful of bagel down with a swallow of sweet coffee. "I told you. We're just friends."

Delaney walked over to the window, opened the curtains, and dropped her bag onto the table. The woman smoking on her fire escape across the alley waved and smiled. Delaney waved back and chuckled.

"When it comes to gay women, there's no such thing as 'just friends' if there's even a sniff of chemistry or sexual attraction."

"You and I are just friends with benefits, and it works for us."

Delaney seemed to hesitate.

"Sure, but we're soldiers. Your baller girl lives in the regular world, with regular people, having regular relationships. If she thinks there's a spark, she'll act on it. Trust me."

Landry sighed. Maybe Delaney knew what she was talking about. *Am I kidding myself thinking I can resist her?* "You make it sound like lesbians can't control themselves."

"So what if I am? So what if we can't?" Delaney threw her arms in the air. "You only live once, right? Even if it does happen to be for two or three hundred years in our case."

"I don't know, buddy. Isn't that the problem? I can't give her what she needs because of our job."

"Sounds like an easy excuse. You're the one always telling me to have a life outside Pulsus, but you've got rules and regulations that mean you're not really fully committing to it. What kind of bullshit is that?"

"Jesus, Delaney, that Ilsa girl has done a number on you." Delaney had always seemed so disconnected from love and emotion. As fuck buddies, they had intense sex, but it was just physical, or so it seemed. It was sport fucking. Landry hadn't taken Delaney to be sentimental about anything. "It almost makes me wish we could've brought her home with us."

"That makes two of us," Delaney said softly.

Landry put her hand on Delaney's shoulder. "What was it like?" She regretted asking the question for a moment, but Delaney was her best friend. If she could ask anyone, it was her.

She turned to face Landry and looked slightly bemused. "What was what like? Love?"

Landry nodded. "Yeah. Love. What's love like?" It felt like a stupid question, but perhaps it would help her figure out what was going on with Jade. She'd never met anyone like her before. Maybe it was just a silly infatuation.

Delaney pulled out a chair and sat, seriously contemplating Landry's words.

"It felt like I couldn't breathe around her, but at the same time, she was my oxygen."

That was beautifully poetic. Landry wanted to ask the obvious follow-up question, but Delaney seemed more vulnerable now than she'd ever seen her before. Then again, Castillo was constantly trying to tell them about the importance of sharing their feelings. The woman had no idea that in order to kill someone, you had to repress your ability to really feel anything. Landry decided to risk it. "What does it feel like now?"

Delaney hesitated again, and Landry wasn't sure if she'd pushed her too far. She scratched at her nose absentmindedly, making Landry think that whatever was going to come out of her mouth, it wouldn't necessarily be the truth. It was Delaney's tell, though she didn't know it. *But why would you lie to me?*

"I'm not sure I've got a handle on it yet." She stood abruptly. "Griffin and Simson are waiting downstairs with Williams. He's going to take us to a quiet place in Central Park to jump back." She picked up the bag and tossed it to Landry. "There's everything you need in there plus the jacket you wanted. Williams said you owe him big for that. He says he had to steal it from one of the players."

"Thanks, buddy." Landry decided not to push it. Delaney was hiding something, but she wasn't sure whether it was about Ilsa or something else. She figured she'd get it out of her eventually. Delaney wasn't one for keeping secrets from her.

"I'll go wait with them."

Delaney didn't wait for a response and was quickly gone from the room. She didn't seem quite right, but there was a whole host of things going on with her that Landry had to cut her some slack for. They'd work it out when they got back to Pulsus and went house hunting on the mainland. She'd stay at a hotel close to Landry's apartment while they looked, and that would give them plenty of time to work on Delaney's nightmares and her state of mind. If only she could see a professional not associated with Pulsus.

Landry turned the bag upside down on the bed and smiled when she saw the navy letterman jacket with its red leather sleeves. She couldn't resist pulling it on and checking herself out in the bathroom mirror. *Perfect.* Landry felt like an excited high school jock getting ready to go out on a date with the prom queen. *The very sexy, athletic, Latin prom queen.*

"Time to go home."

She tossed the jacket aside to take a quick shower and was clean, dressed, and in the hotel lobby within ten minutes. She'd tucked the PRU safely in the inside pocket of her jacket.

"Did you show the doc a good time?" Griffin asked with a filthy grin.

Landry nodded. "She went back to her hotel with Lucy, so yeah, I think she was content with her new start in life."

"And New York was treated to the great Landry Donovan. Can we go home now?"

The sarcasm in Simson's voice was more obvious than a whore on a street corner. Landry thought Simson's animosity had mellowed, but apparently not. She wasn't sure of its source but had wondered if Simson was jealous of her friendship with Delaney. She had to consider how she'd handled Delaney's relationship with Ilsa for the past two years. Now that Landry took the time to really look at Simson, she could all but see her skin crawling with barely repressed aggression.

Landry ignored the comment and addressed Williams. "Delaney says you know a good place for the jump?"

"I do. My car's out front, so it won't take us long."

Landry slipped her arm through his and pulled him toward the lobby entrance. "Let's go."

On the short drive to Central Park, Landry quickly double-checked the details of Williams and Nelson's assignment now that Chernick was in their hands. They were both great handlers, and Landry felt reassured that their part of the mission would run smoothly, particularly given that Chernick had quickly taken to Lucy as well. They'd know soon enough if the mission was fully successful when they got back to Pulsus and endured the high-speed reality catch-up. Landry was a little perturbed that she'd have to go through that before she could check on Jade and the girls in the Pulsus database. Conversely, it also felt strange to be that motivated about non-mission elements. She needed some time to herself to really consider how to balance this work-life thing, now that she'd added a "friend" into the mix as well as the family who'd adopted her. Landry wasn't used to being out of control of anything, or anyone, but the more she let herself have a regular life outside of Pulsus, the more that tightly held control slipped away. *And it's starting to feel like that's not such a bad thing.*

Chapter Thirty-five

July 11, 1942—Central Park, New York City

After saying his good-byes, William disappeared to maintain the perimeter. He'd found a densely wooded area toward the back of Central Park, off the regular pathways, and away from the madding crowd. It wasn't like there was a blinding flash of light that would have New Yorkers running to report aliens landing, but discretion was still the best bet when four people were simply disappearing.

Delaney watched as Landry pressed her finger to the recognition plate on the PRU. The engineers had already set it for the four members of the team, along with the return time, and date. Jumping forward one hundred and thirty-four years meant landing one hundred and thirty-four days beyond the original jump date in 2076. She'd attended the training course when they tried to explain the physics of it to the extractors and operatives, but she tuned out soon after someone said "cosmic strings." Needless to say, it didn't make sense, and it didn't have to. As long as the engineers figured out how to get them to and from the missions, Delaney didn't really give a fuck about the science.

Landry created their time circle, and the blue luminescent threads materialized from its center. Each of the team took hold of a thread, wrapped it around their wrist, and gripped it tightly.

"Ready?" Landry asked.

Griffin nodded, but he didn't seem so sure of himself.

"I won't say the return journey's easier, Griff, but at least your guy's waiting at the other end of this string."

Delaney smiled at Landry's placatory comment. It seemed ironic that she could speak of love when she had no idea how to grasp it when it presented itself. Delaney stopped herself. If she was going back to 1942 for Ilsa, she needed to be over Landry. It wouldn't be fair to disrupt her life, only to find that Delaney's heart was split in two, and even someone as sweet as Ilsa couldn't draw it back together.

"As long as he never finds out where my dick had to go on this mission, I'll be happy. Let's do it."

Simson simply nodded at Landry. Delaney would have to have a serious talk with her. She needed to temper her distaste toward Landry for Delaney's plan to work. And she needed both of them on board. She *wanted* both of them on board. Delaney didn't want to contemplate Landry not working with her, but if she did end up doing it the hard way, Simson would delight in using her particular skill set to persuade Landry to give up the location of the PRU.

"I'm ever ready, Landry. Let's go home."

Landry smiled, and Delaney tried to pull her heart back into her chest. Landry's smile was something else. More than a smile, it was full of optimism and life. *If only it was full of love.*

The team steadied themselves as Landry pressed retrieve, and in order, they began their journey back along their individual strings to May 20, 2076.

CHAPTER THIRTY-SIX

May 20, 2076—Pulsus Island

"Welcome home, Landry."

Her mom was always the first one Landry saw when she emerged from the jump. Sometimes it comforted her. Sometimes she felt smothered. On this occasion, it did nothing but remind her they'd have to talk about the cryptic parting shot about her dad. She offered a blanket, but Landry waved it away, and passed the PRU to the engineer waiting eagerly to reclaim their equipment.

"I'm nauseous, not chilly."

"A month with the Nazis did nothing to lighten your mood, then."

Her mom was joking, but it failed to amuse her. What they'd witnessed, what that period of history meant for millions of people, held no humor for Landry whatsoever.

"Any damage I need to know about that I can't see?" she asked, sounding contrite as she reached to check out Landry's black eye.

"I've got a cracked rib that punctured the skin, but fine otherwise."

"And the rest of the team?"

Delaney emerged from the shredded time curtain.

"Everyone's fine. Just in need of an age rewind."

"And a mind wipe," Delaney added.

Landry wondered if she was referring to the memories of the camp or the memories of Ilsa.

"The pods are ready for you." Elena began to move away, expecting Landry to follow behind. "How did Griffin manage his one and only mission?"

"He did great—wait, what? What do you mean, his 'one and only mission'?"

Elena rolled her head, and Landry heard the audible cracking of her neck. "Griffin won't be coming back, Landry."

Landry said nothing as she allowed the information to process. He took a strand and entered the time circle. If his demise was the only casualty, then they didn't experience retrieval issues. The logical reason was the least palatable. Somewhere before his timeline began, cancer affected it. He simply wasn't born, so as he traveled back to the future, his body turned into nothing.

"You sent him on the mission that killed him?"

"He was the best operative for the job. If he hadn't gone, his whole training would have been wasted, because he simply would have ceased to be here anyway. He knew what would happen, and he wanted to go. He simply didn't share the information with you."

Landry took a moment to absorb what her mom was saying. Griffin had been a great operative, but completing the mission knowing he wouldn't emerge from the time circle, and that he would never see his partner impressed Landry even more. It also made her incredibly sad and returned her mind to Jade and the girls. She had to find out if they were still here, still together.

"So it worked?" Landry didn't want to discuss the mission further with her mom.

Elena smiled broadly. "Perfectly. It went better than we could ever have envisioned. Blumstein completed her first tranche of research and released her findings in 1946, complete with the lead compound required to treat all the major cancers. It only took BodyPose four years to develop the drug, with full FDA approval, and cancer became nonfatal in 1950."

Elena paused, as if wanting a prompt from Landry to continue. She opened the door to the regenerative pod, and Landry removed her jacket before stepping inside. "Don't let anyone take that. I'm keeping it as a souvenir."

Her mom looked puzzled. "You never want reminders of your missions."

"I want this one." Landry replied in such a way as to deter further comment. "So what else did our good doctor achieve?"

Elena grinned like a kitten just discovering it can lick its own pussy. “Blumstein didn’t stop there as we thought she would. She went on to assist a gifted geneticist to identify the mutation that caused cancer in all organs and cells. She didn’t just find a cure to cancer. She helped eliminate it completely.”

Landry smiled as she removed the rest of her clothes and relaxed, naked, into the soft cotton of the pod’s chair. *Way to go, Doc*. “What year will you be retrieving the rest of the team?”

“We’ll get all three operatives in 1953.” She stopped abruptly and closed the pod door. Landry could tell from her voice that she was holding something back.

“Why 1953?” Landry didn’t know why, but her first thought ran to the fact that meant she would only get eleven years with Lucy.

“You saved her to cure cancer, and that’s what she did, Landry. She left a potentially unmatchable legacy. There’s a statue in her honor in Central Park.”

Elena disappeared from view momentarily, and the pod began to warm substantially. Landry felt her body tingle as the sleep gas began to take effect. “Why 1953?” She needed to know what happened.

Elena appeared back at the small window and looked in on Landry. “She died of a heart attack. They were on vacation in Hawaii and nowhere near any medical facilities. There was nothing Lucy could do.”

There was no response to that. Bina had survived the Nazis only for her heart to give up on her at the relatively young age of forty-seven. *Where’s the justice?* As she drifted into a deep sleep so her mind didn’t fight the regenerative process, Landry was thinking of Bina and Lucy. The doc didn’t know Lucy had been put there to keep her happy and on track in her research. Had Lucy fallen in love much the same as Delaney had? Bina wanted something more than her research, and she had exactly that for eleven years. *Jade...*

Though the process had only taken just over an hour, Landry slept hard, and felt as fresh as if she’d had twelve hours. After the high-speed catch-up on how the mission had affected history, Landry emerged from the debrief room and walked straight into the brick wall that was Simson.

"You kept Delaney safe, right?" She kept her voice low so no one overheard.

"Back off, Simson. I always keep Delaney safe."

"Bullshit. If you had her best interests at heart, you would've cut her loose months ago."

Cut her loose? "What the fuck are you talking about?" Landry squared up to her. Simson had the weight advantage by around ten pounds, but Landry was an inch taller. She wasn't expecting Simson to get physical, but she was tired of the constant challenge, and maybe standing toe-to-toe with her would calm her the fuck down.

"Jesus, Donovan, she's in love with you, and you let her follow you around like a lost fucking puppy. If you actually cared about her at all, you'd tell her she means fuck all to you so she could move on and try loving someone else."

The revelation caught Landry off guard. If she had a hundred guesses at what Simson was talking about, she'd never have come up with that scenario. "Don't be stupid. Delaney's in love with Ilsa." *Isn't she?*

"Don't play dumb with me. You know damn well she loves you."

"I don't know what you're talking about. Sounds more like you're the one in love with Delaney, and your jealousy's made you paranoid. Maybe after the debrief, you should head on up to Castillo's department and see if they can fix your head." Landry sidestepped and walked past her, but Simson grabbed her arm.

"Everybody thinks the sun shines out of your ass, Donovan, but you don't fool me, you're just a scared little girl. If we're ever on opposite teams for real, I'm gonna really enjoy fucking you up."

Landry shrugged her arm from Simson's grip. She clenched her jaw, stretched her neck from one side to the other, and smiled tightly. "If we're ever on opposite teams, Simson, you'll lose just like you always did in training."

"Yeah? Maybe one day we'll get to see who's right."

"Sure. I'll look forward to it." Landry walked away. She needed to find Delaney. Simson was talking crazy. *There's no way Delaney's in love with me...is she?*

Chapter Thirty-seven

May 20, 2076—Pulsus Island

We're just friends with benefits and it works for us. Landry's words bounced around in Delaney's head, smashing into her emotions like a wrecking ball around a demolition site. She really didn't get it. And worse yet, Delaney felt like she'd ended up convincing Landry she should go for it with Jade, regardless of the restrictions of the job.

She knew it had to be this way if she had any chance of ever getting over her. If Landry was with Jade, and Delaney was with Ilsa, surely she could put her feelings for Landry to bed, once and for all. *But I don't have to like it. Or Jade.*

The conversation they'd had over Ilsa was bizarre. She'd had to bite her tongue when Landry had mentioned bringing Ilsa home with them. She had no idea how close she was to what Delaney had planned. But she hadn't enjoyed lying to Landry either. Delaney wasn't grieving for Ilsa, because she knew she hadn't lost her. She'd be going back to get her as soon as she had control of Pulsus, and Delaney would show Landry that it was possible to have love and still do their jobs. *Not that she's capable of that kind of love.* Landry had asked that question like she was an AI robot, and human emotions were beyond her comprehension. Maybe that was how Landry stayed so detached during missions, a lack of emotional cognizance making it easier not to be affected by what they did to complete the mission.

Delaney's phone rang, and she saw it was Landry. "Hey, I didn't expect to hear from you today. Are we still apartment hunting this weekend?" Delaney tried to come across light and breezy.

"Yeah, sure. Since you've probably not had the chance to clean your dive up yet, is there any chance you could come over to me tonight?"

This is new. "Can't it wait until the weekend? I was going to hit the sack shortly. I've missed my comfy mattress."

"I'd really like to chat with you today, buddy."

"Okay. I'll be over in an hour." Delaney ended the call and drained the last of the bourbon from her glass. She looked at the bottle, already halfway down, and she'd only been home a few hours. She'd need some strong mints before she went over to Landry's. Delaney wasn't quite sure why grabbing the bottle of Widow Jane and a glass was the first thing she'd done when she got home. It didn't feel like a habit. It didn't feel like a need. She'd had to drink substantially less over the past four years than she had on previous missions and certainly in the lodge she'd shared with Ilsa. And yet, it was the first thing she thought of as she made her way home from the debrief.

Delaney blamed it on missing Ilsa already. Ilsa had kept her grounded, safe almost. When she was around, Delaney didn't really feel an itch for alcohol. She needed to focus on her plan to gain control of Pulsus and to get back to Ilsa. But something felt wrong. Landry sounded serious. She'd promised not to let on about Ilsa, so what was she so desperate to talk about that couldn't wait until Saturday? Surely Simson hadn't let something slip. Delaney was sure she could count on her. Whatever it was, Delaney had to face it head on. She wanted Landry with her on this journey, so keeping her on her side was paramount.

❖

"Nice tat," Delaney remarked, seeing Landry's forearm as she welcomed her into her apartment. "Do you think your mom would design me something? I want something I don't have to get rid of for every mission though. I'm kinda thinking you like the pain of removal and re-application more than the actual tattoo." Delaney knew that wasn't the case. She knew Landry needed it to bring her back to reality after a mission. She wished she could find such an easy solution.

"Ask her next time you see her. Now that she's a lesbian too, she'll probably want to cover herself with them so your timing could be great."

Delaney laughed. "Sounds like you two should go see Castillo for some family therapy."

Landry punched Delaney lightly in the chest. "Fuck no."

She went to the kitchen and came back with a cup of some hot herbal shit she put in front of Delaney.

"Aren't you supposed to ask your guest what they want to drink rather than serving them something that smells like an old woman's bathroom?"

"Funny. It's good for you, cleans out the system, and we could both do with that after this mission, wouldn't you agree?" Landry sat in her large reclining armchair and nursed her own cup of whatever the hell it was.

"I think that'll take more than one cup of this shit, but I'll play along." Delaney took a small swig and made a face to show her distaste. "So, what's this about, anyway?"

"You and Simson. What's going on with that?"

"Whoa, what? What're you talking about?"

"Before the mission, it seemed like you'd spent a lot of…" It looked like Landry was struggling to find the right words. "…time together."

"Yeah, so? My best friend always fucks off to the mainland, so choices are limited. What's the issue?" *And I needed distraction from you.*

"How well do you know her?"

"Well enough. What's with all the questions, Landry? Why don't you just come straight out with whatever's bugging you? I'm tired, and I want my bed."

Landry took a deep breath. "It's ridiculous, I know, but Simson says you're in love with me."

Fuck. "She says what now?" *Shit fuck bastard.*

"Christ, don't make me repeat it."

Yes. I'm in love with you. And Ilsa. It's complicated. "You don't actually believe her, do you?" Delaney slammed her cup on the coffee table. Something about protesting too much came into mind, and she tried to temper her initial reaction. "I mean, you're a great lay, Landry, but you don't have my heart." *You absolutely have my heart...but some of it is Ilsa's too. I'm so fucked.*

"No, of course I don't believe her. I'm just wondering what's going on in her head. Seems to me like she's the one in love with *you*."

That'd be fucking ironic. "We have fun fucking, that's all. Like you and me." *Nothing like I want it to be with you and me.* "I'm pretty sure she doesn't love me. She more or less hates you, but I think that's just jealousy. I think she maybe wants to be you." Delaney was fumbling for solid ground.

"If that's it, then she doesn't like sharing."

"She won't have to now that you're obsessed with your baller, will she? Your days of casual sex are over until you get bored with her." *Fuck, why did I have to say that?*

"Wow, that's pretty harsh. We're just—"

"Friends. Yeah, so you keep saying. I say stop fighting it and fuck her. Maybe it's just because you think you can't have her that she's so tempting. Maybe after you've fucked her, the appeal will wear off, and you can go back to being the illustrious player you really are." *Tone it down, for fuck's sake. She's not gonna keep tolerating me running my mouth off.*

"Go to hell, Delaney. That's not how it is."

Now you're protesting too much. Landry got up, went to the kitchen, and came back with a glass of something stronger than the tea they'd been drinking.

"No glass for me?"

Landry glared at Delaney, her jaw clenching and releasing, clenching and releasing. "No glass for you."

"Look, I'm sorry." *Think. Throw her off.* "I'm still sore from Ilsa. You've got a woman waiting for you to act on your attraction, and I can't follow through on the attraction we share...because she's nearly a hundred and fifty years in the past." *And you might as well be, because you don't see me.* "I'm angry, I guess. I shouldn't have said anything."

Landry swallowed the bourbon. Delaney could smell it, and she was desperate to head to the kitchen and help herself.

"There was something else she said that didn't sit right."

"Yeah, what?" *She'd better not have said anything about my plan.*

"Something about us being on opposite sides, like some day we might have to face off for real, instead of just for the purposes of a mission."

I'm gonna sew her mouth shut. "That's not going to happen, is it? Simson shoots her mouth off without engaging her brain. I don't know, maybe she just wants to fuck you and doesn't know how to ask, like a school kid picks on the kid she's actually hot for."

Landry shook her head, clearly unconvinced. "No, she specifically said she wanted to fuck me up, not fuck me."

"Same difference to her. She likes playing rough." *Leave it be, Landry.*

"I'm not convinced, Dee. Something's going on with her, and I need to find out what. I got a heads-up for our next mission, and she's on my team again. I need to trust her, with my life if need be."

"She's just trying to get in your head, and it looks like it's working. You don't need to worry about your life. I've always got your back." *And everything else if only you'd let me.* "I really don't think there's anything to worry about. She's a team player, always has been and always will be, so you don't need to be concerned about missions." Landry had the power to have Simson removed from their next mission, but Delaney needed her. This was a fuckup that never should've happened. She needed to bring Simson into line. Whatever her obsession with Landry was, she'd have to drop it and get with the program. Both she and Landry were essential to her plan, and Delaney could do without the playground theatrics. It was a tough enough ask to convince Landry to go against her mom, even with the added issue of Jenkin fucking her, so Simson complicating things was as welcome as an inflatable pillow would be for a hedgehog.

"I can't go on a mission with someone I don't trust one hundred percent."

Fuck, no. "Let me talk to her. I think she's just messing with you. I'll let her know you're thinking of kicking her off the team, and I bet that'll do the trick. She had your back in Ravensbrück, and she didn't let you down, did she?"

"Okay, I trust *you,* Dee. Assess the situation and let me know what you think. But be sure. Be absolutely sure."

Delaney stood to leave. She had a craving for the rest of the bourbon bottle she'd left on her kitchen counter. She also wanted to speak to Simson as soon as possible. "Leave it with me, Landry. I'll deal with Simson." Delaney let herself out of the apartment, jogged a few meters, and dialed Simson. "Get your ass over to my place right now."

"Craving something specific, soldier?"

Delaney took a deep breath and clenched her other hand into a fist so tight her knuckles cracked. She wanted to pound on Simson until her arm ached, but not the way Simson would be thinking. "No. You've fucked up, and we have to talk."

"What have I done? I didn't say anything at the debrief."

Her cocksure tone disappeared.

"Just get over to my apartment. I'm not doing this over the phone." Delaney ended the call and nearly pitched the handset across the road into the lake. There was so much more at stake than before. She needed Ilsa. Ilsa was the only cure for Landry. If Landry was capable of love, and she actually fell for Jade, she'd understand why Delaney had to go back to Ravensbrück for Ilsa. It was going to be hard seeing her with someone else, but if Delaney was ever going to clean her blood of her Landry obsession, she'd have to swallow her disdain and wish them the best of luck. It wasn't like she wouldn't be able to pull off her plan without Landry, but having her on board would make it so much easier.

Losing Griffin was just more proof that the Pulsus board couldn't be trusted with the power they held. *No one important in Pulsus would be affected.* That's what they'd been told. Griffin was dispensable. The operatives were all like disposable cutlery to them, throwaway implements they needed to get the job done. When she was in charge, things would be different. *Everyone* would be important. She could only hope Landry would join her. Locking horns with her best friend and would-be lover wasn't something she wanted to contemplate.

CHAPTER THIRTY-EIGHT

May 21, 2076—Mainland, San Francisco

Landry rubbed her eyes and forehead as she waited for her chai latte. She'd hardly slept. Thoughts of Jade, the girls, Delaney, and Simson had driven around her mind like a NASCAR race, each one competing for her attention, bumping the others out of the way. Jade won and the girls came in second. That wasn't unexpected. She'd spent every spare moment thinking about Jade while on the mission. After Delaney left, Landry had searched the Internet for Jade to make sure their cancer success hadn't meant she never existed. Words wouldn't do justice to the relief she felt when images of Jade splashed across her wall screen, along with tales of the amazing run of sixty-point-plus games she was having for the Warriors. Her next search, for Lizbeth and Caitlin's restaurant, La Azucarera, quickly yielded positive results. Problem was, knowing that she was going to see them all the next day made her as excited as a five-year-old on Christmas Eve. A couple of missions ago, she'd started to look forward to seeing the girls, but the added draw of Jade this time was something else entirely.

"Landry. Full-fat chai."

The cardboard cutout barista put Landry's drink on the counter and smiled wanly. Landry wondered if the girl had any ambitions beyond her coffee station. She couldn't imagine working in a place like this. She'd try to slit her wrists with a half-torn coffee cup within a week, she was sure.

She thanked her, turned to go, and walked straight into another customer entering the coffee shop. "Oh, sorry," she said, before looking up and recognizing the stunning azure blue eyes of Dr. Stowe, Priscilla's ER doctor.

"Well, Ms. Donovan, how nice to see you. Your friends tell me you've been out of town. Have you been back long?"

"Just hit the shore this morning." Landry pulled her bag up by its strap as evidence and felt guilty for not calling her. *This is new. Does me having feelings for Jade make me less of an asshole to every other woman?*

"What kind of work takes you away for nearly five months at a time?"

Landry picked up on the hint of testiness in her voice. "The kind that makes it hard to make good on promises to a beautiful doctor."

Stowe raised her eyebrow. "How long will you be in the city?"

"A month this time. Sometimes it's just two weeks." Landry didn't know why she felt like she had to explain herself. It wasn't as if she'd slept with her, made a promise to call her back, and didn't.

"And are you thinking of calling me?"

The doc's voice had lowered to a seductive whisper.

She can't be that pissed with me. Landry was about to reply when her phone rang. By strange coincidence, it was Jade. *Just like last time.* She'd sent a text to her as soon as she got off the Pulsus cargo train. "Do you mind? I have to take this."

Stowe shrugged and joined the end of the long line to place her order.

"So you really weren't kidding about disappearing for big chunks of time. I kinda thought you were exaggerating."

God, I've missed that voice. "You missed me, then?" Landry's tone was teasing, and unmistakably sexual. She realized she was grinning and turned away from Stowe's rapacious gaze.

"Only if you missed me."

Landry's grin grew bigger. She'd missed Jade's smart mouth. *I want that mouth on my neck. I want it everywhere.* "I bought you a present to make up for being away so long."

"And why would you do that? We're just friends…"

There was a pause like she was about to say something else but didn't. Landry imagined her quietly laughing wherever she was. *Where was she?* "Where are you? I'll bring it over."

"I'm at the restaurant. Lizbeth is fueling me up to get me ready for the Conference Finals tomorrow."

"For breakfast? That's a happy coincidence since I'm on my way home right now." Landry looked back at Dr. Stowe. She was beautiful, intelligent, and had an incredible body. *But she's not Jade.* She didn't make Landry's heart race when she spoke. It wasn't dreams of the doc that got her through the dark, lonely nights in Ravensbrück.

"You better hurry if you want to see me. I have to be at the training hall in two hours."

Landry pulled out the pocket watch from the back of her jeans. *Nine a.m.* If she dropped her drink and ran, she could be there in less than ten minutes. She'd be sweaty, and in need of a quick shower, but she had to see Jade as soon as she could. "Enjoy your breakfast. I'll be with you soon enough."

Landry ended the call just as Stowe returned, drink in hand.

"Walk me back to the hospital?"

Her eyes sparkled with the promise of easy sex. Landry threw her cup in the trash and shook her head. "Sorry, Doc, I have to get home." *Don't say it.* "Rain check?" *I said it.*

Stowe tilted her head and smiled faintly. She hooked her finger on Landry's belt buckle, just as she had in the hospital. Though she willed it not to, Landry felt her pussy respond to the doc's touch. *I'm not made of stone.* Deciding to progress things with Jade didn't make her immune to every other gorgeous woman on the planet.

"Since there's more than a fifty-fifty chance of rain in May, I'll give you that." She removed her finger. "But June's a different matter. Don't wait until June."

Landry nodded, though she had no intention of calling the doc, not if she was going to throw the dice and gamble with Jade's friendship. She pulled open the door and jogged up the street without a backward glance.

❖

The combination of the unusually high temperature, a fifty-pound duffel bag, and the San Francisco terrain conspired to drench Landry in sweat by the time she'd completed the mile and a half run home. She was about to slip past the restaurant window and pop upstairs for a quick shower, when Caitlin spotted her from a window seat and knocked on the glass ferociously. Jade was sitting opposite her, looking amazing in a simple loose sweater with her hair falling softly over her shoulders. Landry couldn't help but think how that hair would feel on her stomach as she worked her way down between Landry's legs.

"Get in here," Caitlin shouted and waved frantically.

Landry pulled at the front of her T-shirt to indicate she was sweaty, but Caitlin was already on her feet and through the door to pull her into a bear hug.

"You've been gone for an age. We've missed you." She uncoupled herself. "Why are you so sweaty?"

Suddenly, running seemed too enthusiastic, and Landry was slightly embarrassed. What if Jade was happy with the friend situation? She'd been gone almost five months. That was too long to wait. "Don't you know you sweat more when you're fit?"

Caitlin raised her eyebrow. "I thought that was when you were fat? Anyway, come in. Let Lizbeth fix you some breakfast."

Landry followed her in and approached Jade's table a little gingerly. "Hey."

"Hey, stranger. You look hot."

"Hot sexy or hot sweaty?"

Jade's smile revealed her perfect white teeth, and her eyes sparkled with a hint of lust. "Both."

Landry's pussy throbbed at the way Jade looked her up and down. "I was going to take a quick shower before I came in. Sorry."

"No need to apologize. You look even sexier with a sheen of sweat all over your perfect body." She changed her tone abruptly but was still playful. "Now *I'm* sorry. That's not the way friends talk to each other, is it?"

Landry was about to respond, but Jade continued.

"I'm all done with breakfast." She pushed away the plate, still half-full, and stood. "How about you take me upstairs, and I'll take a self-guided tour of your place while you shower?"

Landry swallowed. Hard. In her head, it sounded like a clap of thunder. Still, she offered no response.

"You can give me your 'sorry I've been a bad friend by being away for one hundred and thirty-five days' present."

You've been counting? "Sure." Landry cursed her sudden monosyllabic spiel. Usually she was so smooth, but Jade knocked her off her game easier than a whore could distract a president. Maybe it wasn't such a bad thing. Maybe slick lines were for one-night stands and not for whatever this was.

"Where are you two going?" Lizbeth looked like she was about to envelop Landry in an embrace but stopped just shy when she saw her glistening with perspiration. "You know I want to hug you, Landry, but this is pure silk. Why are you so sweaty?"

"It's hot, this bag," Landry pulled at the strap, "weighs fifty pounds, and I…walked all the way here."

Lizbeth pursed her lips and tilted her head in obvious disbelief. "I think you ran."

Jade nodded. "I think she did."

Landry let out an exasperated sigh. "Are you two in cahoots now? I'm away for a few months and you get yourself a BFF?"

Lizbeth pulled Jade in for an embrace as if to prove Landry's point. "Us girls have to stick together when the boys go out of town."

Landry huffed, as if bothered by being playfully mis-gendered. Truth was, a woman like Lizbeth could call her anything she wanted and Landry would happily answer. When a woman was that beautiful, they had certain privileges.

"Landry was taking me upstairs to check out her inner sanctum while she cleaned herself up."

Jade winked conspiratorially at Lizbeth, and Landry wanted to grill Caitlin on what the hell had been going on with those two while she was away. As if reading her mind, Caitlin shrugged apologetically.

"Lucky you. It took us ten months to be invited into her apartment even though we only live one floor below."

"It's kind of taken me six."

The two of them stood together, arms linked, and stared directly at Landry. They were toying with her. Landry had to admit she liked it. "I'm going upstairs. You're all welcome to join me."

"Tempting as that is, Caitlin and I have a restaurant full of people hungry for my spectacular breakfasts. We'll leave you to entertain Jade alone and do come down for something to eat when you've worked up an appetite." Lizbeth turned and walked away without waiting for a response.

It was good she didn't wait. Landry had nothing. Except for a hard, deep throbbing between her legs thinking about Jade in her apartment.

"Shall we?" She motioned for Jade to exit the restaurant, and they took the exterior elevator up to Landry's apartment.

Landry pressed her hand to the fingerprint plate to the left of her front door, and it opened automatically. She'd set the air-con remotely when she got back to her Pulsus apartment last night, but given her recent exercise and Jade's presence, she still felt a little too warm. She dumped her bag on one of the sofas in front of the floor-to-ceiling windows and went to the open plan kitchen for a bottle of water.

"Can I get you something to wash down your power pro breakfast?"

Landry turned back to Jade when she didn't answer and saw her running her hand along the black felt of the full-size pool table in the living area.

"I have fond memories of the last time I played pool."

Landry recalled the hot kisses they shared at Jade's team campus and Jade running her hands over her stomach, telling her she wanted to rip Landry's shirt off. She took a chance. "You haven't played pool for five months?"

Jade laughed gently. "Presumptuous much?"

"Hopeful." Landry took a drink of the water. It did little to cool the sensation of her burning skin, desperate for Jade's touch.

"Friends." Jade said the word thoughtfully. "What are you doing, Landry?"

"Taking on some water before I go clean up?" Landry had never felt so unsure of herself around a woman. Jade was either a better player than she was, or she simply wasn't playing.

"Do you really want to play these games with me?"

Landry was at a loss. "How about I give you your present?" She went over to her bag, pulled the Jewels letterman jacket from it, and opened it up to show her.

"Oh my God, where did you get that? *How* did you get that? That must be a hundred and fifty years old! It looks brand new!"

That's because it is. "I figured you already had a Knicks jacket..."

Jade snatched it from Landry's hands and put it on. She looked adorable in it. It was just a little too big for her. The perfect boyfriend jacket. Landry wondered what she'd look like with it on over just her underwear, and she had to clench her sex together in a futile attempt to stop its steady pulsating response to the intoxicating image.

"Does this mean you want to go steady?" Jade reached out, took a handful of Landry's T-shirt, and pulled her a little closer.

"Does it get any steadier than a hundred plus days between dates?" Jade's sweet fig perfume swirled into Landry's nostrils. The scent mixed with Jade's light perspiration instantly connected with Landry's brain, and testosterone surged through her veins.

"How is it your sweat smells so good?"

Jade pressed her leg between Landry's and tilted her head back so their lips were only a few inches apart. Landry sighed deeply, took hold of Jade's jacket lapels, and pulled her closer still. "Research suggests that when you smell *the one*, you can't keep your hands off her."

Jade laid both hands on Landry's pecs and pressed firmly.

"Is that what you are? *The one*?"

Landry bent her head closer so that their mouths almost met. "Do you want to find out?"

"Is this your usual shtick? Because it's very impressive." She ran her tongue over Landry's bottom lip before she sucked it into her mouth and nibbled gently. "If I wasn't just your friend, I'd be in the shower naked with you by now."

The thought of Jade's firm and oh so feminine form stripped bare and pressing against her own made Landry's head spin. "What if I don't want to be *just* your friend?" This attraction was impossible to deny. She'd tried starving the fire of oxygen, and all that had made it do was burn brighter. In Landry's reality, she'd only been away from Jade for just over a month, but it felt like years since her eyes had viewed such exquisite perfection, since the velvety tones of her voice had resounded in her ears. She'd never longed for anyone or anything, but Jade held her attention from the moment she saw her. This was different. *This was...something else.*

Jade's hands drifted downward. She tugged at the bottom of Landry's T-shirt, slipped her hands underneath it, and ran them upward, over the rips of her abs toward her breasts. Her fingertips stopped at Landry's nipples, and she lightly twisted them.

"What do you want to be, Landry?" She whispered so quietly that her voice was barely audible over their heavy breathing.

Jade was channeling pure electricity that tingled over Landry's skin, making Landry want that same touch over every inch of her body. "I want to be the one…" *Don't just say that.* "…who makes you come like you've never come before." Landry placed her hand around the back of Jade's neck and pulled her into a deep, passionate kiss. She broke away, and Jade followed her, desperate for more. "I want to be the one who makes you pass out from too many orgasms." She walked forward until Jade was pressed against the pool table and couldn't back off even if she wanted to. The way she felt in Landry's arms assured her she didn't want to. "I want to be the one who makes your fantasies come true." Landry picked her up and sat her on the edge of the table. She parted Jade's legs and pressed herself between them. "I want to be the one you think of as you fall asleep. The one you dream about." She ran her fingers through Jade's hair and held her neck so her thumb could caress her cheek. "I want to be the first person you think about when you wake."

Jade took the hem of Landry's T-shirt and pulled it up and over her head. She let out a breathy sigh at what she uncovered. "That's a lot of want." Her fingers followed a path from the veins in Landry's hands, up over her tattoo to the hard curve of her biceps. She squeezed them and smiled appreciatively. "Do you have what it takes to deliver on those words?"

Landry leaned in and kissed her hard. "That'll be for you to judge."

Jade smiled and placed her fingertips on Landry's lips. "I have very high standards."

"For a woman of your caliber, I wouldn't expect any less." She sucked Jade's finger into her mouth, and her tongue circled it, suggesting what she might do to her clit. Jade's other hand reached down and unbuckled Landry's belt. She unbuttoned her jeans and slipped her hand inside the shorts Landry was wearing.

"Are you wet from sweat or something else?"

Jade's husky voice traveled straight to Landry's core. She wanted to hear that voice whispering sexy promises to her forever. *Forever?* "What do you think?"

Jade withdrew her finger and used it to circle Landry's hardened nipple. "I don't want to think. I want to feel, and I want to hear you say it." Landry tried to kiss her, but she pulled away and laughed. "Say it."

Landry's jaw clenched. She was so fucking turned on, she wanted to throw Jade on the table and fuck her until the felt was soaked with Jade's sweet juices and would need to be replaced. Women never made her wait. By the time they got to this stage, they were desperate for her to take them beyond what they thought they wanted, and what they thought they could take. Waiting was new, but Landry could feel Jade was going to be worth it.

"You've made me wet. It's a perpetual state whenever I'm around you. Kiss me…please." *And that's unheard of.* Jade's blue-gray eyes were barely visible, edging her dilated pupils, the darkness of which seemed to beckon Landry to crawl into them. She was sure she'd never find her way out if she did, but she really didn't care. She wanted to possess and be possessed. She wanted to be enveloped in Jade's darkness and revel in her light.

Jade let herself sink into Landry's kiss and embrace. She grasped the back of Landry's head and pulled her in hard, her craving obvious. "Would you start with my pool table fantasy?"

Landry nodded and slowly started to remove Jade's letterman jacket. Jade caught her wrists to stop her.

"No, baby. Take me like you want to rip me apart. I feel like I've waited years for you, and I don't want to be alone in this. Make me feel your desperation."

Desperate. Wanton. An all-prevailing, unstoppable desire. Whatever it was, Landry *did* feel it too, and it was more powerful than any desire that went before it. "I want you so fucking bad it's painful."

Landry yanked the jacket from Jade's body and tossed it aside. She pushed her back onto the pool table, pushed her sweater up, and unclipped the front fastening on her bra with ease. Pool balls crashed across the surface, making room for Jade's lithe body. She squeezed

Jade's breasts, while she worked her jeans open with the other hand and pulled them down, along with her panties. The smell and sight of Jade's pussy filled Landry's senses. She slipped two fingers inside her and pressed her mouth on Jade's clit while she cupped her breasts and pinched her nipples with her other hand.

Jade writhed and moaned beneath Landry's touch, and her blatant yearning was intoxicating, driving Landry to push harder, deeper.

"Fuck me, baby. Fuck me like it's the first and last time."

Landry looked up, over the firm, lightly muscled body and olive skin of Jade's flawless physique. It was the view she'd be happy to see multiple times a day for the rest of her life. "It can never be the last time."

Without losing her rhythm, she climbed up on the table, knelt beside Jade, and kissed her. Jade raised her head from the table to meet her and slipped her tongue into Landry's mouth, like she was trying to inextricably connect their bodies. She lifted her hips up and pushed herself harder onto Landry's fingers. Landry could feel Jade tightening around her, and her thrusting became more vigorous and insistent.

"God, baby. Perfect. That's so fucking perfect. Please don't stop."

Landry tried to suppress a smile as their mouths crushed together in their impassioned kiss. As if she'd ever stop. *I need your orgasm more than I need...* Landry remembered Delaney's words. *It feels like you can't breathe around her, but at the same time, she's your oxygen.* She slowed her pace, and Jade broke away from the kiss.

"No, Landry."

No, don't stop? No, don't be scared? "No what?"

"Stay with me, baby."

Landry smiled and kissed Jade softly, as she picked up the rhythm that was taking Jade to the edge. "I'm not going anywhere." She meant it. She really meant it.

She wrapped her hand in Jade's hair and kissed her hard, felt herself dissipate in and around her, only to reform, infused with an unusual and unfamiliar sensation. *I don't want to let go*. Jade called out her name, enfolded Landry in her arms, and begged her to make her come.

"I can't get close enough." Landry pressed her body into Jade's as she brought her closer to orgasm until she came. She yelled Landry's name and dug her short nails into her back, breaking the skin and drawing blood. Landry murmured her pain into Jade's mouth as their kiss rode out Jade's bucking hips before she slowly settled.

Landry lay back on the pool table, and Jade nestled her head on Landry's chest. Jade's fingers followed the undulations of Landry's abs. "You've got the most beautiful body I've ever seen. So much hard muscle, yet your skin is so soft."

Landry stroked Jade's back gently and said nothing. She was trying to make sense of what had just happened. She'd had sex with so many women, of all shapes and sizes, and she'd enjoyed every single one of them. But this, this lifted her up off the pool table and had her feeling like she was lying on a hundred thousand tulip petals. She almost balked at the cheesy imagery that popped into her head, but the tranquility that swathed her soul was a subtle, yet powerful sedative.

"I can see why you're in such demand, Landry. You sure know how to make a girl come." Jade sat up, pulled on her sweater, and edged off the pool table. "Now all you've got to do is decide whether or not this goes beyond a damn good fuck."

Landry opened her mouth to speak, but something stopped her from vocalizing her thoughts. Words seemed inadequate. And if she revealed her feelings out loud, that would make them concrete and tangible. She couldn't retract them.

Jade sighed deeply and pulled her panties and jeans back up. She shook her head, and there was a sadness in her eyes that took hold of Landry's heart with steel-tipped gloves and crushed it without mercy.

"That's what I thought. I have to get to training. Big game this weekend."

What do I say? This was more dangerous territory than the mission in Iraq. "Jade…" *Can't you see it in my eyes?* "I don't know what you want me to say." *I do know, but I can't. It's way too early to be thinking of love.*

"I'm keeping this as a souvenir." Jade pulled the Letterman jacket on. "But if you realize what this is," she whispered, then pressed her finger at Landry's heart and then her own, "call me. Don't be frightened by it just because you can't control it."

She walked away and took one last backward glance before she left without closing the door. Landry lay back on the pool table and looked up at the beams of the ceiling and the light fittings hanging by reinforced steel cable between them. What if the cables failed and the lights crashed down and set fire to her apartment? She'd lose it all. What if her heart was like one of those spotlights? What if Jade took a bolt cutter to the wires supporting it, wrapped around it, protecting it? Would she lose it all? Or gain everything?

Chapter Thirty-nine

May 21, 2076—Pulsus Island

Delaney had sparred with Simson to show the recruits how both fighters could take a beating and still stay upright. Delaney had been a little over zealous, choosing to continue Simson's punishment for mouthing off to Landry with physical recriminations. It ended with Simson in the regen lab to fix some broken bones before they walked to Rik's Place for a perfect end to the day. Simson swiped her card and bought them a bottle of Elijah Craig to enjoy while Delaney filled her in on the sketchy details of their next mission.

"Are we good now that you've given me a code red?"

Code red seemed like a good description, since there'd been plenty of blood. "Sure. We're all square as long as you've learned your lesson and back off Landry."

Simson nodded. "I'll leave her be until you say otherwise. So, this new mission, how many guys did our serial killer dispatch?"

"I did a quick search after Elena gave me the mission outline. There are over three hundred men who were found clearly tortured and murdered over a thirty-year period all over the States." Delaney dropped two ice cubes into her glass and poured another generous measure of the spicy sweet bourbon. She sniffed it appreciatively before she took a smallish sip. She was making a conscious effort to drink less. She wanted to stay the woman she'd been with Ilsa, but it was proving difficult. The nightmares hadn't abated, and she'd decided they wouldn't until her plan had been put into action. The vivid dreams were her motivation almost as much as getting back to Ilsa. She was sure that she'd been affected by the things they'd done, because she was the only one strong enough to know what they had to do about it. Until then, a little of this stuff was needed to take the edge off and help her catch little slices of sleep.

Simson raised her eyebrows and looked impressed. "Wow. But we've only got to save one? Are we being authorized to kill the killer if we find them?"

"Yes, and, no, of course not. That's not our assignment, remember? We've got narrow parameters for our work, don't we?" Delaney didn't want to say too much. As usual, there weren't many patrons in the bar, but she still didn't want to discuss her intended coup anywhere other than the inside of her apartment, where she could be sure there was no surveillance.

"What's so special about this guy…Muniz, did you say?"

"Lyman Muniz. A biophysicist who would've probably gone on to invent a sustainable and economic alternative to fossil fuels. He was one of Jenkin's buddies."

"Probably? Aren't they supposed to be absolutely certain given that it costs eight hundred million dollars per mission?"

Simson wasn't exaggerating. Each mission *was* that expensive, but no one would expect time travel to be as cheap as buying a Muni card. "Given the potential gains, they're willing to take a chance on this one. Plus, we're bringing him back with us, so Pulsus will own the tech that saves the world from melting. This one's more like an investment, I guess. They'll spend eight hundred million saving him, but make billions once he finishes inventing, researching, whatever the hell he's going to do."

Simson sipped at her liquor. "What're your thoughts on that? Seems a little off our sphere of activity."

Delaney emptied her glass and clambered out of the booth, pulling the bottle with her. "Let's take this to my place and talk some more." It was time to fill Simson in on her strategy to take control of Pulsus, and Rik's Place wasn't the right location for that particular conversation.

❖

"This is exactly what I've been afraid of. The board is out of control. Look at what happened to Griffin. They knew he wouldn't come out of the time circle if he went on the mission, but they sent him anyway. There were at least five other operatives who could've gone in his place, and you can't tell me that all of them had some form of cancer story in their lives." Delaney drained the glass and slammed it down on the table. "Now we're running missions for their financial gain."

Simson refilled Delaney's glass. "I'm so bummed about Griffin. I really liked the guy. So what're we going to do about it?"

Delaney liked that Simson used "we." It signaled her complete buy-in and loyalty. "This mission is the perfect chance for us to set our takeover in motion. We're going back to 2035. At the same time, the Cagle gang was running their business from Boystown, Chicago. One of their departments was mercenaries for hire: top quality, ex-military, and highly trained."

Simson grinned and nodded enthusiastically. "Our own little army."

"Exactly."

"Where does Donovan and getting the PRU fit in?"

Delaney cracked her neck and emptied her glass again. "We need the PRU to take our band of mercenaries back to Pulsus to enact our hostile takeover. When Landry jumps to 2035, I'll explain what we're doing and why. I'll ask her nicely for the PRU."

"What about her mom? She practically runs Pulsus with Jenkin. How will you get her to go against her mom?"

"She hates Jenkin. She thinks she manipulated her mom into a relationship. I'll use that to convince her to join us, and then she'll give me the PRU."

"And if she doesn't?" Simson's mouth curled into a twisted smile.

Delaney didn't want to say the words she knew would light Simson's face like a Christmas tree. She didn't want to think of her best friend turning against her when she needed her most. "Then you'll have to persuade her to give it to me."

Simson's smile turned into a full-on open-mouthed grin. "You know what my persuasion techniques are, don't you?"

Delaney could smell Simson's excitement at the prospect of getting her hands on Landry and torturing her to get the location of the PRU. The last thing Simson would want was for Landry to give it up freely. She took a deep inhalation of her Cohiba and nodded slowly. "You'll do what you have to do to get me the PRU."

"And you won't stop me?"

Simson was incredulous. She knew Delaney was in love with Landry, but she also knew she was in love with Ilsa. Delaney recalled the damage she'd seen Simson inflict on countless recruits. The torture methods she'd employed in Colombia had given some of the most experienced drug lords new ideas. She could only hope that Landry would either give up the PRU immediately or break before Simson did irreparable damage. "I won't stop you. If Donovan won't join us, then she's against us. There is no middle ground. I have to have the PRU, and if the only way to get it is to let you loose on Donovan, then so be it."

"It'll take time. She won't break easily. I hear she was tortured for seventy-five hours on the Iraq mission and still didn't crack."

Simson laced her fingers together. She was practically rubbing them with glee.

"That's true. Everything you've *ever* heard about Donovan is true, and there's so much more you've not heard. You'll have all the time you need. I just need the PRU."

Simson held her glass up in a mock toast. "She'll be my Michelangelo. My masterpiece."

Delaney swallowed the last of the bourbon straight from the bottle. *If I can't have Landry, maybe my only way forward is to destroy her.*

CHAPTER FORTY

May 24, 2076—Mainland, San Francisco

Landry and Delaney had looked at five apartments and houses yesterday, and she'd been enamored with none of them. The last one they were viewing today belonged to one of Jade's teammates. She was moving out of the city into a seven-million-dollar house on Edward's Avenue, Sausalito, and she needed to lose this place in Dolores Heights. Jade had offered to show them around, and Landry saw her waiting, perched on the hood of the latest Ferrari Spider. Landry wished Delaney wasn't there so she and Jade could have sex with the warmth of the engine on her hands and the spring sunshine on her back.

Landry introduced them, and when Delaney wasn't particularly friendly, she figured it was because she was bored with the house search.

"You were great last night. Some of your three-pointers were unbelievable." They hadn't seen each other since Landry had come home, and they'd had the most amazing sex on her pool table. They had plenty of phone and text contact, but Jade hadn't pressured Landry in any way about the "L" word. She'd kept the conversations light, flirty, and fun, and it hadn't felt awkward at all, which was quite the feat, considering the situation. If anything, it'd been Landry wanting to talk about what had happened between them, but she didn't really have the first clue how to broach the subject.

"For your size, you're surprisingly good at them."

Jade laughed. "Thanks. I haven't heard that before."

Landry smiled at the way Jade brushed off Delaney's barbed comment. She wondered if anything got to her or if she was just so practiced at deflecting criticism, it was impossible to tell if anything actually hurt.

Jade opened the door and turned off the alarm system. She gave them the full real estate agent spiel as they toured the three floors of the property, and every statement was met with a pointed remark from Delaney.

"*I love how close this place is to Dolores Park.*"

"Maybe you should live here then."

"*There are five garages underneath the house, off to the side, if you've got cars or motorbikes.*"

"How many vehicles does one person need?"

"*It was built in the 1900s but was split into three condos in the fifties. The previous owner purchased all three units and restored it to its former size and glory.*"

"So it could fall down at any minute."

"*The outdoor deck has recently been re-varnished, and all the furniture is for sale with the house.*"

"Sounds like you've got a fallback career when you get too old for basketball."

Jade didn't react to the sarcasm in Delaney's final statement. "Thanks. What do you plan to do when you're too old to be a soldier?"

Delaney smirked. "I'm going back to the deck for a better view."

Landry caught hold of her arm as she left. "Why are you being such an asshole?" she whispered as Jade wandered away to the kitchen.

"I haven't got stars in my eyes, Landry. Doesn't make me an asshole."

"Apparently, it does. You've done nothing but make snide comments the whole time we've been here. If you don't like the house, let's go, and we can stop wasting Jade's time. I'm sure she's got better things to do than this, and we've got plans tonight, so what's your problem?"

Delaney shrugged her arm away from Landry's grasp. "No problem, stud. Go get her." Delaney walked off, leaving Landry deciding which one of them to go after. *It wasn't a tough choice.*

Jade was pulling a bottle of water from the fridge.

"Share with me?" Landry slipped her hands around Jade's waist from behind.

"How long has Delaney been in love with you?" she asked as she turned to face Landry.

"Why do people keep saying that? We've been friends a long time, and we've worked a lot of missions together. We're just close. That's all." *Is everyone else seeing something I'm missing?*

"Have you ever fucked her?"

Landry spat out the water she was drinking. "What the—? Why?"

"Answer the question—have you fucked her?"

"Yeah, but—"

"But nothing. The woman's in love with you." Jade took the bottle back. "I can't blame her, not after what you did to me, but I don't know how you can't see it, Landry. Her pores are seeping jealousy."

"Firstly, what I did with you was different from anything I've ever done with any woman before you." Landry's breath caught in her throat when Jade smiled at her words. "And secondly, you've heard the term 'friends with benefits.' That's all we are—were. Soldiers relieving tension with no fear of emotional entanglement."

Jade gently stroked Landry's face; her fingers caressed her throat and traveled down to her chest. "Maybe that was the case for you, hotshot, but she's all entangled in your funk, and she's fallen hard."

"She's in love with someone else, someone from our last mission." Landry blurted the sentence out and realized how desperate she sounded. Delaney couldn't be in love with her. All they'd ever had was hard and fast sex. They'd never cuddled. There was no spooning. There'd never been any foreplay.

"And you think you can't be in love with two people at the same time? Or that she's not trying to get over you by saying she's in love with someone else?"

Fuck. Landry thought about the time Delaney *had* tried to slow things down, and there were times she'd wanted Landry to stay the night after they'd fucked. *It can't be.* "I don't know anything about love. I've never been in love before—" Landry stopped herself.

Jade might as well have read her mind. "Before now?"

She winked and smiled, and Landry's breath caught in her throat. Landry echoed Jade's words from earlier that week. "Presumptuous much?"

Jade played along. "Hopeful."

"Are you still coming over tonight so I can cook you my special, one and only dish?"

"I'll know if it's one of Lizbeth's and you've just warmed it up, you know."

"I do know, because your new best friend would straight up *tell* you that's what she'd done." Landry heard the heavy footsteps of Delaney's engineer boots on the oak floor. "So you're coming?"

"Oh, I hope so." She flashed a wicked smile before she looked over Landry's shoulder at Delaney. "Seen enough?"

"Yeah. I've got to get back to base, Landry. Drop me at the station?"

"Sure." She shrugged and followed Delaney out of the building.

Delaney jogged down the front steps and turned to look at the house. "Tell your friend I'll take it. I can have the money transferred to her account today."

Jade looked at them both and raised her eyebrows. She locked the door. "I didn't realize working for Uncle Sam paid so well."

Delaney laughed and shook her head. "Is that who Landry told you we work for?"

What are you playing at, Delaney? "No. It isn't." She glared at Delaney, but smiled when Jade looked at her.

"She's kept more or less silent about the who. I suppose I made an assumption that you work for the government."

"Have you seen Landry's building? She couldn't afford that on a government salary."

Oh shit. Landry shook her head and put her finger over her mouth to signal Delaney to shut the fuck up.

Jade looked puzzled. "I've seen her apartment. What do you mean, building?"

Delaney's smile grew broader when she obviously realized she knew something Jade didn't. "The apartment? She owns the whole building, sweetheart."

Jade didn't miss a beat. "Perhaps you'll tell me all about your work tonight over dinner, in *your* building."

Landry felt the competition heat up suddenly, but she really didn't want to believe everybody was right, and Delaney *was* in love with her.

"In the perfect little family restaurant?"

Landry closed her eyes and waited for Jade's response.

"Oh no." She sounded so innocent, but her voice was laced with possessive undertones. It wasn't a quality Landry had ever found attractive before, but from Jade, it made her pussy twitch. "I'll be dining in the penthouse restaurant. Has Landry cooked for you before?"

That was naughty. Delaney knew Landry never took women to her home. Delaney had never seen the inside of Landry's bedroom in her place on Pulsus, and she'd met her in the restaurant yesterday, rather than her apartment. And even though Landry's apartment had three bedrooms, Delaney knew better than to ask to stay over and had booked a hotel close by.

Jade knew all of that. She knew exactly how special she was to be invited into Landry's retreat. Delaney had been an ass to her though, so Landry had to admit, she deserved it. No pithy retort was forthcoming though, and Delaney just walked away.

"I'll see you back at base, Donovan."

Since when do you use my last name? Landry looked down the road at the disappearing Delaney and back to Jade, whose mischievous eyes and smile sparkled brighter than the L.A. sun. *Do I go after my friend or stay with...my lover?*

"You should go after her. You're breaking her heart."

Landry couldn't tell if Jade was serious or not, but she'd resolved to confront Delaney again. How come she was the only one who hadn't seen Delaney was in love with her? "Should I?"

"Of course...if only to explain that she should concentrate on the other woman in her life, because you're already being pinned down by me."

Landry laughed. "You're too tiny to pin me down." She wanted to explain why that wasn't possible and briefly wondered what it might be like to share *everything* with Jade, including the details of her work. Her mom would go ballistic, and Pulsus would probably kidnap and keep her prisoner on the island for the rest of her life. But what would it be like to have that trust in someone, to have a sounding board, or someone just to come home to and complain about a bad day, or an awful mission?

Jade pulled Landry close to her and leaned in to whisper in her ear. "You might be tall and muscle-bound, but I can show you some moves that'll have you on your back and happy to be so." She stepped back. "But maybe we're getting ahead of ourselves. You should go after your temperamental friend, and I'll see you at your place tonight."

"But this isn't a test, and I won't lose points if I leave you to go calm Delaney?" Landry was half joking, but honestly, she wasn't sure if this was a pass/fail situation.

Jade smiled widely. "I'll see you tonight. Go."

Landry placed her hand around Jade's neck and kissed her. "I'm going to work you out."

"We'll see if you have the patience for that."

Jade jogged down the steps, got into her car, and drove off, leaving Landry to catch up with Delaney. All Landry wanted to do was jump into her own car and follow Jade wherever she went. She was intrigued to know exactly how Jade planned to get her on her back.

CHAPTER FORTY-ONE

May 24, 2076—Mainland, San Francisco

Landry was in love with Jade. There was no getting away from it. Delaney couldn't deny Jade was a nice piece of ass, and she had a quick wit, but Delaney wondered if she had the chops to hold Landry's attention long-term. How could their relationship ever really stand up to the test of Landry not being able to discuss her work, of her being away for six months, or longer, and not knowing where she'd been or what'd happened to her?

That's not my problem. When she rescued Ilsa, she'd be able to share her work with her, and she was hoping Ilsa would want to be a big part of it. All Delaney had to do was concentrate on her relationship with Ilsa, and that would be much easier once the next mission was complete, and she could go back for her. With Ilsa by her side, ignoring her feelings for Landry wouldn't be so much of an issue.

"Has being an asshole made you work up much of an appetite?"

Landry's approach had been silent. Either that, or Delaney was so caught up in her own thoughts, the world had faded into the background. It'd been a long time since she'd been among regular people without being on a mission. It was a bit overwhelming, and Delaney couldn't wait to get back to her hotel room to pack and head back to Pulsus.

"Ha fucking ha. I'm not hungry, but I could use a drink. Being around all these civilians is unnerving."

"I'll take you for tea but nothing stronger."

"Christ, Landry, doesn't choosing a place to live here earn me a real drink?"

"Nope. There's a great Japanese garden in Golden Gate. I'll get my car."

Delaney sighed. She and Landry hadn't hooked up since the beginning of the Mexican drug cartel mission. Being around her wasn't helpful, but it was a hard habit to break. Delaney loved Landry's company, but if she was constantly around her, how could she make the transition from wanting to be her lover to accepting just her friendship? That had been easier to swallow when friendship was something Landry offered only a few people. Friendship had always meant more to Landry than love, but it looked like her relationship with Jade was changing her perspective. *Then again, she has come after me rather than staying with Jade.*

"Fine. As long as you don't make me drink the same herbal shit you gave me the other night."

Landry smiled and punched Delaney on the shoulder. "I won't… I'll make you try some *other* herbal shit instead."

On the way to Golden Gate, they chatted mainly about the house Delaney had just committed to buying, but she could feel something wasn't quite right with Landry. When she'd accidentally brushed Landry's hand as they both reached to change the music at the same time, Landry had pulled away abruptly. Had Jade picked up on something and told Landry she too thought Delaney was in love with her? Simson's claim had been relatively easy to discredit, but she wasn't sure Landry would believe her a second time.

They walked in awkward silence to the Japanese tea garden, and Delaney let Landry order her some fancy beverage from the hostess dressed in a traditional kimono, with the obi-jime tied tightly to create an impossibly minute waist. Delaney wondered how she managed to breathe.

Landry was first to speak. "I've been wanting to say that I'm sorry I was so hard on you about Ilsa. I'm glad you managed to experience love while you were in that shit-hole."

Now her weirdness made sense. Landry wasn't ever comfortable with apologizing. Not that she was often wrong about much, which was both infuriating and inspiring to Delaney. She struggled to find the appropriate response. "Thanks."

"How have you been coping, you know, with the nightmares? Were they better in Germany?"

Delaney smiled briefly. "Not really, but it was nice having someone comfort me." Delaney thought about Ilsa wrapped in her arms. She'd wake at the sound of Delaney's yelling and gently stroke her face until she awoke. Then she'd curl up into Delaney's arms, and her soft breathing would sometimes soothe Delaney back to sleep. *I want that again.*

"How's sleeping alone?"

Blunt. "It sucks." *It always sucked when you left my bed after sex, too.* Delaney wasn't sure where Landry was going with her questions, so she kept her responses short. She didn't want to trip herself up and ruin everything. Their hostess came back with cast iron teacups and pots. Delaney picked hers up to examine it. "This looks like something a kid would drink from."

Landry poured some of the tea into her tiny iron cup. "Imagine it's a shot of bourbon then."

Delaney still detected an edge to Landry's voice. The apology obviously had nothing to do with the recently developed atmosphere. "So you'll come to my housewarming barbeque then?" Maybe a change of subject would be sufficient to distract Landry from whatever she was chewing on.

"Sure. You'll invite Jade?"

I'd rather pull down my pants, sit bare-assed on the grill, and offer my rump steak to guests. "Of course. She found it for me. Would be rude if I didn't."

"You didn't seem to mind being rude to her at the house."

So you're bristling because I hurt your pretty girl's feelings. "Didn't look like it bothered her."

"Why *were* you such an asshat?"

Delaney took a sip of the too-hot tea and burned her lips. She took a swig of the cold water their hostess had also placed on the table and looked away. Delaney wasn't doing a great job of keeping

Landry's focus off the topic she really wouldn't be able to handle her tackling. With a master's in psychology, Delaney expected Landry was reading her like the clichéd book.

The question took physical form and hung between them. Landry simply stared at Delaney and waited for her response. "I don't know. I guess I don't know how to be around civvies anymore."

"Really? So it's got nothing to do with you having deeper feelings for me, then?"

Fuck shit. "Fuck, Landry, this again? I told you, Simson was bullshitting you. How big is your fucking ego that you think I'm in love with you?" *Fuck shit fuck.* She could see from the look in Landry's eyes that she wasn't fooling her this time.

"It's not just Simson, Dee—"

"Who then? Your girlfriend? Can't she handle you having a best friend? You can tell her that jealousy doesn't look good on her." Delaney raised her voice a little too loud, and the family at the adjacent table looked at her disapprovingly. She stopped scratching at her nose and smiled to placate them.

"You're lying to me, Delaney. Did I lead you on? I thought we were both clear what we did was sport fucking?" Landry's language caused the family's mom to glare in their direction again.

So she'd finally figured it out, with a little help from Jade and Simson. Delaney decided there was little use in protesting further. If she admitted it, if it was out in the open, maybe it would help her get over it. If she could tell Landry the things that really revved her engine, she'd stop being so fucking sexy, and Delaney could focus on Ilsa.

"I don't know what to tell you, Landry. I can't help the way I feel, and believe me, I've tried. I never meant to fall in love with you, just like you never meant to fall in love with Jade, I guess."

"Don't bring Jade into this. This is about you and me. How long have you felt this way?"

From around the time I first saw you in recruit training. "Not that long."

"You should've told me. We could've stopped fucking. I don't want to be responsible for messing with your heart."

"You were never messing with my heart, Landry. I knew you didn't and wouldn't ever feel the same. I was happy to at least have sex with you, since that's all that was offered." She laughed, but Landry didn't join her. "Look, now that you know, can't we just forget about it? I was in love with Ilsa, and I've put that aside." *Liar.* "With a little help from you, I'll be able to do the same again. Maybe I'll end up with a really hot neighbor and she'll fall for me like Jade obviously has for you." *Or I bring Ilsa back home to stay in my fancy new house, and we live happily ever after.*

"This ruins everything, Delaney. Why did you have to…fall for me at all?"

"It doesn't change anything. We haven't fucked for a while now, and you knowing doesn't mean I expect you to fall in love with me. Just give me some time to get over you, that's all."

Landry sipped at her tea, narrowed her eyes, and looked thoughtful. When she did that, it was impossible to tell what the hell she was thinking, good or bad.

She smiled. "Maybe Jade can fix you up with a woman as well as the house."

"That might be an idea. I suppose trying a civilian relationship wouldn't be the worst thing. You could be on to something with this 'life outside Pulsus' thing."

"Seriously though, how do I make this easier for you?"

By helping me bring Ilsa back. "I'll let you know when I figure it out."

Landry nodded. "Okay, buddy, however you want to do this, just talk to me."

"Sure." *I'll talk to you when we're on our next mission, and hopefully, you'll come down on my side. I'd hate to see Simson bust up your gorgeous face.*

CHAPTER FORTY-TWO

May 24, 2076—Mainland, San Francisco

Landry had taken a ridiculous amount of time to get ready for Jade's arrival. She always liked to look good for any night out when the goal was to meet and bed a woman, but this was a night in. Her first. And it wasn't just with any woman. It was with someone who seemed to have cast a line into her chest and snagged her heart like an accomplished Atlantic Ocean whaler. Now she'd left Landry's heart dangling on a harpoon, deciding whether or not to make a last-ditch attempt for freedom, or embrace the charms of sweet captivity.

In the end, she'd gone for her favorite button-down black shirt, teamed it with a dark blue tie, dark wash True Religion's, and she'd stayed barefoot, rather than adding more height that would dwarf Jade. Landry thought her drool might be off-putting when she answered the door to Jade, who was wearing a simple white long sleeve sweater dress, that ended mid-thigh, and knee-high boots. She wore a long wool royal blue coat with a stand up collar, and Landry wanted to slip her hands inside it and pull her close enough to feel her heart beat.

They had dinner, sat an unbearable distance apart, and talked about everything other than the L word. Jade asked about Delaney and smiled knowingly when Landry revealed she was right about Delaney's feelings for her.

"I tell you, a woman's intuition is never wrong."

"Then how come I didn't see it?" Landry's question was genuine. She was bothered she hadn't picked up on it. She was highly intelligent and extremely well trained in the psychology of people.

How had she missed Delaney's love for her when everyone else around them seemed to have seen it?

"Perhaps you don't want to acknowledge that love even exists."

"Studying psychology as a fallback career?"

"Nope, just a hobby. And you're a complicated study, Landry Donovan."

"Am I?"

"No, not really, but everyone likes to think they're hard to work out." Jade laughed and it was musical. "Just kidding. Yes, you are."

"In what way?"

Jade pushed back her chair and got up from the table. She sat on the leather sofa by the window, and the soft wall lights cast shadows on her flawless, beautiful face. Her eyes sparkled enticingly, and Landry felt herself being further enchanted.

"You seem determined to keep people at a distance, even though you've got a wonderful, loving, and open heart."

Now it was Landry laughing. "How the hell do you work that out?" She joined Jade on the couch and sat with one leg stretched out and the other bent at the knee, touching Jade's leg. She needed the proximity desperately.

"Don't be coy. Let's talk about this building of yours. The one that Caitlin and Lizbeth think they're renting from some guy who's so loaded, he hasn't hiked the rent for years, despite the value of the property and surrounding area going through the roof."

Jade paused, obviously awaiting Landry's response, and her hand, which had been gesticulating her point, came to rest on Landry's thigh. Landry touched her tongue to her upper lip and sighed gently. She was so fucking hot for Jade, she was considering whether spontaneous combustion might be a possibility.

"You can't tell them I own it."

"Why? Because you're an international drug dealer, and it's been bought with blood money?"

Landry grinned widely. "You have an overactive imagination."

"And *you* have an unusually high income and a mysterious occupation you can't tell anyone about. Your best friend was extremely dismissive about the government job. *Is* there something I need to worry about?"

"No, of course not. There are some very rich philanthropists out there. Baby, that's all I can say."

"Then I guess that'll have to do for now. You were telling me why the girls shouldn't know who their mysterious benefactor is—"

"Raising a child is an expensive business. They don't need to be wasting their hard-earned money on unnecessarily high rent. And they don't need to think they owe me anything either."

"Caitlin already owes you her life."

"You can't say that. I stopped her from getting a bad beating, and there's nothing to say it would've gone any further." Landry didn't want Caitlin to idolize her, but since that night, both she and Lizbeth propounded her as their hero to anyone who would listen.

Jade squeezed Landry's thigh. "Actually, you're wrong. All of the people involved are now in prison for murder."

Landry looked at her disbelievingly. "How on earth do you know that?"

"I researched them after Caitlin told me about the attack. They did exactly the same thing to another woman six months later, except no tall, handsome stranger stepped in to save her."

This new knowledge saddened Landry. Senseless violence disturbed and angered her, especially when it was aimed at women. "Still, they don't need to know." Landry put her hand over Jade's. "Will you promise me you won't say anything? Ever."

"You know if you just wore glasses, no one would realize you're a superhero?"

Landry looked at her in exasperation. "Jade..."

"Fine. I won't say anything. But back to my point, what about the hospital bills you paid for them?"

"So, not only a spare time shrink, but also a private dick? I have the money, and they don't. It seemed like the right thing to do, and again, I don't want them thinking they owe me anything."

Jade's hand slipped along Landry's thigh until it rested lightly on her crotch. "I'm not criticizing, baby, I'm proving my point. You try to keep people at a distance, but you'd give them the world if they needed it."

Landry said nothing. She could feel the red-hot heat of Jade's hand through the denim of her jeans, and she ached to be inside her again. Jade reached over and pulled out Landry's pocket watch. Landry felt her breath on her neck and took a deep one of her own, trying hard to control the need that threatened to devour them both.

"What's with the pocket watch—what's the story behind it?"

She turned it over and over in her hand. Landry wanted Jade's hand inside her shirt, squeezing her breasts. "I inherited my dad's collection. He loved them, but I don't use them because I don't want to break them, I guess. Delaney found this one for me on our last mission, mainly for the quote on the back."

"*Yeshuat Hashem what?*" She quickly gave up on the Yiddish pronunciation. "What language is that?"

Jade's thumb traced the intricate stenciling on the watch case. Landry wanted to be the watch. "It's Jewish-German. It means that no matter how grim the situation is, salvation could be just around the corner."

"Salvation? I didn't peg you as the religious type."

"Oh, I'm not. Not at all. But I like the idea of always having the hope that rescue or recovery can come along in an instant."

Jade smiled and placed the watch back in Landry's pocket. "You wear it, but you haven't looked at it once this evening."

"That's because you're such wonderful company. I don't want to know that time's running out."

Jade looked puzzled. "How is it running out?"

Landry sighed, not really wanting to think about tomorrow or any other day. What she wanted to do was enjoy and relax into what was happening tonight. "You have a basketball game. I have another mission to go to in a few weeks. I'll be gone maybe two months." She paused, unsure. *Do I say this and risk ruining everything?* "I have to say again that it's possible I don't come back at all. Time escapes us."

Jade reached for Landry's face and caressed her cheek. "So we shouldn't keep wasting it, then?" She leaned in and kissed her hard, wanting, her hand pressed firmly on Landry's crotch.

"I was hoping you might say something like that." Landry dropped her knee, wrapped her hand around Jade's neck, and pulled her into her lap. She drew her fingers up the outside of Jade's naked thigh and stopped at the hem of her dress.

"There's just the small thing of where you think this is going, Landry. I don't want a 'friend with benefits' gig. What do you want from me?"

Landry looked deep into Jade's eyes and saw something she'd never seen in the eyes of another woman. Tomorrow. And the next day. "Everything. I want everything from you."

"And if I give you everything, what do I get in return?"

"All of me…if you want it."

"I'll take it, if you're sure that's what you can give."

Landry nodded. "I'm sure. And you can handle my job?"

Jade nodded tentatively, pressed her lips to Landry's, and traced her tongue over them. "Do we get the bed this time?"

Landry slipped one arm under Jade's knees and the other around her back. She shuffled to the edge of the sofa and stood. Jade giggled a little, probably at Landry's strength, and began to undo her tie.

"If the soft give of my bed is what you'd like, your wish is my command." Landry walked past the kitchen to the end of the corridor and pushed open the bedroom door with her foot.

"To say you never have women here, that's an awfully big bed."

"I move around a lot in my sleep. I even sleepwalk." Landry let Jade down onto her feet.

"If you do it in your sleep, how do you know?" She pulled Landry's tie from around her neck and tossed it onto the bed.

"I wake up in strange places. In front of the curtains, in the kitchen, in the shower. It's one of the reasons I never sleep anywhere other than here." Landry ran her fingers through Jade's soft hair and kissed her neck.

"Any ideas why you do it?" Jade asked as she began to slowly open Landry's shirt.

"Usually when something's on my mind and I can't resolve it. I woke up putting the duvet over the pool table last night."

Jade laughed and continued to unbutton Landry's shirt; her perfectly manicured fingers moved deftly and sensually over her body. "What was on your mind last night?"

"You were. You've been on my mind night and day since we met."

"Smooth line."

"Thanks."

Jade pulled Landry's shirt from her jeans and slipped it from her shoulders. She kissed and nibbled Landry's chest and murmured appreciatively into her skin. "I know I told you last time you were half naked in front of me, but your body is stunning. I don't think I've ever been with a woman with so much muscle. Have you always been this big?"

"I had a rough childhood, so I bulked up. It doesn't bother you?"

"God, no. I've always loved women with big muscles. I've just never had one."

Jade worked open Landry's buckle and began to open her jeans. Landry watched, mesmerized, growing even hornier when Jade unzipped them and slipped her hand inside to cup her pussy through her briefs. Landry reached down, pulled up the hem of Jade's dress, and removed it in one fluid movement. She swallowed hard at the vision of Jade in matching Victoria's Secret white lace bra and panties and the unbelievably sexy way they contrasted against her olive skin.

"I never realized I was such a cliché," Landry whispered between the kind of steamy kisses that seem to defy the earth's gravitational pull. The kind of kisses Landry thought were only imagineered for the movies.

"Meaning?"

"I've been with lots of different kinds of women, but seeing you in that dress, and in that lingerie, makes me think I only *ever* want to see you looking like that."

Jade smiled and bit Landry's neck gently. "I have to admit to a similar sin. Your shirt, tie, and jeans outfits make me twitchy." She dropped to her knees and pulled down Landry's jeans as she did so.

Landry stepped out of them, and Jade pressed her mouth to Landry's briefs. Her hot breath swept straight to Landry's sex, and she wrapped her hand in Jade's hair, keeping her in position. "Now you're making me wish I had something else to offer you."

Jade nibbled at the soft cotton and traced her tongue over Landry's hardened clit. "Maybe next time, handsome." She pulled Landry's shorts down, grasped her hips, and tongued between Landry's lips.

Landry moaned, and her legs buckled slightly. "There's no way I can stand if you're going to do that."

Jade stood, grabbed Landry by the shoulders, and pushed her onto the bed.

Landry edged farther onto it and smiled. "You're pretty strong for a little one."

"Told you I'd be able to get you on your back." Jade got onto her knees on the bed, spread Landry's legs, and lowered her mouth onto Landry's pussy.

"It's not really a position I'm familiar with."

Jade raised her head. "You'll get used to it."

Landry relaxed into the cool cotton sheets and concentrated on the growing throbbing between her legs. Jade licked from the base of her pussy upward and circled her clit slowly and firmly. She slipped both arms under Landry's legs and rested her hands on her stomach. She looked up and met Landry's gaze.

"Close your eyes and relax, baby."

"I need to see you."

Jade's eyes showed she was smiling as she returned to Landry's sex. She reached down and rested her hand on Jade's head. Her other hand rested on Jade's fingers. The pressure built, quicker and more intense than Landry was used to when she played with herself. It was very rare she let any of her short-term lovers suck her off. Landry was more than happy giving and rarely had the patience or time to allow a woman to learn how to get her off. She felt herself getting incredibly slick, and Jade's rhythm had her approaching her orgasm in no time. She moaned and pushed her hips into Jade's face. She moaned in response, never breaking contact. Just as she was about to come, Jade slipped two fingers inside her and began to fuck her, without missing a stroke with her tongue. They met each other's gaze again, and Landry could see the longing in Jade's eyes, the need to make her come just as Landry needed Jade's orgasm. The throbbing became too intense to hold, and she let go, releasing herself, and her love to Jade.

Jade didn't stop. She continued to lick, suck, and fuck until Landry couldn't take any more and pulled away, the pleasure too much. She lifted her head, and Landry could see her chin and mouth slick with her wetness.

"Wow, baby, you're juicy."

Landry laughed, slightly embarrassed. "You're to blame for that." She reached down and felt how wet she was. "I've never come that much, even for myself."

Jade wiped her mouth, crawled up, and lay over Landry's body. "I like that. I like doing something no one else has ever done to you."

Landry held Jade in her arms, marveling at how right she felt there, how well she fit. *Like the jigsaw piece you can never find that completes the puzzle of your life*. They lay silently. Not an awkward silence where both parties are desperately searching their minds for something interesting to say post-coitus, but the kind of silence that comes from being completely, and inexplicably, at ease, so much so that inane conversation is redundant.

"I like listening to your heart beat."

It beats for you. Oh, fuck, does it? That's so fucking cheesy. "Yeah? Is it tuneful enough to keep you interested long-term?" *Less cheesy, that's better.*

"I don't see why not."

Landry flipped Jade onto her back and straddled her. She unclipped her front fastening bra, released Jade's full breasts, and bent down to take her nipple into her mouth. Jade writhed beneath her and moaned loudly.

"And might this keep you interested long-term?" Landry asked, as she slipped her hand inside Jade's panties, and her fingers inside her pussy. She lay beside her and sucked Jade's nipple into her mouth.

Jade let out a breathy gasp and took a handful of Landry's hair. "I don't see…why not."

Landry worked her fingers deeper into Jade and used her other hand to pull the panties off altogether. She left them wrapped around one ankle, and though it seemed a little tawdry, Landry found it incredibly erotic.

Jade groaned and pushed her body onto Landry's fingers, daring her to go deeper and harder. Landry looked into Jade's blue-gray eyes, and the raw honesty she saw in them took her breath away. She'd wanted most women to close their eyes when she was fucking them. She had no desire to see if the cliché that they were the windows to the soul was true in the throes of sex. All Landry wanted was to know they'd had a great time and an even better orgasm. Making women come fed a need that originated from God knows where. But this need was a whole new ball game.

She picked up the pace in response to Jade's grinding and the tightening grip she had in Landry's hair.

"Baby, I'm gonna come. Fuck me harder."

Landry smiled at Jade's demand, glad that her honesty bled into her sexual need. "Fuck, you're even more beautiful when you're about to come."

Their thrust and pull synced perfectly. Jade's breathing quickened, and she begged for Landry to pump faster. She lifted her hips from the bed as she orgasmed, and Landry slipped beneath her. As she came down, she rested on Landry's lap, and powerful tremors shuddered through her. Landry kept her fingers inside Jade and began again just as she'd settled on Landry's stomach.

"Oh, fuck." Jade grabbed at Landry's body and dug her nails into Landry's shoulders.

She started off slow and hard, building back up to the rhythm that had sent Jade over the edge. Her body writhed on top of Landry's, allowing her to catch nibbles of Jade's body as she rose up and down. She was quick to come again, and shortly after, once more. Landry noticed how the evening light through her bedroom windows danced like diamonds on the light sheen of sweat that covered Jade's body. She wished for technology that could capture what the eye saw without the need for bulky photographic equipment.

Landry slowly withdrew her fingers and began firm movements over Jade's clit. Once again, she responded, and another powerful release flowed through her body. Landry raised her hand to her nose to breathe in Jade's scent and sighed deeply.

"You smell amazing." Landry probably couldn't describe it, if asked. Pure didn't have a scent signature. *Pure love?* She *did* know it was the sweetest aroma that her brain had ever processed.

Jade giggled, a little shy. "You're dirty."

"You like me that way."

"I do. And you make me *very* glad I'm multi-orgasmic."

Jade rolled off Landry and lay at an angle with her head on Landry's chest, so she could look up at her.

"I have no idea how this is going to work, baby." Landry ran her hand from Jade's shoulder to her hip and rested there. She really didn't know, but she *did* know she wanted to try.

Jade outlined gentle circles on Landry's chest. It was alien but felt wonderful. Previously, Landry enjoyed a firm caress and had no time for the tender touches. Now it seemed like she'd let Jade do whatever the hell she wanted to her. Her heart felt exposed and yet simultaneously protected, and she had no desire to build another wall around it. Most probably, Jade would be able to run a bulldozer straight through it anyway.

"We don't need all the answers, handsome. We just need each other, and the rest will fall into place."

Landry experienced a wave of calm sweep over her. Lying here with Jade was quite possibly the most peaceful she'd ever felt in her entire life. In the years after her mom had died, her memories echoed of a life that had been chaotic, and the only order she found was in the military. Her new memories, of a life *with* her mom, were disordered in a different way she couldn't figure out because she hadn't really lived that existence. In both of them, her life meant little to her. She went on missions, first for her country, and then for Pulsus, with little regard for the personal consequences. Suddenly, with Jade, there was a life to share and to cherish. There was meaning to the time between missions, and she wanted to hold Jade in her arms forever.

"Will you stay the night with me?" Landry felt a catch in her throat, but still managed the words she'd never spoken.

"I'd love to, baby, but I can't. I have to catch a flight to L.A. in the morning for the final playoff game, so I need to get home for an early night."

Landry clenched her jaw shut and closed her eyes. She didn't want to say anything she might regret, but this knockback was demanding she brush Jade off immediately.

"If you promise to let me sleep, you could stay with me…"

The breath Landry caught in her throat released. "That's a mammoth ask, but if it means I get to wake up and you're the first thing I see, it'll be worth it."

"See how good you are at this romance thing already? You've got all the right lines, baby." Jade kissed her and climbed off the bed. "It's a fifty-minute drive, but if we're quick, we could probably get a few more orgasms in before I have to sleep." She winked, and her wicked smile had Landry jumping off the bed to follow her.

❖

As they headed out of the city on the 101 across Golden Gate Bridge, the traffic thinned considerably. Jade led the way in her Spider, having challenged Landry to keep up with her Italian supercar in her "old-fashioned American muscle car." After Marin City, Highway One was more suited to the Ferrari, but Landry's driving skills had her hot on Jade's tail.

"Did you want to be a race car driver when you were a kid?" Landry asked over Bluetooth. She'd thought Jade might find it silly if Landry suggested they stay talking to each other while they drove in separate cars. Instead, she thought it was sweet and promised Landry an extra special treat when they got to her place on the beach.

"What's the matter, hotshot, can't you keep up?"

Landry laughed. "I'm doing okay. You haven't lost me yet."

"Losing you is the last thing I'm trying to do, handsome. I've only just found you."

The highway was dark, and their headlights were the only lights for miles. They were so alone.

"Is there a pull-in anywhere on this road?" Landry asked, unable to disguise the absolute lust in her voice.

"Why?" Jade played along.

"Fresh air sex is very fucking hot."

"Another night, baby. What I've got in mind, I can't do to you on the hood of either of our cars."

Landry grinned and let out a husky breath. "Damn, you're a sexy bitch."

"You're going to spend the next few decades finding out how—fuck!"

The rest happened so fast. Jade shouted and then screamed. She continued to scream as she lost control coming out of the hairpin bend by Lone Tree Creek. Her car skidded off the road and careened down the deep valley.

"Jade!" Landry slammed on her brakes and held it steady as the back end threatened to spin the car. *Please keep screaming, baby.*

"Baby!"

The Ferrari rolled and smashed into a tree. Jade's screaming stopped abruptly. Landry brought her car to a halt, headlights facing along the valley toward Jade's car. She threw the door open and tried to get out but her seat belt stopped her. "Fuck." She released the restraint and jumped out. "Jade!" Landry called out, the phone connection still open, but there was no answer. She listened hard for breathing, whimpering, any sign of life, but she couldn't hear a sound.

"I'm coming, baby." Landry ran down the steep incline toward Jade's car. With the force of the impact, it was highly likely the car might blow up. "Jade. Talk to me, baby. Tell me you're okay."

Landry's breathing faltered as she reached the Ferrari, lying on its roof. The door had burst open with the collision, and Jade was half-hanging from her seat, with her belt keeping her in. The thick branches of the tree had forced themselves through the windshield and the driver's side window. Landry could see one had penetrated deep into Jade's thigh, and her blood had turned her white dress ruby red. Her immediate concern was that it might have punctured an arterial vein.

"God, no." *This can't be happening.* She leaned in and held her ear to Jade's mouth. Her breathing was shallow and labored, but at least she was breathing.

She knew she couldn't pull the branch out. The best chance of saving her leg at all would be to saw through it, wrap the wound around it, and take her to a hospital. "It's going to be okay." Landry was trying to convince herself more than the unconscious Jade.

Landry paused. They were almost an hour from the hospital. It was likely by the time they got there, the badly damaged nerves would be dead from the trauma. Her leg lost. Her basketball career over. She was only thirty minutes from the Pulsus train stop, though. *What am I thinking?* Take her to Pulsus. Fix her up. *Then what? How do I explain the car, the accident? My job?* Her mom could fix her. She could regenerate the leg tissue. *Would that be my career over?* It was strictly forbidden to even speak to anyone outside the organization about their work, let alone bring someone to the island.

Landry scrambled back up the bank, opened her trunk, and pulled out her tool kit. "Stay with me, baby. I'm here. We'll get through this." She continued to speak to Jade as she ran back down to the car. Landry pulled out a laser saw and carefully sliced through the branch three-inches above Jade's thigh.

She went back to her kit bag and pulled out a can of skin sealant. It was another Pulsus invention that shouldn't be off the island, but Landry didn't give a damn. She sprayed around the branch and tossed it back into the bag before she put the bag on her back.

"I'm going to take care of you, baby. Don't worry about a thing." Landry leaned under Jade's unconscious body, supported her as she released the seat belt, and gently took her down from the seat. She carried her up the ridge, placed her in the backseat of the Mustang, and got back in the car to drive to the station. Landry took a deep breath as she turned the car around before making the most important call of her life.

"Mom, you have to do something for me. I've never asked you for anything, and I never will again. But I need you to do this for me. I need you to say you will before I even ask you."

"What's happened, pumpkin? Are you in some kind of trouble on the mainland?"

"Please, Mom. Just tell me you'll help me."

"I'll do anything you need me to, you know that. You know you don't even have to ask."

"Meet me at the regen lab in forty-five minutes. Don't tell anyone else."

"Landry, what's this about? You're scaring me."

"Please, Mom, no questions. Just say you'll be there. I need you like I've never needed you before."

There was a short pause on the other end of the line. "I'll be there, Landry."

"Thank you."

Landry ended the call and glanced through the rearview mirror at the unconscious body of her lover.

The woman she'd just spent the night making love to.

The woman she loved.

The woman she'd risk everything to save.

EPILOGUE

Soundproofing. Such a wonderful invention.

Nelida Staton ran her hand over the walls, loving the feel of the aluminum foil, and the spongy give of the construction beneath her fingertips. She turned to quietly study the young man she'd acquired earlier that day. He wasn't screaming yet, but in time, he would. For now, he could remain sleeping, entirely unaware of the horror to come. *His horror. My pleasure*. He was naked but for the harness and shackles that entwined his body. His wrists were bound together behind his back, and he was secured upright by a nylon harness looped under his arms, connected to the steel frame at the very top of the unit.

She caressed the curves of the transparent polyethylene plastic container, as lovingly as if it were her lover, though she couldn't remember the last time she'd taken one of those. With this as her hobby, she had little need or time for the demands of a sexual partner.

He began to stir. *Showtime*. She adored this part. The slow return to consciousness, and the drowsy look in their eyes as they thought, then hoped, and occasionally prayed, they might be experiencing a particularly vivid nightmare. The recollection of their capture usually followed, and then came the abuse. How long it took for the abuse to dissipate, and the pleas to begin was, she believed, an indication of the caliber of the man she was holding hostage. Too short a gap was the telltale sign of a weak and cowardly man. Too long, and she was dealing with an imbecile, someone who failed to realize how utterly out of control they were.

She kept records of all of them. The words they used, and the tone with which they delivered them. How they begged, and for how long. The excuses, the reasons they should live. Some were imaginative, but many centered on the age-old justification of having a family that would miss them terribly. She was sometimes disappointed with the inanity of some as the realization of their imminent demise finally hit them. But mostly, she felt invigorated by their entreaties.

When she was between projects, she would flick through the pages to her favorites, tabbed with turquoise sticky notes, and try to recall how they sounded, in life and in the throes of death. It took up to forty-eight hours for the tank to do its work and reduce its occupant to liquid. The shock killed some, with their bodies simply shutting down as their heart gave in. Others took satisfyingly longer before they died, as they felt themselves dissolve. And the screams. The screams were always magnificent. The way the process tore them from the mouths of her captives was something she never could've hoped to experience when she first dreamt of doing this.

"You fucking bitch. Get me out of here."

Nelida laughed softly. "In time, my love, all in good time."

About the Author

Robyn Nyx is an avid shutterbug and lover of all things fast and physical. Her writing often reflects both of those passions. She writes lesbian fiction when she isn't busy being the chief executive of a UK charity and co-director of Global Wordsmiths, which she runs with her soul mate and fellow scribe, Brey Willows. They have no kids or kittens, which allows them to travel to exotic places at the drop of a hat for "research." She works hard to find writing time, when she's not being distracted by blue skies and motorbike rides.

Books Available from Bold Strokes Books

Escape in Time by Robyn Nyx. Working in the past is hell on your future. (978-1-62639-855-9)

Forget-Me-Not by Kris Bryant. Is love worth walking away from the only life you've ever dreamed of? (978-1-62639-865-8)

Highland Fling by Anna Larner. On vacation in the Scottish Highlands, Eve Eddison falls for the enigmatic forestry officer Moira Burns, despite Eve's best friend's campaign to convince her that Moira will break her heart. (978-1-62639-853-5)

Phoenix Rising by Rebecca Harwell. As Storm's Quarry faces invasion from a powerful neighbor, a mysterious newcomer with powers equal to Nadya's challenges everything she believes about herself and her future (978-1-62639-913-6)

Soul Survivor by I. Beacham. Sam and Joey have given up on hope, but when fate brings them together it gives them a chance to change each other's life and make dreams come true. (978-1-62639-882-5)

Strawberry Summer by Melissa Brayden. When Margaret Beringer's first love Courtney Carrington returns to their small town, she must grapple with their troubled past and fight the temptation for a very delicious future. (978-1-62639-867-2)

The Girl on the Edge of Summer by J.M. Redmann. Micky Knight accepts two cases, but neither is the easy investigation it appears. The past is never past—and young girls lead complicated, even dangerous lives. (978-1-62639-687-6)

Unknown Horizons by CJ Birch. The moment Lieutenant Alison Ash steps aboard the Persephone, she knows her life will never be the same. (978-1-62639-938-9)

Divided Nation, United Hearts by Yolanda Wallace. In a nation torn in two by a most uncivil war, can love conquer the divide? (978-1-62639-847-4)

Fury's Bridge by Brey Willows. What if your life depended on someone who didn't believe in your existence? (978-1-62639-841-2)

Lightning Strikes by Cass Sellars. When Parker Duncan and Sydney Hyatt's one-night stand turns to more, both women must fight demons past and present to cling to the relationship neither of them thought she wanted. (978-1-62639-956-3)

Love in Disaster by Charlotte Greene. A professor and a celebrity chef are drawn together by chance, but can their attraction survive a natural disaster? (978-1-62639-885-6)

Secret Hearts by Radclyffe. Can two women from different worlds find common ground while fighting their secret desires? (978-1-62639-932-7)

Sins of Our Fathers by A. Rose Mathieu. Solving gruesome murder cases is only one of Elizabeth Campbell's challenges; another is her growing attraction to the female detective who is hell-bent on keeping her client in prison. (978-1-62639-873-3)

The Sniper's Kiss by Justine Saracen. The power of a kiss: it can swell your heart with splendor, declare abject submission, and sometimes blow your brains out. (978-1-62639-839-9)

Troop 18 by Jessica L. Webb. Charged with uncovering the destructive secret that a troop of RCMP cadets has been hiding, Andy must put aside her worries about Kate and uncover the conspiracy before it's too late. (978-1-62639-934-1)

Worthy of Trust and Confidence by Kara A. McLeod. FBI Special Agent Ryan O'Connor is about to discover the hard way that when you can only handle one type of answer to a question, it really is better not to ask. (978-1-62639-889-4)

Amounting to Nothing by Karis Walsh. When mounted police officer Billie Mitchell steps in to save beautiful murder witness Merissa Karr, worlds collide on the rough city streets of Tacoma, Washington. (978-1-62639-728-6)

Becoming You by Michelle Grubb. Airlie Porter has a secret. A deep, dark, destructive secret that threatens to engulf her if she can't find the courage to face who she really is and who she really wants to be with. (978-1-62639-811-5)

Birthright by Missouri Vaun. When spies bring news that a swordswoman imprisoned in a neighboring kingdom bears the Royal mark, Princess Kathryn sets out to rescue Aiden, true heir to the Belstaff throne. (978-1-62639-485-8)

Crescent City Confidential by Aurora Rey. When romance and danger are in the air, writer Sam Torres learns the Big Easy is anything but. (978-1-62639-764-4)

Love Down Under by MJ Williamz. Wylie loves Amarina, but if Amarina isn't out, can their relationship last? (978-1-62639-726-2)

Privacy Glass by Missouri Vaun. Things heat up when Nash Wiley commandeers a limo and her best friend for a late drive out to the beach: Champagne on ice, seat belts optional, and privacy glass a must. (978-1-62639-705-7)

The Impasse by Franci McMahon. A horse packing excursion into the Montana Wilderness becomes an adventure of terrifying proportions for Miles and ten women on an outfitter led trip. (978-1-62639-781-1)

The Right Kind of Wrong by PJ Trebelhorn. Bartender Quinn Burke is happy with her life as a playgirl until she realizes she can't fight her feelings any longer for her best friend, bookstore owner Grace Everett. (978-1-62639-771-2)

Wishing on a Dream by Julie Cannon. Can two women change everything for the chance at love? (978-1-62639-762-0)

A Quiet Death by Cari Hunter. When the body of a young Pakistani girl is found out on the moors, the investigation leaves Detective Sanne Jensen facing an ordeal she may not survive. (978-1-62639-815-3)

Buried Heart by Laydin Michaels. When Drew Chambliss meets Cicely Jones, her buried past finds its way to the surface—will they survive its discovery or will their chance at love turn to dust? (978-1-62639-801-6)

Escape: Exodus Book Three by Gun Brooke. Aboard the Exodus ship *Pathfinder*, President Thea Tylio still holds Caya Lindemay, a clairvoyant changer, in protective custody, which has devastating consequences endangering their relationship and the entire Exodus mission. (978-1-62639-635-7)

Genuine Gold by Ann Aptaker. New York, 1952. Outlaw Cantor Gold is thrown back into her honky-tonk Coney Island past, where crime and passion simmer in a neon glare. (978-1-62639-730-9)

Into Thin Air by Jeannie Levig. When her girlfriend disappears, Hannah Lewis discovers her world isn't as orderly as she thought it was. (978-1-62639-722-4)

Night Voice by CF Frizzell. When talk show host Sable finally acknowledges her risqué radio relationship with a mysterious caller, she welcomes a *real* relationship with local tradeswoman Riley Burke. (978-1-62639-813-9)

Raging at the Stars by Lesley Davis. When the unbelievable theories start revealing themselves as truths, can you trust in the ones who have conspired against you from the start? (978-1-62639-720-0)

She Wolf by Sheri Lewis Wohl. When the hunter becomes the hunted, more than love might be lost. (978-1-62639-741-5)

Smothered and Covered by Missouri Vaun. The last person Nash Wiley expects to bump into over a two a.m. breakfast at Waffle House is her college crush, decked out in a curve-hugging law enforcement uniform. (978-1-62639-704-0)

The Butterfly Whisperer by Lisa Moreau. Reunited after ten years, can Jordan and Sophie heal the past and rediscover love or will differing desires keep them apart? (978-1-62639-791-0)

The Devil's Due by Ali Vali. Cain and Emma Casey are awaiting the birth of their third child, but as always in Cain's world, there are new and old enemies to face in post Katrina-ravaged New Orleans. (978-1-62639-591-6)

Widows of the Sun-Moon by Barbara Ann Wright. With immortality now out of their grasp, the gods of Calamity fight amongst themselves, egged on by the mad goddess they thought they'd left behind. (978-1-62639-777-4) boldstrokesbooks.com

Bold Strokes Books

Quality and Diversity in LGBTQ Literature

SCI-FI

E-BOOKS

MYSTERY

EROTICA

YOUNG ADULT

Romance

W·E·B·S·T·O·R·E

PRINT AND EBOOKS

Lightning Source UK Ltd.
Milton Keynes UK
UKOW04f2304060917
308712UK00001B/15/P